Dead Man for the Defense

Shawn kicked open the courtroom doors.

Veronica Mason gazed at Shawn with new hope. The spectators in the gallery looked like they were at a football game and Shawn had run onto the field just as the home team was about to score. Behind the bench, a graying Jerry Garcia look-alike in black robes stared openmouthed at the interruption.

"I object!" Shawn shouted.

The judge pounded his gavel so hard his small gray ponytail bounced up and down. "What do you mean, you object? Who are you?"

Shawn glanced at the judge. And *saw*. Saw the crystal pyramid holding down a stack of papers. The leather thong around his neck disappearing under his black robe.

"I'm Oliver Mason, and I'm here to say my wife did not kill me!"

psych

A MIND IS A TERRIBLE THING TO READ

William Rabkin

AN OBSIDIAN MYSTERY

OBSIDIAN
Published by New American Library, a division of
Penguin Group (USA) Inc., 375 Hudson Street,
New York, New York 10014, USA
Penguin Group (Canada), 90 Eglinton Avenue East, Suite 700, Toronto,
Ontario M4P 2Y3, Canada (a division of Pearson Penguin Canada Inc.)
Penguin Books Ltd., 80 Strand, London WC2R 0RL, England
Penguin Ireland, 25 St. Stephen's Green, Dublin 2,
Ireland (a division of Penguin Books Ltd.)
Penguin Group (Australia), 250 Camberwell Road, Camberwell, Victoria 3124,
Australia (a division of Pearson Australia Group Pty. Ltd.)
Penguin Books India Pvt. Ltd., 11 Community Centre, Panchsheel Park,
New Delhi - 110 017, India
Penguin Group (NZ), 67 Apollo Drive, Rosedale, North Shore 0632,
New Zealand (a division of Pearson New Zealand Ltd.)
Penguin Books (South Africa) (Pty.) Ltd., 24 Sturdee Avenue,
Rosebank, Johannesburg 2196, South Africa

Penguin Books Ltd., Registered Offices:
80 Strand, London WC2R 0RL, England

First published by Obsidian, an imprint of New American Library,
a division of Penguin Group (USA) Inc.

First Printing, January 2009
10 9 8 7 6 5

Copyright © NBC Universal Inc. *Psych* is a trademark and copyright of Universal Studios. 2009 All rights reserved.

The Edgar® name is a registered service mark of the Mystery Writers of America, Inc.

OBSIDIAN and logo are trademarks of Penguin Group (USA) Inc.

Printed in the United States of America

For Carrie

Prologue

1988

*T*he morning was perfect. A cool breeze blew off the
bay and tempered the warmth that was already radiating off the sun-soaked hills. In a few hours the coastal fog
would burn off, and the heat would force Henry Spencer
to put down his tools, pick up a beer, and spend the rest of
the day in the comfort of his air-conditioned living room
watching the Dodgers blow another easy one. But for now
he couldn't imagine why anyone would want to spend this
glorious day doing anything besides painting trim, patching rain gutters, and performing all the basic house maintenance that had been put off during the long, wet winter.

There was a crash of paint cans from the open garage.
"Are you all right, son?" Henry shouted. He got a muffled
grunt back in return.

Henry knew his boy didn't share his enthusiasm for
the day's tasks. Shawn had begged him to put off cleaning
the garage for another week. Fishermen had caught an
enormous great white off the Santa Barbara coast, and it
was on display at the pier today only. Shawn was desperate to get a look.

But the boy had to learn—work first, play later. He'd already put off this task three weeks running, and Henry finally put his foot down. Shawn accused his father of ruining his life, but Henry knew he was actually saving it. Shawn was so smart and so charming at ten years old, it would be all too easy for him to skate through the rest of his adolescence without ever accomplishing anything. He needed to learn good work habits now if he was ever going to become a man.

Henry picked up the paint scraper and bent down to attack the peeling woodwork above the foundation. As he turned away from the garage, he caught a flash of motion out of the corner of his eye. He jumped up just in time to see a bicycle tearing up the driveway toward the garage. Shawn's bicycle. And though the rider had a baseball cap pulled down to hide his face, Henry still managed to recognize his own son.

"Shawn!"

The bicycle sailed into the garage. Henry ran over to the driveway just in time to see Shawn's best friend, Gus, hurriedly taking his place on the bike as Shawn jammed the cap over his head.

"Hi, Mr. Spencer," Gus said. "I just got here. On this bicycle. With this cap on my head. In fact, that was probably me you saw riding up the driveway just now."

"Was it?" Henry said.

"Oh, yes," Gus said. "Because Shawn's been here all morning, working away. Look at the excellent job he's done stacking your paint cans."

Gus pointed to a stack of cans. Henry had to admit it was meticulously shaped.

"If you just got here, how do you know what Shawn's been doing?" Henry said.

Gus froze, searching for an answer. Shawn pulled the cap off his head and put it on his own.

"Fine, you caught us," Shawn said. "Gus was cleaning

out the garage while I went to see the shark for both of us."

"I'll deal with you in a minute," Henry told his son, then turned to Gus. *"You wanted to see the shark as bad as he did. Why would you let him take advantage of you like that?"*

Gus looked puzzled. Apparently he had never thought of it that way. *"Shawn said if he went, he could describe the shark to me in such detail, it would be just like I saw it myself. But if I went, all I could say was it was great. And white. So this way we both have the experience."*

"And Gus gets to improve his valuable can-stacking skills," Shawn said. *"I'm not taking advantage of him if we both win."*

"So you get to do what you want, and Gus gets to do what you don't," Henry said.

"Exactly," Shawn said. *"It's a win-win."*

Henry sighed. Military school. That was the ticket. A few years of strict discipline might teach Shawn the lessons he resolutely refused to learn from his father. The only thing that stopped Henry from picking up the phone and enrolling him today was the fear that a few years with Shawn might end up undermining the entire military.

"You are grounded for the next four weekends," Henry said.

"Dad!"

"I don't care if the Loch Ness Monster is hanging at the pier. You will spend the next four Saturdays and Sundays working around the house under my direct supervision," Henry said. *"And you're going to start right now. Not only are you cleaning out this garage—I want you to scrub the oil stains off the floor."*

Shawn stared down glumly at fifty years of accumulated grime, searching for a way out. A quick glance at his father's face told him there wouldn't be one. Not today, at least.

Gus gave Shawn a consoling pat on the shoulder and started toward the door.

"Where do you think you're going?" Henry said.

"I guess I'll go see the shark," Gus said.

"I guess you'll stay here and help Shawn with the garage," Henry said.

"But you just said Shawn was taking advantage of me," Gus said.

"He was," Henry said. "And he's going to keep doing it until you learn to stand up to him. Think of this as your first lesson."

Chuckling, Henry walked out of the garage. Behind him, he could hear the two boys arguing over whose fault this was. As he picked up his paint scraper, the arguments were drowned out by the sound of boxes being dragged out onto the driveway.

The day was perfect. The sun was hot, the breeze was cool, and Henry had two boys cleaning out his garage. Talk about a win-win.

Chapter One

The speed was exhilarating. Intoxicating.

The plastic letters on the hatchback spelled out TOYOTA, but as Gus piloted the blue Echo down State Street, it might as well have been a Ferrari. He stomped down on the gas and felt 105 horses galloping under the hood. The four cylinders screamed like an F/A-18 Hornet in a Blue Angels formation. Gus knew if he cracked down the window, the blast of wind would blow his hair right off his head—if he didn't keep it buzzed close to his scalp just for such an occasion. At the very least, it would whip his Donald Trump Collection power tie out the window. God only knew if the clip-on would be strong enough to keep it in the car.

Even so, Gus was tempted. It would be worth the risk to face the primal force of nature's fury. But to crank down the window meant taking one hand off the wheel, and ahead in the distance, he saw danger.

Danger that would require all his driving skill.

As the light changed from green to yellow, a flock of schoolkids stood on the corner, waiting for the WALK sign. If they spread out in the crosswalk, there would be no way to avoid plowing into them. Gus took his foot off the gas.

There was a strangled scream from the seat beside him.

"It's okay, Shawn," Gus said. "I see them."

Under his perpetual one-day stubble, Shawn Spencer's face was turning red. He seemed to be having trouble forming words. Extreme speeds work like that on some people, Gus knew.

"The light just turned yellow," Shawn said. "You can make it!"

"You mean run the light?" Gus said.

"You don't need to run it. You can walk and still get through before it changes."

Gus' foot hovered over the gas. Shawn's hand shot across the gear shift and pushed down on Gus' knee.

"A woman's life is at stake. Punch it!"

Gus struggled to keep his foot airborne. "Don't touch the knee."

"Then speed up."

The hand pressed down on his knee. Gus had to risk taking one hand off the wheel to pry it off. But Shawn's fingers were curved around his patella, and he couldn't peel them away.

"Do you have any idea how fast we're going?" Gus said.

"Yes. Thirty-three miles an hour."

"*Eight* miles over the legal limit. If there's radar working, we're in trouble."

"We're already in trouble. That's why you need to speed up."

"First, take your hand off my knee."

Shawn scowled, but his hand retreated back to his side of the cabin. Up ahead, the light changed to red.

"We could have made it," Shawn said.

"We're not going to be able to help Veronica Mason if we're killed in a car crash," Gus said.

"She's not going to care if we're dead if we don't get to the courthouse before the jury comes back."

"Maybe you should have thought of that when we got the call, instead of watching TV all morning."

"It wasn't TV—it was HBO," Shawn said. "More specifically, it was *Into the Blue*."

"Jessica Alba is not taking off her bikini no matter how many times you watch that movie."

"Are you sure? Because I'm thinking there might be a bonus every tenth time."

"You explain that to Veronica Mason when she's sitting on death row. Maybe you can watch it with her in her cell," Gus said.

"They don't give you a TV on death row. You get a Bible, and if you're lucky, you can train a rat to be your friend."

"She's already got a rat for a friend."

"Really?" Shawn said. "You're going with the rat thing?"

The light changed to green and Gus hit the gas. The car chugged through the intersection and began to pick up speed. Shawn's hand hovered over Gus' knee, but after a stern look, he pulled it away.

"You promised a month ago you could prove she was innocent," Gus said. "Now she's about to be found guilty, and you haven't done anything except play Centipede."

That wasn't exactly true. In the weeks since Veronica Mason first stepped into the beachside bungalow that housed their psychic-detective agency, Shawn and Gus had pored over every shred of evidence against her. They'd gone undercover as plumbers, pizza-delivery drivers, and piano tuners to question other suspects. And besides, Shawn wasn't just playing Centipede. He was competing. He'd finally beaten Donald Hayes' world record of 7,111,111 points, even if that had involved adding up the scores of a dozen separate games and then multiplying by eight.

"I was trying to get into our client's mind," Shawn said. "Centipede was the first arcade game ever written by a woman, and still one of the few to appeal to a female audience. Now would you please speed up?"

Gus glanced down at the speedometer. He was already thirty percent over the limit. But one look at Shawn showed him how much his partner was worrying about this case. Maybe it was worth the risk of a ticket.

When it started, it all looked so promising. Gus and Shawn were luxuriating in the glow of a string of successful cases. Which for Gus meant celebrating by rearranging their extensive DVD collection, moving from standard title-based alphabetization to a more intricate breakdown by genre, star, national origin, and release date. Shawn was busy studying the bra ads in the *Santa Barbara Times*. As Gus wrestled with the thorny question of whether *Mannequin 2: On the Move* should be filed with the Kristy Swanson collection, the "inanimate object becomes a hot chick" section, or the "sequel so bad it killed the franchise" area, the door opened. Gus looked up and saw a dollar sign standing in the doorway.

Actually, it was a young woman. In any other circumstance, Gus might have noticed her fiery red hair, blazing green eyes, and flawless skin, her long tan legs, and perfect shape. He certainly would have noticed the way her blouse hung open at the top, one button too many left undone. But after their unbroken string of solved cases, Gus was waiting for the Big One, the high-profile wealthy client who could put them at the very top of the local PI pyramid. This woman was obviously what he'd been looking for. He hoped that Shawn saw her the same way.

"Is this the detective agency?" the woman asked, her voice trembling.

Gus jumped out of his chair.

"Welcome to Psych," he said, holding out a hand. "Come in. I'm Burton Guster."

With a sinking heart, Gus saw her take a quick glance around the office at the frat-boy-with-a-credit-card decor: the leather armchairs, the wide flat screen, the comic books scattered over the coffee table.

"This is a mistake," the woman said. "You can't help me. No one can."

"Many people think that before they come to us," Gus said. "Before they meet Shawn Spencer."

"Is he really psychic?"

Gus heard a moan of pain from behind him. Shawn lay spread-eagle in his desk chair, arms flung out at his sides, legs up on the desk, eyes screwed shut.

"I'm sensing something." Shawn rose out of the chair as if yanked up by unseen strings and stared into the woman's eyes. "There's been a murder."

"Yes," she said. There was a flicker of hope in her eyes. *Keep it coming,* Gus thought. *You've almost got her.*

"I'm sensing that you were not the victim," Shawn said.

The hope flickered out and died. "I'm sorry. I shouldn't have come here."

Gus dived for the door, throwing himself between the woman and the exit. "You have to understand that Shawn sees the spirit world so clearly that sometimes he can't tell if he's addressing a living person or a ghost."

"Often I need to use my hands to be sure," Shawn said, extending his arms toward her.

"Shawn!"

"But not this time," Shawn said, dropping his arms. "I sense there was a murder."

"Yes, you sensed that already," Gus said. "Maybe you could sense a little more."

"Maybe I could," Shawn agreed.

"Maybe you should," Gus said. "Like now."

Shawn put his fingertips to his forehead and sniffed the air.

"I was wrong," Shawn said. "You *were* the victim of this crime. Not only has someone you loved deeply been taken away—you have been blamed for it. Unfairly, cruelly blamed by a world jealous of your talent, your beauty, your capacity for love."

The woman froze, then turned to Shawn. She started to tremble, then fell back in a swoon. Gus leapt forward to grab her before she could hit the floor, and guided her to the couch, where he laid her down gently. Shawn nudged him out of the way as he kneeled by the couch, taking her hand. She opened her eyes, then sat up quickly as she remembered where she was.

"I'm sorry," she said. "It's been so long since . . ."

"Since anyone understood you?" Shawn said.

She nodded, tears forming in the corners of her eyes.

"I see a wedding," Shawn said. "A man who is much older—"

"Not so much," she murmured. "Only forty-three years between us."

Shawn turned to Gus, disgust on his face. Forty-three years—*yuck*. Then turned back to the woman on the couch.

"To the outside world, it seemed like a lot," Shawn said. "But to two souls who'd been destined to be together, a matter of days."

"Yes." She closed her eyes, reliving her happier times.

"I see months of happiness. I see you honeymooning on his private jet."

"Yes."

"And on his private island."

"Yes."

"Off the coast of his private country."

Her eyes opened. "What?"

"I see your wedding bed, spread with rose petals, the eager bride emerging into the chamber and lifting her—"

Gus felt his face getting hot. "Maybe you should see something else," he said.

Shawn shot him a look. "I'll just hold on to that part of the vision for now. Then I see darkness. A return to his mansion on the cliffs overlooking the crashing seas. And in the window, this strange, evil woman, laughing maniacally as the flames rise around her and—"

"There wasn't a fire," the woman said.

"That's *Rebecca*," Gus said.

"It is?" Shawn said. "Yes, it is. That's your husband's name."

"Her husband was named Rebecca?" Gus said.

"I'm sensing that your husband's name was Laurence Olivier. No—Oliver. And you are Veronica."

"That's right," she said.

As infuriating as Shawn could be, Gus loved watching him do this—take tiny details that no one else ever noticed and use them to understand vast truths. He had no idea how Shawn had figured all this out and was looking forward to the explanation that would come once their new client was gone.

"You and Oliver had days of bliss. And then he took ill. The end was tragically fast, leaving you all alone with only his billions to keep you company. But what came next was even worse. You were accused of the crime. And while you assumed your name would be quickly cleared, the police found evidence pointing right at you."

"Yes!"

"And worst of all, no one would believe that you'd never hurt Rebecca—"

"Laurence," Gus said.

"Oliver," she said.

"Oliver. When in truth you wouldn't even mind going to jail, if only it didn't mean people would believe you capable of hurting the only man you ever loved."

"It's like you read my mind," Veronica said.

"Yes, much like that," Gus said.

"I don't read minds. I read auras," Shawn said. "And your aura is the most innocent I've ever seen."

"Can you help me?" she said.

"I guarantee it," Shawn said.

"Because I've been to every other detective in town, and no one has been able to find anything that wasn't incriminating," she said. "And my trial starts on Monday."

"Like I said, I guarantee it," Shawn said. "You don't have to pay us anything until we clear your name."

"Except for a small retainer," Gus said quickly.

"Which we'll waive in your case."

Gus felt his face getting hot again. Only this time it wasn't embarrassment.

"The other detectives—"

"Don't have a direct link to the spirit world the way I do. Although in your case, it should be a link to Heaven, so I can communicate with the other angels."

"Thank you," she said, squeezing Shawn's hand.

Gus could barely wait until the door closed behind her before he exploded.

"You guarantee it?"

"Don't we guarantee every case?"

"No!"

Shawn sat down behind his desk and picked up the newspaper. "We should start. It's a great marketing idea."

"Unless we fail and we have to give the client's money back."

"Don't be ridiculous," Shawn said. "We can't give her her money back because we didn't take any in the first place."

Shawn flipped through the pages of the paper, then tossed it to Gus. A gorgeous model in a skimpy bra and skimpier panties smiled serenely up at him. "What does this tell you?" Shawn asked.

"That she's Fit For The Cure," Gus said, reading the copy on the bra ad.

"True, although they never say the cure for what. I think it's the high price of *Maxim* magazine. But that's not what I meant." Shawn took the paper and flipped it over, then gave it back to Gus.

There was a small picture of their new client. Over it, a headline read "Model Wife or Murderess: Veronica Mason Trial Starts Monday." Gus quickly skimmed the story, which included all the details that Shawn had "psychically" intuited and many he hadn't mentioned. Oliver Mason was a pillar of the Santa Barbara community since his days as quarterback of the high school football team. He'd married the head cheerleader shortly after graduation, leaving many broken hearts behind, and begun a career in aviation that made him a billionaire. His first wife had died of cancer two years ago. Last summer he met Veronica in a restaurant where she was working as a waitress, and a month later they were married. Shortly after their honeymoon, Mason collapsed and died of an apparent heart attack. At first the death was ruled as natural causes, but an autopsy revealed a massive amount of the stimulant epinephrine in his tissues. With that discovery, the Santa Barbara police, led by Detective Carlton Lassiter, opened a murder investigation. They only had one suspect, and when they found multiple used "epi-pens"—one-shot epinephrine auto-injectors used to treat anaphylactic shock—in Veronica's medicine cabinet, she was arrested and charged with her husband's murder. The rest of the article was filled with quotes from people who had known and loved Mason.

"So she did it," Gus said.

"Buddy, why so cynical?" Shawn chided. "Why would she kill him?"

"For a billion dollars and a private island?"

"He was decades older than her. If she wanted his money, she could have waited a few days for him to kick off from natural causes like Anna Nicole Smith did. Only without the whole posing for *Playboy* and dying of an overdose part. Which is too bad—the *Playboy* part, anyway."

"She was twenty-five. He was sixty-eight. He could have lived twenty more years easily."

Shawn stopped to do the math. "Twenty-five and forty-three is ... Well, it's really gross, however long he had to live. The point is, the police arrested the first suspect they could find, and they never looked any further. She's obviously innocent."

"You just want to believe that because her blouse was unbuttoned down to her knees."

"Be that as it may, we've got to prove she's innocent. Or we're never going to get paid."

So they got to work. Gus had to admit there was an element of brilliance to Shawn's plan. With the trial going on right now, as soon as they came up with the evidence, they'd be able to burst into the courtroom and prove both her innocence and their genius on live TV. There was only one problem. In all the weeks the trial dragged on, Shawn and Gus found nothing. Not one thing that would undercut the prosecution's claim. Now both sides had presented their cases, the jury had deliberated, and the verdict was due to be announced this morning. In a matter of minutes, their client was going to be sentenced to life in prison, and Shawn and Gus were going to lose their only chance for a payday.

Gus made a hard right onto Anacapa Street and saw the fake Spanish-Moorish palace that was the Santa

Barbara courthouse. Shawn pointed at an empty space right in front of the steps.

"Park there," he said.

"It's red," Gus said, scanning the street ahead for another space. There was nothing.

"We're here for five minutes, you're not going to get a ticket."

"We're right in front of the courthouse."

"And no one's going to be stupid enough to park in a red zone where he knows there are going to be cops coming and going all day, right?" Shawn said.

"Right," Gus said.

"So why would meter maids even bother to patrol here?" Shawn threw his door open and jumped out of the car. "You coming?"

With a heavy sense of foreboding, Gus slid the Echo into the red zone, locked his door, and followed Shawn across the flagstones through the whitewashed archway and past a pair of heavy wooden doors. By the time Gus caught up with him, Shawn was standing in the vaulted hallway, frozen outside the door to courtroom number three.

"Something wrong?" Gus asked.

"Just going over the plan one last time," Shawn said. "Making sure every piece is in place. Every angle is covered. Every contingency is . . . contingencied."

"Great," Gus said. "What is the plan?"

"No idea," Shawn said, and kicked open the massive wooden doors.

Chapter Two

Every head in the courtroom swiveled to stare as Shawn marched down the aisle between benches packed with spectators. At the defense table, Veronica Mason gazed at Shawn with new hope. Under a low-cut blouse, her perfect breasts heaved as she breathed a sigh of relief.

"Man," Shawn whispered to Gus, "does she ever button all the way up?"

"I wouldn't know," Gus said. "I thought we cared about her innocence, not her cleavage."

"I can care about lots of things at the same time."

Veronica's was the only friendly face in the room. The spectators in the gallery looked like they were at a football game and Shawn had run onto the field just as the home team was about to score. Behind the bench, a graying Jerry Garcia look-alike in a black robe stared openmouthed at the interruption into his courtroom.

"I object!" Shawn shouted, striding toward the wooden gate separating the spectators from the trial's participants.

The judge pounded his gavel so hard his small gray ponytail bounced up and down and his beard trembled. "What do you mean, you object? Who are you?"

Shawn glanced at the judge. And *saw*. Saw the crystal pyramid holding down a stack of papers. The leather thong around his neck disappearing under the black robe.

"I'm Oliver Mason, and I'm here to say my wife did not kill me!"

A shocked whisper went through the crowd. In the jury box, the forewoman, a saggy matron in a black dress, went ashen, the verdict sheet trembling in her hand. Bert Coules, the Santa Barbara district attorney, jumped up from his chair.

"Your Honor!" Coules shouted. A former Army Ranger, Coules still sported the buzzed hair and buffed body of the military's most elite. When he looked at Shawn, Gus could almost see his eyes narrowing into sniper scopes.

"Veronica loved me," Shawn said. "You must not convict her!"

The judge stared at Shawn. "Young man, this is a court of law. If you're making some kind of joke, I will jail you for contempt."

"Do not blame this young man," Shawn said. "He is only a vessel for my spirit. I have taken over his body to speak through."

The gavel hung in the air as the judge studied Shawn closely. "You're a medium?"

"I used to be, but I think I've gained a few pounds," Shawn said.

Gus shoved him. Shawn shoved back.

"Your Honor, this is ridiculous," Coules said.

"It's unorthodox—I grant that," the judge said. "But many people believe that communication with the spirit world is possible."

"Idiots," Coules said. "The same brain-dead ex-hippies who believe that crystals cure cancer and—"

The judge pulled the leather thong out from under his robe, revealing the gleaming crystal hanging from it.

"—and if we're going to take this 'medium' seriously, I demand some proof that he really is channeling Oliver Mason," Coules said quickly. "Let him tell us something about his wife that only the deceased would know."

"That's fair," the judge said, tucking his crystal pendant back under his robe and turning back to Shawn. "If you are channeling Oliver Mason, you must know all sorts of secrets."

"Secrets," Shawn said. "Yes, lots of them."

"We only need one," the judge said.

"One, right," Shawn said. "You know, it's amazing what being dead does to your short-term memory. Maybe if I had a couple of minutes to think ..."

"Our client is about to be found guilty, and we're parked in a red zone," Gus whispered furiously. "Think of something now."

"We're waiting," the judge said.

"I think we've waited long enough," Coules said. "He's obviously a phony."

Shawn pressed his fingers to his forehead. "My wife has a small birthmark on her right breast, just above the nipple."

The judge glanced over at the female guard who brought Veronica to the courtroom every day. "You've seen the accused change from her prison jumpsuit into street clothes?"

"I have, Your Honor," the guard said.

"Does she have such a birthmark?"

"She does, Your Honor," the guard said.

"I'm impressed," the judge said. "Mr. Coules?"

"It's in the shape of a strawberry," Coules said, "and there's a freckle at the top that looks like the stem. I guess I'm Oliver Mason, too. And so is every man in this courtroom. Including you, Your Honor."

The judge banged his gavel. "I warn you, Counselor—"

"Come off it, Judge, I saw you looking when she was on the stand," Coules said. "You'd have to be a lot deader than Oliver Mason not to. Now will you please get this fraud out of here?"

The judge sighed as if he'd just learned at sixty that there is no Santa Claus. He banged his gavel desolately. "Bailiff, remove the medium."

The bailiff bolted up the aisle like a defensive end looking for a quick sack. He grabbed Shawn around the waist and started to haul him toward the exit.

Gus followed. "I told you to stop thinking about her cleavage."

The judge cleared his throat. "I apologize to the jury for this interruption. Have you reached a verdict?"

As he struggled to free himself from the bailiff's arm-lock, Shawn saw the jury forewoman stand up again. She raised the verdict form and began to read.

"We have, Your Honor," she said with a quaver in her voice.

Shawn looked at the forewoman and *saw*. Saw the savage pen stroke under the verdict that almost tore through the paper. Saw the ring on her finger—a class ring, Santa Barbara High School, class of 1958. Saw the Med Alert bracelet dangling off her wrist—allergic to bee stings. Saw the small smile of triumph on her face as she sneaked a glance at Veronica.

"On the charge of murder in the first degree, we find the defendant—"

"I'm sorry!" Shawn howled. "I'm so sorry I hurt you!"

The judge gaveled again. "Quiet!"

"I've been quiet too long," Shawn said. "I should have spoken up in high school—when I broke your heart."

"How long does it take to get one guy out of a court-room?" Coules said.

The bailiff yanked Shawn toward the door. Shawn grabbed on to a bench. "But it was the second time that was unforgivable. After my first wife died, I knew you thought we'd finally be together. But I married this wait-ress instead."

The forewoman gasped. The judge glared at her. "Do you know this man?"

"No," the forewoman said. But her face had gone pale.

The bailiff lifted Shawn off the ground, trying to break his grip on the bench. "And I know you didn't mean to kill me when you stuck me with the epi-pen you carry in case you're ever stung by a bee. Just like the one you undoubtedly have in your purse right now."

"Bailiff, release that man," the judge said.

The bailiff let go of Shawn, who crashed to the floor.

"You wanted to provoke a minor heart attack so you could save my life and prove that we were meant to be together. But when I died, you knew who was really responsible—it was Veronica, who had weakened my heart with her intense sexuality. Every time I saw her cleavage, it took another year off my life."

"Enough with the cleavage," Gus whispered.

"Bailiff, I'd like to see the forewoman's purse," the judge said.

The bailiff walked over to the jury box and held out his hand. The forewoman reluctantly gave him her large leather bag.

"And since you knew that Veronica was ultimately to blame for my death, you planted several of your epi-pens in her belongings so that justice would be done," Shawn said. "When you were put on this jury, it was like justice itself was congratulating you for a job well-done. When in fact it was probably just a close friend some-where in the court system."

A wiry woman in a floral-print dress jumped up from her seat in the back of the galley so fast she nearly knocked over the bench full of spectators. She leveled a shaking forefinger at the forewoman.

"You lied to me!" the woman said. "You told me you just wanted to get on the jury to get a book deal!" Fighting off tears, she ran out of the courtroom. At a signal from one of the prosecutors, a guard went after her.

The judge dug through the forewoman's purse and came up with a small black cylinder, roughly the size and shape of a ballpoint pen. He held it out to Coules.

"Does this look like the murder weapon to you, Mr. Coules?" he said.

Coules took the epi-pen and stared at it.

A tear ran down the forewoman's face. "I always loved you, Oliver. And you said you loved me. That night under the bleachers—that's why I . . . I know you meant it. Wait for me—I'll join you in the spirit world and we can have eternity together."

"Bailiff, take this woman into custody," the judge said. Then he turned back to Coules. "I assume you won't mind dropping the charges against Mrs. Mason."

"No, Your Honor," the prosecutor said.

The crowd burst into cheers. Veronica leapt up from her seat and hugged her defense attorney. "Thank you," she said.

"You're welcome . . . I guess," he said, trying to figure out what had just happened.

Shawn gave a quick shudder as if he'd just woken up from a deep sleep. "Where am I?" he said. "What am I doing here? Why am I lying on the floor?"

Gus helped him back to his feet. "Good plan. Well contingencied," he whispered as they headed toward the door, fighting their way through a throng of people begging to know who Shawn was. Gus made sure each one of them got a Psych business card.

They finally got into the hallway, where another mob surrounded Veronica Mason. Now that the fear of prison was gone from her face, she was more beautiful than ever. As the crowd swept them past her, Veronica leaned over and whispered in Shawn's ear.

"Call me," she said. "I've got a birthmark even Oliver didn't know about."

And then the crowd swept her down the hallway from them. Shawn watched her go, then turned to Gus with a satisfied smile.

"I think we've made a new friend," Shawn said.

"I think you've made a new enemy."

They turned to see Bert Coules, the DA, looming over them. His fists were clenched, and a vein in his temple throbbed.

"Hey, Bert," Shawn said. "Good work in there. Think how well it would have gone if you'd tried the right person."

"She was the right person," Coules said. "You just let a murderer walk free."

"The forewoman confessed," Gus said. "You heard her."

"I heard a pathetic, lovelorn spinster desperately falling for a con dreamed up by a cheap fake," Coules said.

"I am not cheap," Shawn said. "I'm reasonable. Maybe you should try my services next time."

Coules' eyeballs looked like they were going to explode out of his head. "No, Mr. Spencer, you are going to try mine," he said. "Unless you are the most law-abiding person in Santa Barbara County. Because if I discover you've committed the tiniest infraction of the smallest regulation, the entire office of the district attorney is going to find a way to make you serve the sentence Veronica Mason should be serving."

Chapter Three

"**G**us, this is just one of those things that no one could have anticipated."

Shawn and Gus trudged along the endless stretch of chain link, heat radiating up from the melting asphalt and burning through the thin leather soles of Gus' best dress Oxfords.

"No one except a psychic," Gus said, staring through the metal links at the acres of cars. "Too bad neither of us knows one."

"Gus, Gus, Gus," Shawn said, "that would have been a truly cutting comment if I actually believed I had psychic abilities. But since we both know I don't, you've got to dig a little deeper."

"Thanks for the advice," Gus said. "Almost as useful as the last bit you gave me."

"I know you loved that fanny pack, but its day was over."

"I mean about the street signs," Gus said. "Specifically about the signs that said, 'No parking—violators will be towed.' Specifically that we should ignore the signs because meter maids would never patrol outside the courthouse."

The day had been going so well. After Shawn's triumph in the courtroom, they were mobbed by journalists. They spent two hours giving interviews that would lead to tons of free publicity. One of the reporters even asked who Gus was.

But when they finally got outside the courthouse, everything started going downhill. First was the shock of finding an empty curb where Gus' Echo used to be. And then the greater shock of realizing that the curb wasn't completely empty. Detective Carlton Lassiter was standing there, a grim look on his face.

That wasn't the real problem. Detective Carlton Lassiter almost always had a grim look on his face. He was the lead detective of the Santa Barbara Police Department, and he took his job every bit as seriously as he took himself. Shawn's easy attitude toward crime fighting had the same effect on him as a roll in a field of poison oak.

The real problem was that Bert Coules was coming up to Lassiter, and his look was anything but grim.

"Look, Gus, your car finally got its wish," Shawn said. "It's been turned into a real boy."

"Close," Coules said. "Not the boy part, of course. But the turning into what it's always wanted to be. In this case, a heap of scrap metal."

"You can't," Gus said. "My car didn't do anything wrong."

"It didn't?" Coules said. "I thought it solved the Oliver Mason murder case and then withheld the identity of the real killer until it could be used to embarrass the entire Santa Barbara DA's office."

"My car would never do that," Gus said.

"Be that as it may," Lassiter said, "it was parked in a tow-away zone. You left us no choice but to tow it away."

"Oh, there were other choices," Coules said. "Personally I favor arresting you both for reckless endangerment. If there was a fire in this courthouse, that car could have been blocking the exits."

"But it wasn't!"

"I'd be willing to let a jury make that decision," Coules said.

Lassiter stepped between them and handed Gus a ticket. "The police felt it was sufficient to write you up for a violation. You can collect your car once you've paid the ticket and the towing fee."

"Better do it fast, though," Coules said. "Hate to see them crush it for scrap by mistake."

"Shawn, do something!"

"If we can't get to a crime scene, how are we going to solve your cases for you, Bert?" Shawn said.

"I meant do something useful," Gus whispered furiously. "Like apologize."

"Oh, that," Shawn said. "Sorry, Bert. I assumed you were capable of prosecuting the right person. I won't make the same mistake next time."

Gus groaned. "Please, if you have to punish someone, punish Shawn. The Echo didn't do anything."

"Tell it to the boys at the impound lot," Coules said. "But you'd better start walking if you want to make it before they close. It's about eight miles from here."

"Walking?"

"You don't have a car. And I wouldn't even think about trying to hitch your way over there." Coules gave Lassiter a significant look.

Lassiter sighed apologetically. "California Vehicle Code section 21949-21971, article 21957 specifically forbids soliciting a ride from the driver of any vehicle. And while I probably shouldn't give away department secrets, I believe that all patrol cars have been ordered to step up enforcement of that particular provision today."

And with one last wave, Coules stepped off the empty curb and headed across the street to the police station. Lassiter stood in the street, uncomfortably trying to decide if he had anything to say. Finally he decided against speech and followed Coules. Gus sank down to the curb.

"You're not going to let him get you down?" Shawn said.

"I'm not letting him do anything," Gus said. "He did it all without my permission."

"He's hazing us," Shawn said. "It's a sign of respect. Welcome to the brotherhood of crime solvers."

"I hope one of the other brothers has a car, because we don't have a way to get home."

"What kind of attitude is that?" Shawn said. "It's a beautiful day. We're young, healthy, and strong. And Santa Barbara has been repeatedly voted best pedestrian city in the USA."

Gus stared up at him. "Are you saying we should walk to the impound lot?"

"Of course not."

"Good."

"There's no point in us both going. So I'll wait in the coffee place on Anacapa. You know, the one with the waitress you think likes you but who really has a thing for me."

"My car was towed because of you. You're going with me to get it back."

"Okay, okay. But we're not going to walk. I'll call my father and ask for a ride."

Gus sighed, then got wearily to his feet and started walking down the street.

Shawn called after him, "Where are you going?"

"To get your phone. It's in my glove compartment."

Those were the last words Gus said to Shawn for eight long miles. Eight long *vertical* miles up a narrow, twisting road. Because the impound lot lay at the top of a high hill looking out over all of Santa Barbara and the bay.

On a cooler day, Gus might have wondered who would have been crazy enough to build a wrecking yard on a lot that could be developed into multimillion-dollar-view homes. But the heat of the sun made it clear why that had never happened. The canyon directly below the yard was Santa Barbara's most active landfill, and the stench of rotting garbage made breathing almost impossible.

Now they were finally at the impound yard, and Shawn was still trying to get Gus to respond.

"So you really think this is my fault?" Shawn said. "You're going to blame me?"

Gus grabbed the fence and pressed his face against the links. Autos stretched out across acres. In the middle of the lot, like the god the cars all worshipped, a yellow crane towered over the car crusher.

Gus searched the lot for a sign of blue.

"No," Gus said. "I'm going to blame myself. You've been taking advantage of me since we were kids. It's my fault for letting you."

"Well, as long as you're not blaming me," Shawn said.

In the far distance, Gus saw a glint of blue metal. The roof of his Echo seemed to be calling to him for help.

"There it is," Gus said. "It looks so lonely."

"It's got all those other cars to play with," Shawn said. "It's probably having a great time—won't ever want to come home."

Gus thrust his finger at Shawn's face. "We're getting the Echo now." Without waiting to see if Shawn was following, he turned and marched down the fence toward the impound lot's entrance.

A small tin building stood at the far end of the fence. A sign on the door designated it as the office, which was helpful since otherwise it might be mistaken for the punishment box at an Alabama prison camp. Gus pushed open the door and was met by a searing blast of hot air.

"Close that damn door," a voice growled from inside. "You're letting the air-conditioning out."

Gus slipped into the shack, Shawn following him before the door could slam shut. As soon as the door closed, the temperature inside seemed to double.

"Now I know what one of those chickens feels like inside the rotisserie," Shawn said. "I think I'll wait outside."

Gus didn't answer, but the laser beams shooting out of his eyes welded the door shut. Or at least, that was the effect his glare had on Shawn.

"Or I'll stay here and enjoy the steam," Shawn said, looking around for a place to sit. Two drooping Formica chairs leaned against one corrugated wall, their molded plastic forms melting out of shape; a low table between them held a copy of *Popular Mechanics* jauntily promising that mankind would finally walk on the moon within no more than ten years. Across from this luxurious waiting area, its proprietor leaned on a sagging counter covered with dust-crusted plastic signs. At least Gus assumed this was the proprietor—it could have been a ton of potatoes sewn into a filthy jumpsuit.

As Gus and Shawn approached the counter, the potatoes stood up, leaving a man-sized grease mark on the scarred surface. Long hair drizzled from his scalp, tangling into a longer beard.

"Bathrooms are for employees only," he growled, then settled his bulk down on the counter. "No exceptions."

"I promise I won't ask," Gus said, trying desperately not to imagine what the employee restroom might look like. "I'm looking for car. It's a blue Echo."

"License plate?"

Gus pulled out his wallet and slid his vehicle registration across what little part of the counter wasn't taken up by the attendant's forearms. Heaving a sigh deep enough to rearrange most of the smaller spuds in his jumpsuit, the attendant leaned down and pulled a laptop computer out of a drawer, then typed Gus' information on the keyboard.

"That will be six thousand dollars," the attendant said.

"Six thousand dollars!" Gus heard the shriek coming out of his mouth before he could close it. "That's not possible."

"For that much money, you should just get a new one," Shawn said.

"That's a *company car*, Shawn. Do you have any idea what that means?"

"That you don't even own it, so we shouldn't care if it gets crushed?"

"Not exactly," Gus said. "It means I've been entrusted with the responsibility to take care of a valuable piece of equipment owned by Central Coast Pharmaceuticals for use on my sales route. And that it's my sworn obligation to return it to them in exactly the shape I received it, aside from routine wear and tear." He turned back to the potatoes. "There must be some kind of mistake."

"Yeah, and you made it eighty-seven times," the potatoes said. "Parked in front of a hydrant at the corner of Anacapa and Cruzon."

Gus pulled the laptop across the counter and stared at the screen.

"That's where that coffee place is," he said. "But I never park on the street when I go there. Why would I when there's a huge lot right down the street?"

"Because you hate cold coffee," Shawn said. "And when you've got to drive it all the way back to the office, every second of cooling counts."

Gus turned to him, realization, then rage, boiling up inside him. "You did this!"

"Only because I care about your health," Shawn said. "Once a cup of coffee drops below a hundred fifty degrees, all sorts of bacteria start growing in there. I couldn't take a chance on giving you food poisoning."

Gus pointed at the screen. "You parked there an average of twenty-seven minutes each time."

"Do you think I just pulled that hundred-fifty-degree number out of the air? I was consulting with top coffee professionals."

"You were flirting with the waitress!"

"Yes, but . . ." Shawn stopped. "You know, I've got no way of justifying that one."

Gus turned back to the potatoes, his voice trembling. "I need my car. Please."

"Six thousand dollars. Cash only."

Gus glanced hopefully into the wallet in case multiple thousands of dollars had spontaneously appeared there. Inside he found the crumpled two-dollar bill he hadn't been able to spend, since most cashiers had never seen one before and refused to accept it as real money, and a certificate that would have gotten him a free Frogurt Plus with only four more purchases if the store hadn't gone out of business a year ago.

Gus turned to Shawn. "Do something!"

"Like what?"

"Like something you'd do if it was your car!"

"I really don't think this is the right time to upgrade the sound system."

"Shawn!"

Shawn gave Gus a reassuring pat on the shoulder, then stepped in front of him. He looked at the potato-shaped man behind the counter—and he *saw*. Saw the way he pinched the burning ash out of his cigarette before dropping the butt into the ashtray. Saw the calluses on his hand, permanently blackened by dirt. Saw the fading red scar around his wrist.

Shawn doubled over, clutching his forehead. Then straightened like a marionette wielded by a stroke victim. "I'm hearing something," he moaned. "It's a voice from beyond . . . and it's singing to me." As if controlled by a force from above, Shawn's right arm drifted up, and his hand unfurled, leveling an accusing finger at the man behind the counter. "Singing to you."

"I don't want anyone singing to—"

" 'Gonna use my arms, gonna use my legs, gonna use my fingers, gonna use my toes,' " he moaned. " 'Gonna use my, my imagination.' "

"You're gonna use your feet to get the hell out of my office, you know what's good for you," the potatoes said.

"Wait a minute," Shawn said. "That's the wrong song. They're sending me a new one."

"Maybe they could just send the six thousand dollars instead," Gus said.

Shawn arms flailed around his head. " 'Such a drag to want something sometimes. One thing leads to another I know.' "

"What the hell is that?" the potatoes growled.

"Sounds like the Pretenders' greatest hits," Gus said.

Shawn jerked again. "That's still the wrong song. They're trying to tell me something, but they can't find the right melody."

"Maybe they should look at the back of the CD box," Gus said.

"Yeah, like the Forces Beyond don't have an iPod," Shawn said, then reared back, as if hit by a psychic sound wave. "I hear it. . . . They're singing to me. Listen."

Intrigued against his will, the potatoes leaned across the counter. "I don't hear anything."

Shawn sang unsurely, as if a voice beyond was dictating to him. " 'I found a picture of you, oh oh oh oh. What hijacked my world that night. To a place in the world we've been cast out of.' " He broke off and turned to Gus. "Little help here."

"What?"

"I need backup!"

"And I need my car."

"Just sing, damn it."

"Fine. 'Oh oh oh oh oh.' "

" 'Now we're back in the fight. We're back on the train,' " Shawn sang. Then he froze. He turned to the potatoes. " 'We're back on the chain gang.' "

The man behind the counter stared at him angrily. "Concert's over, punk. Get out of here."

"The song doesn't lie," Shawn said. "You were on a chain gang. Which means you were convicted of a class-A felony in Arizona, the only state with an active chain gang program."

Gus didn't stop to wonder how Shawn had figured it out. He stepped up to the counter. "And now you're working for a city-approved garage, which means you must have given them a fake name to pass the background check."

"As the official psychic to the Santa Barbara Police Department, I have an obligation to turn you in," Shawn said. "But you've been so kind to us, I hate to see you fired, maybe jailed for perjury. If only I'd never come here today, I never would have found out."

"The only reason we came here is to get my car," Gus said. "If we had it back, it'd be like we were never here at all."

"It's a big yard, must be thousands of cars here," Shawn said. "No one's going to notice if one blue Echo is missing."

The potatoes thought that over. "It is a big yard, and there are thousands of cars here," he agreed. "No one's going to notice if one blue Echo has a couple of bodies in the trunk."

"Good, then we're—" Gus said, then broke off. "Bodies?"

The potatoes moved so fast they barely realized he was reaching under the counter before the barrel of the shotgun was leveled at them.

"Got a song for this, pretty boy?" the potatoes said.

Shawn and Gus dived below the counter as flame erupted from the shotgun and a rain of pellets tore holes in the corrugated wall.

"Okay, this is not how I planned things," Shawn said.

"I'm certainly glad to hear that."

"All he had to do was give you back your car," Shawn said. "It wasn't like it was his car. Hell, it isn't even like it's your car, technically."

"It's still my responsibility!"

"Exactly. Your responsibility, not his. So why is he trying to kill us? Because there's something going on here. Something he's willing to kill to cover up."

Shawn was right—they had stumbled onto some major criminal enterprise. That was the only explanation for the potatoes' behavior. As a detective, Gus knew he should care about this. He should be working through the clues, piecing together the puzzle, unmasking the mystery.

"I don't hear any singing!" the potatoes said, slapping two more shells into the gun.

On the other hand, what good would solving one more mystery do for Gus if he was dead? "So let him cover it up. We'll pretend we don't know anything about his massive criminal conspiracy if he lets us live."

"Think he'll buy it?"

"He wouldn't have to buy it if you hadn't parked in front of a fire hydrant eighty-seven times," Gus said. "I can't believe I'm going to die because you wanted to flirt with a waitress."

"Ironic, isn't it?" Shawn said.

"It's not ironic at all," Gus said.

"Dude, it's so like a black fly in your chardonnay."

"How many times do I have to tell you that's not ironic, either?"

"Rain on your wedding day?"

" 'Irony' is the use of words to convey a meaning that's opposite to their literal meaning," Gus said. "That stupid song came out fourteen years ago, and we still have this exact conversation at least once a week."

"Yeah," Shawn said. "Ironic, isn't it?"

Gus threw his hands up in despair—and felt hot metal just above his head. A quick glance confirmed his fear. The shotgun's barrel was pointing down at them. All the way at the other end of the gun, the potatoes gave them a cheery smile.

"I didn't realize how much I missed having music in this place," he said. "After I kill you, I'm going to buy a radio."

Gus grabbed the gun barrel and pulled. He nearly screamed in pain as the blazing metal burned his hands, but he wouldn't let go.

"Run, Shawn," he said. "One of us has to keep on living."

Shawn didn't move. "I can't leave you here to die. Not when it's at least a small part my fault that you're here in the first place."

"A small part!"

"Okay, since you're giving up your life to save me, I'll let you have this one—it's all my fault. Shake on it?" Shawn extended an open hand to Gus.

"My hands are a little busy here," Gus said. Above them, the potatoes was yanking on the gun's barrel, trying to get it away from him.

"I'm not leaving until we shake hands," Shawn said.

"Then you're crazy."

"Let go of my gun," the potatoes grunted, giving the stock a yank that nearly pulled Gus off his feet.

"Absolutely," Shawn said. "Let's shake on it."

Gus stared at Shawn's outstretched hand, baffled. The potatoes yanked at the gun again, and suddenly Gus understood. "Oh, *shake* on it."

"If you don't let go of my gun, I'm going to come around and beat it out of you," the potatoes shouted, then gave the stock another hard pull. Just then, Gus clasped Shawn's hand and gave it a hearty shake. Of course, to do that, he had to let go of the barrel first. The gun flew upward, blasting hundreds of tiny holes in the tin roof as the potatoes toppled over backward.

"Now run!" Shawn shouted. Gus hadn't waited for him to explain the rest of the cunning plan. He was halfway to the door before Shawn was on his feet. Somewhere behind him he knew the potatoes was pulling himself up on his spud feet and reloading the shotgun. Gus could feel the muscles in his back rearranging themselves into the concentric circles of a practice target, and he needed to put the bull's-eye out of range.

In college, Gus had tried out for the track team to impress a girl his roommate had described as "fast." With the sure, if completely mistaken, knowledge of a date with the most beautiful woman in the northwest quadrant of campus as his reward, Gus ran faster that day than he ever had before, missing the qualifying time for the four hundred meter by less than a minute.

If only he'd had a shotgun pointed at his back in college, Gus might have had a chance to learn just how little interest the "fast" girl actually had in runners. Because Gus was blasting through that qualifying pace. He could feel the hot asphalt slamming into his feet through the thin leather soles of his English dress shoes as if he were barefoot, and he didn't care. His calves were coiled springs, propelling him violently forward with every step.

In the distance behind him, Gus could hear someone calling his name. If he'd stopped to think about it, he would have known it was Shawn, probably begging him to slow down a little to let him catch up. But he wasn't going to stop for anyone, not even his best friend.

It wasn't fear driving Gus anymore. Not completely, anyway. It was the exhilaration of the run—the sense of speed, of freedom, of life itself. He felt that if he could increase his pace just a fraction, he could achieve escape velocity, actually lift off the earth and into orbit. He'd be flying.

"Gus, stop!" Shawn was shouting somewhere in the far distance. Gus ignored him. Couldn't Shawn see he was about to fly?

"Gus, car!"

When Shawn shouted, Gus was at least thirty feet in front of him. Since sound travels at seven hundred seventy miles per hour, it took his voice at least one-thirty-fifth of a second to reach Gus. Maybe a fraction more, since he was accelerating away from Shawn, and there was the Doppler effect to consider. Even after Gus heard Shawn's voice, it would have taken at least another .028 of a second for the meaning of the word to penetrate his brain. Even if he could have shaved a couple of milliseconds off, there was no way Gus could have altered his direction in the time necessary. He was in midstride, both feet off the ground. The best he could do was twist his trunk around so he could see down the length of road he was crossing.

So he could see the bright red Mercedes S500 slaloming down the street as its driver pounded the brakes. So he could smell each particle of rubber scraped off the smoking tires as they left sharp black skid marks on the faded asphalt. So he could appreciate the glint of sunlight off the shiny Mercedes logo heading straight for him.

For one second, Gus knew exactly what he needed to do. If he could somehow keep himself in the air, postpone his descent for just one fraction of a second, he could clear the car's hood and land on its opposite side with catlike grace.

Gus squeezed his eyes shut and willed all his strength into his ankles. If they didn't sprout small wings to keep him aloft like the Sub-Mariner's, it wouldn't be for lack of trying.

A second passed, and Gus realized he hadn't been smashed against the windshield like a bug. He opened his eyes and saw the car screeching to a stop behind him. He did it. He flew. He looked down at his ankles to see if the wings had sprouted there.

There were of course no wings. But that wasn't the problem. He'd lived this long without feathered ankles. The real problem was the other thing he didn't see down there.

The road.

Or any solid ground.

All he saw was the battered gray metal of the guard rail disappearing under his feet. And then the long, long drop to the garbage dump below.

Chapter Four

The asphalt was surprisingly soft under Gus' back. When he was running, he could feel every pebble and shard of glass piercing the soles of his shoes. But now that he was sprawled out over the pavement, it felt soft, smooth, and pliable. Gus stretched out a hand and probed the ground with his fingers. The asphalt compressed under his touch as if it were stuffed with down.

Gus tried to understand what was happening. There was a faint possibility that he had developed super-strength to go along with his newfound ability to fly. But the aches in his muscles, the pounding in his head, and the screaming pain from his rib cage were suggesting strongly that he was not about to be sworn into the Legion of Superheroes. Which made it far more likely that what he was feeling under him was actually not the road where he'd fallen. He probed the surface again, and this time recognized the slip of sheet over mattress.

He was in a bed. But how did he get here? He might convince himself that he'd dreamed the whole thing, Veronica Mason's trial included, if there was an inch of his body that didn't hurt.

Using all the strength he could muster, Gus forced his eyelids open. A giant head filled his vision, sandy brows nearly brushing his own eyeballs. Gus let out a scream.

The giant head screamed, too, and moved away quickly. Gus' eyes fought to focus.

"Dude, you're awake," Shawn said.

Gus squinted against the light and was able to make out Shawn's beaming face over his.

"I was just checking to see if you were still breathing," Shawn said.

"What happened?"

"You were," Shawn said.

"Before that," Gus said. "How did I get here?"

"Someone tried to kill us."

Gus tried to recapture his last, fleeting memory. A red Mercedes flitted across his consciousness before his subconscious hauled it back with the other moments too painful to remember.

"With a car."

"With a shotgun."

There was something about a gun tickling the edges of Gus' brain. For some reason, he envisioned what could only have been the mascot for the University of Idaho's skeet-shooting team; a giant smiling potato holding a shotgun. And then it all came flooding back. The Echo. The shack. The attendant.

"He tried to kill us!"

Gus fought the screaming pain in his shoulders and moved his arms across his body, checking for spatter pattern. There didn't seem to be any.

"Don't worry, buddy," Shawn said. "Nothing but soft-tissue damage. At least that's what a fleet of doctors tells me."

"Doctors?"

For the first time, it occurred to Gus to wonder exactly where he was. He managed to shift his eyes away
from Shawn's face, even his ocular muscles aching with
the strain, to see the dull fluorescent tube throbbing on
the ceiling, the small TV bolted to the wall, the cheery
sailboat painting hanging over the institutional sink.
He flexed his fingers over his chest and noticed that his
starched button-down business shirt had been replaced
with a flimsy sheath of slick, flameproof polyester.

"I'm in the hospital?"

Shawn patted him proudly on the shoulder. It felt like
a sledgehammer on Gus' bruises. "And they were worried about potential brain damage. I knew your brain
was too strong for that."

"Who was worried?"

"And I was right. They all agreed that everything was
going to be just fine. As long as you woke up before—"
Shawn checked his watch. "Hey, right under the wire.
Good timing, buddy."

"What if I didn't wake up now?"

Before Shawn could answer, Gus heard the sound of
a door opening across the room.

"Shawn?" It was a woman's voice. Gus risked dis-
lodging several vertebrae and twisted his neck so he
could see the door. A pair of blazing red shoes, the toes
more sharply pointed than the four-inch spike heels, appeared in the threshold. Gus could hear the heels digging divots out of the linoleum with every step. Forcing
his head higher, Gus could make out a long stretch of
tanned, muscular legs. He put his hand under his chin
and forced his head up farther. The bare legs seemed
to go on forever. Finally, far above the point where any
normal piece of clothing would have ended, Gus saw a
flash of hem. Blazing red hem.

The legs turned and moved assuredly toward the
couch.

"I got the paper," a female voice said. At least, those were the words she used. The voice itself seemed to be promising something much more enticing than the *Santa Barbara Times*.

"Thanks," Shawn said, then turned back to Gus. "You and Tara haven't been formally introduced. Although you have kind of met already. Well, you might have seen her as you sailed over her windshield."

Shawn moved out of the way, and Gus' entire field of vision was filled with the image of Tara's upper thighs. He struggled to pull himself to a shaky sit so he could finally see what she looked like. And immediately wished he'd closed his eyes and slipped back into his coma.

The woman was almost as tall as Shawn, at least in those absurdly high heels. Her long hair was as black as crows' feathers; her ice blue eyes burned out from lashes that were even blacker. Her lip gloss flashed the same fierce red as her minidress, although the gloss seemed to cover a few more square inches of skin. Tara's lips parted in a smile, and Gus felt a mixture of terror and attraction he hadn't experienced since Natasha Henstridge used her tongue to turn a suitor's brain into shish-kebab in *Species*.

"I'm so happy you're awake," she said in a voice that seemed to promise joys and punishments Gus had only imagined when he was absolutely certain no one could ever read his thoughts. "We were so worried. When you went over the edge like that, I thought my heart was going to stop."

"Thanks," Gus said, then grabbed the only part of Shawn he could reach, the tail of his shirt. "Could I speak to you alone for just one moment?"

"We are alone," Shawn said. "Well, alone with Tara, which is better than being alone alone."

"Shawn!"

Shawn gave him a disappointed sigh, then turned regretfully to the woman in red. "Not quite himself. Needs a moment to put on his face."

"I certainly understand," Tara said. "I'll be in the waiting room, reading about how amazing you are."

Gus watched the legs amble out the door, then hissed at Shawn, "Do you know who that is?"

"She just told you," Shawn said. "Her name is Tara Larison and—"

"Did she mention she's also the devil's daughter?"

"We haven't really talked much about her family. She did say she has a cousin in medical school. That's why she could be so sure you were alive after we found you."

"Shawn, she looks just like Satana," Gus said.

"Isn't that a kind of raisin?"

"That's a 'sultana.' Satana is the daughter of Satan, raised in Hell and banished to earth to live as a succubus."

"When did you start going to church?"

"Every Sunday when I was little," Gus said. "My parents insisted I pray for forgiveness for all the things you talked me into doing. But this isn't from the Bible. It's from *Vampire Tales* number two."

"That would be one of your lesser-known holy books."

"The whole story didn't come out until *Marvel Preview* number seven."

Shawn stared at him. "You're saying she's a character from a comic book."

"Not just one. She was all over the Marvel Universe."

"Gus, I know you hit your head, but you should be able to tell a few things about Tara. Like for instance she isn't printed on cheap paper. When she talks, her words don't appear in balloons over her head. And after long and hard study, I can guarantee she exists in at least three dimensions."

"I know she's not an actual comic book character,"

Gus said. "I am awake enough to realize that. But if someone chooses to look just like the incarnation of all evil in the world, shouldn't that send some kind of message?"

Shawn sat on the bed next to Gus, sending a shock wave through the mattress that made all of Gus' muscles scream in pain. He started to pat his friend on the shoulder, but Gus' obvious flinch made him reconsider.

"Maybe," Shawn said. "But so should this. When you went over that cliff, she nearly went with you, she was trying so hard to catch you. She's the one who guided the ambulance to where you'd fallen. She dug through garbage to make sure you were comfortable until they came. And she never stopped fighting for you. She insisted on staying here until you were awake. She badgered the doctors and nurses into giving you the kind of treatment they usually only give to people they actually care about. If you'd needed that surgery, I think she would have scrubbed up and joined in the operation."

"What surgery?" Gus said.

"Nothing you have to worry about now," Shawn said. "And that's in large measure because Tara fought so hard for you."

Gus felt the familiar pang of guilt he experienced every time he caught himself judging another human being on physical appearances. And then he felt the equally familiar pang of irritation at feeling guilty about making that kind of judgment. Ever since his mother had caught him making fun of Bobby Fleckstein's new glasses in second grade and made him sit in the corner for ninety minutes, Gus had felt guilty every time he made a snap judgment about another person. And since his careers as a pharmaceuticals rep and a detective both depended on his ability to size up a new contact immediately, Gus spent a lot of his time feeling guilty. And irritated.

"Okay," Gus said. "I guess she isn't really here to regain her powers so she can return to Hell and battle her father for the kingdom."

"Glad we got that out of the way," Shawn said. "You can come back in now, Tara."

Even after his gracious concession, Gus half expected her to materialize before them in a puff of sulfur. Instead she clacked her way in, spike heels turning the floor into a cribbage board behind her.

"I didn't realize how amazing you were," Tara said, waving the newspaper.

"Not many people do," Shawn said. "But I'll be happy to make sure that you are one of the select few."

"I mean what you did at that trial," Tara said. "You told me you were there to give justice a helping hand. But this is much more than that."

"I start out trying to lend an appendage, but once I'm involved, my whole body gets into it," Shawn said. "If you'd like a further demonstration of the principle, I'm sure it can be arranged."

Gus tried to focus enough to read the headline on the newspaper. No matter how many times he squeezed his eyes shut, every time he opened them he saw the same words: "Veronica Mason Innocent." Of course that would be the lead-in story in any afternoon paper. But Santa Barbara didn't have an afternoon paper.

Gus snatched the newspaper out of Tara's hand and felt lightning bolts of pain shoot up him arm. He squinted through the tears of pain clouding his eyes and tried to make out the date above the headlines. "Shawn, this is tomorrow's paper."

Tara let out an excited gasp. "You get newspapers from the future?"

"Ever since a man named Lucius Snow saved my life as a child," Shawn said. "He gave me the gift . . . and the great responsibility that comes with it."

"That's amazing," Tara said.

"That's not you," Gus said. "It's Kyle Chandler in *Early Edition*."

"Next you're going to tell me I don't coach high school football in small-town Texas, either," Shawn said. "That poor Jason Street. What's he going to do with his life now that he's in a wheelchair?"

"Shawn! This newspaper is from Wednesday. The trial was on Tuesday."

"And on Thursday, it's dollar day at BurgerZone."

"What I'm trying to say, Shawn, is how long was I unconscious?"

"Not that long," Shawn said.

"How long?"

"Remember *Titanic*?"

"Sure."

"About that long."

"That was only four hours," Gus said. "She hit me before lunch."

"Sorry," Shawn said. "How long it *felt*."

"Oh, my God."

Tara kneeled down next to the couch and took Gus' free hand. "It was a long, long night, and a longer morning," she said. "But Shawn was with you every minute of that time."

"And now we're going to get the guy who did this to you," Shawn said.

"The impound attendant?"

"Exactly. He's hiding something, and he thought he could scare us away by waving his shotgun at us."

"Actually, I think he thought he could scare us away by killing us," Gus said.

"Either way, he was wrong. And we're going to take him down."

"Did the police find out anything?"

"The police?" Shawn said. "What do they have to do with anything?"

"Didn't you call them to say he'd tried to kill us?"

"So they could bungle the case the way they did with Veronica Mason's?" Shawn asked. "This guy is ours, and we're going to make sure he pays for what he did. We're going to spend every minute of every day uncovering his criminal conspiracy. We're never going to stop until— Hey!" Shawn shoved the newspaper at Gus, pointing at a small boxed headline in the bottom right corner. "Look at that."

Gus focused on a small headline that read "Local Businessman to Invest in Area, details page six."

"Way to focus, Captain Attention Span," Gus said.

"Just look," Shawn said.

Gus managed to stretch his arms far enough apart to open the paper to the correct page. At least it was the page indicated by the tease. All Gus saw was a large ad promising that the junior partner in a major mattress company would commit suicide if he were forced to sell his stock at the insanely low prices his senior colleague had promised.

" 'You're killing me, Larry?' " Gus read.

"Oh, we're killing him all right—but Larry's got nothing to do with it." Shawn pointed to a small article running directly under the mattress chain's generous delivery policy.

" 'A venture capitalist has pledged to invest several billion dollars in the Santa Barbara economy, helping local companies compete on a national playing field,' " Gus read.

"Keep reading."

" 'Santa Barbara native Dallas Steele, who spent the last ten years as the managing partner of a New York investment bank—' " Gus stopped. "Dallas Steele? From high school?"

"Check the photo," Shawn said.

Gus peered down at the tiny article. There was nothing but type. "There is no photo."

"Exactly!"

Lost, Gus dropped the paper and stared at Shawn's beaming face. Tara beamed beside him. "I don't get it," he said.

"No, he didn't get it and we did," Shawn said. "That jerk Dallas Steele comes swaggering back into town—"

"I don't remember him being a jerk."

"That's the brain damage talking," Shawn said.

"You said there was no brain da—"

"He was the biggest phony at Santa Barbara High," Shawn said. "With his perfect hair and perfect GPA and perfect football season and perfect girlfriend."

Tara looked confused. "He doesn't sound phony to me. He sounds like the real thing."

"That's the worst kind of phony. The genuine kind."

"You're right," Tara said. "No wonder you hated him."

"He was always nice to me," Gus said. "I mean, when you tried to rent me to the football team as a tackling dummy, he talked me out of it."

"Depriving you of badly needed income, to say nothing of extra PE credit," Shawn said. "And all so he could say he'd helped out some geeky loser."

"He never called me a loser."

"Everyone called you a loser, Gus," Shawn said. "It was the parachute pants. Anyway, there's only one loser now, and that's international phony Dallas Steele."

"It says here he's a multibillionaire."

"And he's still not happy," Shawn said. "He's got to come back to Santa Barbara and lord it over us all. And that might have worked, if it wasn't for us meddling kids. We knocked him right off the front page. He's probably sitting in some palatial estate right now, leafing forlornly through today's paper, wondering exactly how his high school nemeses Shawn Spenser and Burton Guster bested him."

Shawn held up his hand for a high five. Gus tried to reach up for it, but his arm wouldn't rise above his rib cage. He didn't really understand why he was supposed to be fiving, anyway. Dallas Steele was a billionaire investor, and Gus had spent the last day in a near-vegetative state because he couldn't scrape up the cash to ransom his company car.

"And just think how he'll feel when he reads that we've crushed a criminal conspiracy that reaches into the highest levels of Santa Barbara society," Shawn said triumphantly. "We may even take out some of his neighbors."

Gus wasn't sure that people in Steele's economic bracket actually had neighbors, except in the way astronomers discuss neighboring galaxies. But that didn't seem as important as the other question banging against his skull. "What conspiracy is that?"

"The phony impound man," Shawn said. "We know he's a criminal. We know he's hiding something."

"That doesn't mean there's a conspiracy reaching into the highest levels of Santa Barbara society," Gus said. "Maybe he's a loner. Or maybe his partners are even lower down than he is."

"You can't have the ultimate bad guy being some poor schmuck," Shawn said. "Your really good villains are the wealthy elite."

"You were watching another *Law and Order* marathon when I was unconscious, weren't you?"

"That has nothing to do with it," Shawn said. "You want your hero to go up against the entrenched power structure, a lone knight in dented armor tilting at the windmills of wealth and influence in what's supposed to be a class-free America."

"Didn't we just free the widow of a multimillionaire by scamming a confession out of a woman wearing Wal-Mart's bargain line?"

"Is that a trick question?"

Gus was spared answering by the arrival of a nurse, who shooed Shawn and Tara out of the room. After a moment she was joined by a doctor, who gave Gus a quick once-over and approved his release. Gus spent the next fifteen minutes filling out insurance paperwork and the following forty-five coaxing his fingers into bending sufficiently to button his shirt. At least it was a fresh shirt. Sometime in the night Shawn must have stopped by Gus' place and picked up a change of clothes for him.

When an orderly wheeled him to the hospital's front door, Shawn and Tara were waiting by her red Mercedes. They kept waiting as he made his way across the sidewalk. Each step was an agonizing ordeal, as he forced stiffened and bruised muscles to contract and relax. After what felt like another hour, he made it over to them.

"Tara's offered to take you home, bud," Shawn said.

"It's the least I can do. If there's anything else, please let me know."

"Thanks, but you don't have to," Gus said. "You've already done so much."

"Anyone would have done the same thing."

"For a complete stranger? I don't think so."

"Well, we're not strangers anymore," Tara said. "I'd like you to think of me as your friend."

"Works for me," Shawn said.

"In that case, there is one thing I'd like to do before I go home," Gus said, gritting his teeth against the pain. "If you wouldn't mind driving back up that hill, I want to see the man who really is responsible. And put an end to his criminal enterprise, no matter how high or low it reaches."

Shawn looked like he was going to argue; then he re-laxed into a grin. He turned to Tara. "Do you mind mak-ing one quick stop?"

Gus sprawled out across the red leather of the back-seat as Tara piloted them back to where she'd first seen him. Normally he would have used the travel time to work out an action plan with Shawn. But no matter how helpful Tara was being, it didn't feel right to discuss their process in front of her. So Gus used the trip to experi-ence every minor bump in the road as a wave of pain coursed through his entire body.

Which turned out to be just as beneficial a use of time as planning would have been. Because when the Mer-cedes pulled up across the street from the impound of-fice, he heard Shawn mutter a confused expletive. Pulling himself up in the seat, Gus looked out the window.

The area in front of the shack was surrounded by police cars. Uniformed officers and plainclothes detec-tives stood outside the front door. Two EMTs loitered by their open, empty ambulance.

"What's going on?" Gus said.

Shawn surveyed the scene. "I'd say you're not the only victim of the criminal conspiracy. Looks like they've taken out one of their own. Or as they say in *Law and Order—chung chung.*"

Chapter Five

In cooking, no procedure is simpler or more foolproof than roasting a chicken. You turn the oven on to 350 degrees, slap the bird in a roasting pan, and pull it out after an hour or so. Of course there are plenty of ways to improve this basic recipe, but as long as you follow these easy steps, you'll end up with a tasty dinner.

Even with a dish this basic, there are ways to destroy it. Let's say you set the oven to something like 120 degrees and leave the bird in for a couple of days. You might think of it as slow roasting. But you won't be cooking the chicken so much as speeding up its decomposition. And if you've forgotten to remove all those quick-to-spoil innards from the cavity, you'll end up with a dish that's almost as toxic as it is disgusting.

Whoever killed the attendant at the impound yard apparently didn't know the rules for successful roasting. He had left his victim's body in the 110-degree metal shack overnight, and he definitely hadn't done any cleaning beforehand.

Which is why seven of the eight members of the Santa

Barbara Police Department called to the scene were still
standing outside the shack's door, their faces covered
with handkerchiefs, paper bags, or take-out coffee cups
when Tara's red Mercedes pulled up across the street.
And why the eighth, one of the techs from the crime
lab, blasted out onto the tarmac, fell onto his knees, and
heaved just moments after he'd gone in.

Shawn leaned back over the front seat. "I guess our
work here is done. Want to go home?"

"What do you mean our work is done? We haven't
done anything."

"The guy who tried to kill us isn't going to be trying
again anytime soon. And it's not like we can wreak any
good vengeance on him now."

Shawn was right. They could go home. For a moment,
Gus imagined what it would be like to ease his aching
muscles into a warm bath. And to stay there for a month.
But then he remembered why his muscles hurt in the
first place.

"We're detectives, not rubber duckies," Gus said.

"Duckies?" Shawn said.

"Never mind," Gus said. "Let's break this thing
open."

Shawn beamed at him. Those were exactly the words
he wanted to hear. He threw open his door and marched
across the street.

"Isn't he amazing?" Tara said.

"Yeah, amazing," Gus said, struggling to pull the door
handle all the way back. "Would you mind helping me
out of here?"

Tara slid out of the driver's side and opened the back
door for Gus. He grabbed the handle over the window
and hauled himself to the doorway, then realized he was
stuck. His top half was already leaning out toward the
pavement, but his legs were trapped in the well behind
the front seat, and he couldn't lift them over the thresh-

old. In about two seconds, he was going to tip over and fall face-first onto the asphalt.

"Little help here," he called.

Tara grabbed his shoulders just as he was beginning to topple. Gently, she eased his trunk back into the car, then lifted his feet over the threshold. She held out a hand to help him get up, but he waved it off.

"I'm okay now," he said. "Thanks."

"Would you like me to help you across the street?"

Gus looked at the gaggle of police officers standing outside the shack. The open ambulance waiting for a body. He remembered how he had felt when he saw his first corpse. There was no need to put this poor woman through that.

"You've done enough," Gus said. "In fact, you might as well go home. We can get a ride with one of the detectives."

"I can't do that," she said, taking his arm.

Despite the apparent fact that his neck had lost the ability to swivel, Gus scanned the road in both directions, making sure there was no car within a quarter of a mile before he headed toward the impound lot.

"Sure, you can. I'm sorry I dragged you all the way out here."

Tara looked puzzled. "You didn't drag me here. Shawn did."

He felt like the Tin Woodsman—his muscles seemed to be rusted solid, but once he started moving they eased up considerably. "It was really both of us who—"

"No." There was an edge of steel in her voice that Gus hadn't heard before. He didn't understand where it was coming from. "Shawn dragged me here. That's why I was here to see you fall. I was answering his call."

"How could he call you? His phone was in my car, and my car was impounded," Gus said.

Her ice blue eyes bored into his. "Shawn doesn't need

a phone to call me. He's a psychic. He beams his thoughts directly into my mind."

Gus stopped dead in the middle of the street. He would have, anyway, if his body hadn't been experiencing a sense memory of his last journey over this particular stretch of road and propelling his legs forward without any input from his brain. "He does?"

"No matter where I am or what I'm doing."

Gus realized he had made it to the other end of the street. So why did it feel like he had just stepped into quicksand? "Does Shawn know about this?"

"He's the one beaming me his thoughts," she said in a tone that suggested Gus had just come out of a short yellow bus, not a red Mercedes.

"But have you discussed this with him?"

"Did you talk to your feet before you sent them the mental order to cross the street?" she said.

Actually, today he had. But he knew what she meant. He needed to talk to Shawn about this right away.

"Are you getting any beams from Shawn right now?"

She thought it over, cocking her head like a puppy to aid her reception. "Nothing."

"That's what I was afraid of," Gus said. "All those police radios are interfering with the signals."

"I didn't know they could do that," Tara said. "It's never been a problem before."

"It's a new invention," Gus said. "With all the bandwidth going to cell carriers, the cops have switched to psychic frequencies for their radios."

"I'd better get closer to him then."

"No!" Gus said. "I mean, he's asked me to relay a request—an order—to you."

"I didn't hear him do that."

"Exactly," Gus said. "That's why I have to tell you that Shawn wants you to—Shawn orders you—to wait by the car."

He waited for a moment for her to process this. Then she smiled and went back across the street. Forcing his legs to go faster, Gus walked over to the shack's front door, where seven of the police were still standing frozen as the crime scene tech finally managed to get up off his knees.

"Good to see your new cologne's going over as well as the old one, Lassie," Shawn said.

"I thought he was responding to one of your jokes," Lassiter said. "It's how they make me feel."

Gus stepped up before Shawn could respond. "There's something we need to talk about."

"Not just yet, Gus," Shawn said. "Detective Lassiter was just going to demonstrate what makes him Santa Barbara's finest."

"You really think I won't go in that shack?" Lassiter said.

"I will if you will," Shawn said.

"You most certainly will not," Lassiter said.

"Shawn," Gus whispered fiercely, "there's something you need to know. Now."

"The Santa Barbara Police Department doesn't need your help on this one," Lassiter said. "Which you might have been able to figure out by the simple fact that nobody asked for it."

The other police detective pulled the handkerchief away from her face, revealing the bright eyes and easy smile of Juliet O'Hara. Except that right now her eyes were slightly dimmed by tears, and her smile was anything but easy—the stench was proving stronger even than her own fierce will. And her will rarely lost a test of strength. The youngest detective on the squad, O'Hara was almost always underestimated by men who saw her pretty face and assumed she was soft. It annoyed her, but she'd learned how to use their assumptions against them. "Yes, Carlton, somebody did."

She turned to Shawn. "You could have returned one of my calls."

"Sorry. I've been away from my phones."

"Then how did you know to come here?" she said.

"Jules, Jules, Jules," Shawn said, "do you really need to ask?"

Lassiter looked at her as if she'd gotten up before she'd finished her time in the naughty spot. "You called him?"

"I did."

"You don't have the authority to authorize an unauthorized consultant. You need to have that cleared by Chief Vick."

"Her exact words were, 'Do whatever you want as long as you don't make me come to that hellhole,' " O'Hara said.

"And what is it you want to do, Juliet?" Shawn said. "I mean, deep down."

"I want to clear this case so I never have to smell this smell again," she said.

"You heard the lady, Lassie," Shawn said. "Let's solve us a murder. What do we hear from the CSI boys?"

District Attorney Bert Coules stepped out from around the side of the shack. "Mostly retching," Coules said. "Occasional vomiting. A lot of moans."

Shawn listened for a moment. "Yes, I see what you mean. But before they lost focus, what were they saying?"

Gus pulled Shawn aside. Or he tried to. He couldn't quite get up the strength to actually exert a force, but Shawn noticed him brushing at his shirtsleeve.

"There's something you need to know," Gus said.

"And I'm about to learn it from the lovely detective."

"I sure hope not," Gus said, as Shawn stepped away from him.

"It's a mess in there," Coules said.

"You're not looking so good yourself," Shawn said. "Got a little spot on your suit there."

Actually, there were several spots on the DA's suit. His knee was stained with grease. His jacket was flecked with a goo whose origin Gus hoped he'd never learn.

"Metal building, hot sun, dead body, check," Coules said. "You investigate a crime scene, you're going to get dirty. You stay much cleaner if you just make up your facts."

"And this place was a mess before the guy was dead," O'Hara said. "Apparently, it hadn't even been swept in the last decade. Which means every fingerprint that's ever been left is still there."

"That's not going to stop us from finding the killer," Lassiter said.

"Not when the victim works for the City of Santa Barbara," Coules said. "That's why I'm here now, and why I won't let this case drop until it's solved and the perpetrator is behind bars. At the district attorney's office, we believe that anyone who's willing to harm a member of our local government is targeting democracy itself. And I will not let that stand. Do you understand, Detectives?"

"We'll take the prints and run every single one of them, even if it's the entire population of Santa Barbara," Lassiter said.

Gus felt Coules' eyes boring into him. He tried to remember how many fingerprints he and Shawn might have left in the shack. Including the ones he must have left on the barrel of the shotgun. Not that he and Shawn had done anything wrong. They were the victims. But would that stop Coules from coming after them?

"And I bet it is," Gus said. "Every single citizen. We'll be amazed at the prints that are in there. Probably even people who have never been in the area. Just thought about stopping by."

"That would include you two, then, wouldn't it?" Coules said.

"Us?" Gus squeaked.

"You were certainly thinking about stopping by yesterday," Lassiter said. "Just think, if you'd made the walk, you might have run into the killer. Your laziness might have saved your lives."

This was the moment. All Gus had to do was say three simple words: "We were here." Sure, there would be an investigation, but they didn't kill the man, so what did they have to worry about? Even if Bert Coules was looking for vengeance after his humiliation at the Veronica Mason trial, he'd never actually charge them with the murder. And if charges were filed, what jury would convict them? A miserable year or two, a few hundred thousand dollars in legal fees, and it would all be over. If only Gus could bring himself to say those three simple words.

"It only looks like laziness," Shawn said. "But it's really more of a Zen survival thing. Or a Spidey sense. It's hard to tell the difference between the two sometimes."

Gus whispered furiously to him, "What are you doing? We should tell them."

"After we've solved the murder," Shawn said. "This is *our* case."

Detective O'Hara cleared her throat. "Other forensic evidence is going to be mostly useless for the same reasons. From what I understand, the place is absolutely disgusting, even without the body. One of the techs tried to describe the bathroom to me, and was seized by another fit of vomiting."

"Sounds like my kind of place," Shawn said. "Let's do this thing."

"You really think you're man enough to step through that door?" Lassiter said.

"Shawn's man enough for anything," a female voice behind them said. They turned to see Tara coming up to the door, looking stern. "And he doesn't like it when his masculinity is questioned."

"Good thing he hired a hooker to defend his honor, then," Coules said.

"I am not a hooker," Tara said. "I just dress like one because Shawn likes it."

"That's absolutely untrue," Shawn said.

"No?" O'Hara said, studying Tara's tiny dress. "Didn't you try to get me to wear an outfit like that when I went undercover at that convent?"

"First of all, that was a joke," Shawn said. "And second—what I mean to say was that it's absolutely untrue that I order Tara to dress a particular way. Not that it's untrue that I like it."

Lassiter shook his head in disgust. "I'm glad we cleared that up. Now why don't you ask your friend to leave? In Santa Barbara, we don't bring dates to crime scenes."

"So for Lassie we can add crime scene to the list, along with restaurants, movie theaters, and the beach," Shawn said. "As for Tara, she's not my date. She's my . . . new assistant."

"I thought Guster was your assistant."

"Hey!" Gus said. "I am no one's assistant. Shawn and I are associates."

"Really?" Lassiter said. "That must be why I always see you running behind Spencer, doing exactly what he wants."

Gus wanted to argue, but words wouldn't come. He knew there was a mistake in something that Lassiter had said, but he couldn't find it.

"Can we get this over with?" Detective O'Hara said. "That body isn't getting any fresher."

Chapter Six

"I confess!" Gus screamed. "I did it! I killed that man! Now please, please let me out of here!"

No one moved to take Gus into custody. No one even looked at him. That was probably because Gus had only confessed in his mind. But another two minutes in the shack, and he'd admit to anything if it would get him one breath of sweet fresh air.

The stench in the office was overwhelming. It was so strong it blasted through his sense of smell and filled all the others. Gus could taste it, see it, hear it. When he took a step, he felt it pushing back against him.

A quick glance at the others showed he wasn't the only one reacting this way. Bert Coules was pressing his handkerchief to his face so strongly it looked like it was about to pass through his sinuses and out the back of his skull. Lassiter was trying to pretend the smell didn't bother him, but he was breathing in short, shallow gasps, and his feet kept edging toward the door whenever he didn't exert conscious control over them. O'Hara seemed to have simply decided to hold her breath until they were out again. Even Shawn had gone pale under the beard stubble.

Gus was glad Lassiter hadn't let Tara into the shack. She might be crazy, but she certainly didn't deserve this kind of suffering.

There was one person in the office who didn't seem to notice the stench, but he had an excuse, being its principal cause. The attendant was sprawled on the ground behind the counter, a cloud of black flies buzzing around his head like a halo. His eyes stared up at the holes in the tin roof, which seemed particularly odd as he was lying on his stomach.

"It's pretty clear what happened," Coules said.

"Good, let's get out of here." Gus started toward the door, but Shawn hauled him back.

"Justice comes before comfort, Gus," he said.

"And nausea comes before vomiting," he said. "You want proof of that, keep me in here for a while."

Lassiter moved to the front wall and pointed at the cluster of small holes the buckshot had punched in the metal. "Is this what you're talking about, Bert?"

"Oh, my God, you're right," Gus said.

"Yeah," Coules said. "It's evidence that—"

"It's *air*," he said, pushing Lassiter out of his way and pressing his face up against the wall.

"How about you, Spencer?" Coules said. "Any psychic visions to tell you what happened here?"

Shawn halfheartedly raised his hands to his head, then dropped them again. "If spirits liked hanging around this kind of stench, they would never have left their bodies in the first place."

Coules walked over to the counter. "You don't think so? Maybe they'll talk to me." He pressed his index fingers to his forehead and winced. "Ooh, ooh, I feel it. I'm getting a vibe. I'm getting a feeling."

Shawn turned to Gus, a troubled frown on his face. "Is that really what I look like?"

"Yes, that is the thing that bothers me the most right now," Gus said, turning his attention back to the air holes.

"What's that, spirits?" Coules said, dropping his hands away from his face. "Someone came in here. He was angry. Maybe he was angry because his car had been towed. He was yelling, maybe even threatening the attendant."

"That's not how it works," Shawn said. "You're just making this stuff up."

"Yes, but the difference is I'm doing it based on the evidence. The victim felt threatened and pulled out his weapon, a shotgun he kept under the counter. His first shot was a warning. That's the one that put the holes in the wall."

"God bless him for that," Gus said from his spot by the wall. He'd never felt so grateful to someone who'd tried to kill him.

"But the killer wasn't scared off," O'Hara said. "In fact, he attacked. I'd guess he leapt over the counter and knocked the victim off his feet."

Lassiter pointed up at the ceiling. "That's when the second shot went off. The gun was now empty, and the killer grabbed it and threw it away. Then he bent down and savagely twisted the victim's neck, killing him."

Gus saw one dim light of hope in the DA's scenario. "The killer must have been a big guy to break his neck like that."

"It doesn't take size or strength to kill like this," Coules said. "That's the first thing they teach you in the Special Forces. It's just a matter of knowing the right way to twist."

"So it could have been anyone," Shawn said. "The pool of suspects is infinite. It's hardly even worth investigating anymore—unless you found something like a computer listing of the last people who came in to get their cars."

Lassiter was checking out all the drawers behind the counter.

"Don't bother," Coules said. "I already checked. Killer must have thought of that."

"Then there really is no way to solve this," Gus said. "Let's go."

"That would be true," Coules said, "except for one small detail. The shotgun isn't by the body. That means that somebody must have tossed it away from the victim—and that wouldn't be the victim himself, now, would it? So we find the gun, run whatever prints are on it, and our suspect is as good as in the gas chamber."

"That's very good thinking, Lassie," Shawn said.

"What do you mean, it's good thinking?" Gus whispered anxiously. "It's bad thinking. Very bad. Or have you forgotten which nonmurderer left his fingerprints all over that gun?"

"I forget nothing, my friend," Shawn said. "Like the fact that in this tiny shack, no one's found the gun yet. Which means the killer probably took it with him. So you're safe."

Gus breathed a sigh of relief. Or he would have, if he could have persuaded his lungs to inhale the toxic air in the shack. Then he saw a glint of light reflecting off metal in a far corner of the office. "I'm safe—unless Lassie decides to look behind that filing cabinet."

Shawn followed Gus' gaze. The shotgun's barrel peeked out from behind the cabinet. "What do you know? Lassie really nailed this one. Who'd have thought it?"

"I would have," Gus said. "I knew this was going to happen. I'm going to the gas chamber for a crime I didn't commit."

"Would you rather be executed for something you did do?" Shawn said. "At least this way you can feel morally superior to the rest of the guys on death row."

"Shawn!"

"Stay cool, buddy," Shawn said. "All we've got to do is distract him before he finds the gun."

"So start distracting."

Shawn gave it a quick thought, then doubled over and let out a screech. "I'm hearing a voice. It's speaking."

Lassiter didn't bother to look up as he searched the office. "That's nice. Tell them they're too late."

"It didn't work," Gus whispered to Shawn. "Try something else."

"Like what?"

"I don't know. Like he was a member of a criminal conspiracy that reached to the highest echelons of Santa Barbara society."

"And let them have the glory of busting the case wide open?" Shawn thought again, then jerked backward. " 'I found a picture of you,' " he sang.

" 'Oh oh oh oh oh oh,' " Gus added.

Lassiter peered down at the floor to examine a large stain. "I don't like music when I'm working."

"That didn't work either," Gus said.

"Which is really odd. My fifth-grade music teacher said my voice had a rich, strong timbre."

"Shawn!"

"I'm thinking."

"There's no time for thinking. We need a way to distract Lassiter now!"

Actually, there was some time left. Lassiter was studying the filing cabinet, and it would be at least fifteen seconds before he would walk around it and see the gun's barrel.

Shawn and Gus were so focused on Lassiter they hadn't noticed the door to the shack creep open and

Tara slip in. They didn't notice her walk up behind Juliet O'Hara. They didn't see her tap the young detective on the shoulder. They had completely forgotten about her until they heard her voice from behind them.

"Excuse me, Detective," Tara said. "I have no choice in this matter."

"In what matter?" O'Hara said, turning toward her.

Now Shawn and Gus did turn to see what was happening. Gus wondered momentarily how she'd managed to get past the uniforms manning the crime scene tape, but a quick glance at her legs made him realize how persuasive a woman like Tara could be to a middle-aged cop counting down the days to his twenty.

Lassiter looked up from his search to see Tara take O'Hara forcefully by the shoulders, then lean in toward her for a long, slow kiss.

For a moment, there was no motion in the shack, with the exception of Tara's face moving toward Detective O'Hara's. Gus felt a blush starting at his toes and working its way up to the top of his skull. He glanced over and saw Shawn staring with the same look he'd gotten when they walked into the wrong auditorium at the multiplex and discovered Mickey Rourke teaching Kim Basinger tricks far different from the ones they'd planned to see Mr. Miyagi teaching Ralph Macchio. Even Lassiter seemed to be unable to move, except for letting his jaw drop even closer to the ground.

"Shawn!" Gus whispered. "This is the distraction."

"No." Shawn's eyes began to glaze over. "The rest of the physical world is a distraction. This is what matters. This is the only thing that has ever mattered."

"Shawn!"

Shawn managed to pull his eyes away from the spectacle. "Right, murder, conviction, execution. Got it."

He moved across the room just as Detective O'Hara recovered from her shock. She shoved Tara violently away from her just as their lips were drawing together. "What the hell do you think you're doing?" she demanded. "I could arrest you right now for assaulting a police officer."

"I didn't have a choice," Tara said. "It was what Shawn wanted."

"I have no doubt of that," O'Hara said. "Does he want you thrown into prison, too? Wait. I can imagine the answer to that one. Shawn!"

Lassiter emerged from behind the filing cabinet, holding the rifle's stock in his gloved hand. "I've got the killer right here."

Coules glowered at him approvingly. "You let my office know the instant you pull a print off that gun," he said. "We're going to teach this murderer you don't take out an employee of the city of Santa Barbara."

"Maybe we could start the lessons outside," Shawn said. "I don't know if you noticed, but it doesn't smell very good in here."

Lassiter shrugged and headed for the door. Gus and Tara followed. Once they were out in the air, they paused to take several deep breaths. The stench of garbage rising from the landfill seemed like perfume.

"That was amazing, Tara," Shawn said.

"I was only following your orders," Tara said.

"My orders?"

"That's what I was trying to tell you," Gus said.

Lassiter threw the shotgun at one of the crime scene techs, then started yelling at the two uniforms manning the tape. Shawn and Gus couldn't hear what he was saying, but when the cops all turned and glared at them, Gus was certain that they'd already recognized his prints on the barrel.

"I think we may have worn out our welcome here," Shawn said.

They started back to the car, but before they'd gotten halfway across the street, Shawn stopped. Detective O'Hara was standing apart from the other cops. Her face was red, although whether it was from embarrassment, anger, or the effort of holding her breath for the entire time they were in the shack it was impossible to say.

"Can you give me a minute?" Shawn said.

"It'll take me twice that to get in the car anyway," Gus said.

Shawn turned back and walked to Detective O'Hara. "You okay, Jules?"

She glared up at him. "Was that fun for you?"

"As a matter of fact—" He broke off when he saw the anger in her eyes. "No, no fun. Not at all."

"I've fought so hard so long to get respect as a woman in this boys' club of a department. I always thought you were on my side, that you saw me as a cop as well as a woman. But today you proved me wrong. You did more damage to my reputation than anyone ever has."

"Jules—"

"Just get out of here, Shawn. I'm sorry I brought you onto this case. Now you're off it."

"Jules!"

She turned and walked back to Lassiter. Shawn watched her go, then turned to head back to the car.

Gus finished wedging himself into the backseat as Shawn walked around the car and got into the front. "So what is it you needed to tell me about?" he asked Gus.

Gus leaned up and whispered into Shawn's ear, "It's about Tara."

Tara started the engine and slammed the gearshift into drive, seemingly oblivious to their conversation.

"What about her?"

Gus checked to make sure she wasn't listening, then whispered again. "She thinks you're beaming your thoughts into her head."

Gus waited for Shawn to react. To draw back in horror, maybe, or to snatch the keys out of the ignition, or even to leap out of the moving car like Mannix. For some reason, he didn't do any of those things. Instead, he gave Gus a reassuring smile.

"Don't worry about that," Shawn said. "I know all about it."

"You do?"

"Of course," Shawn said. "I'm the one beaming my thoughts into her."

Chapter Seven

Gus pressed himself against the wall, then peered out through a crack in the curtains. The red Mercedes sat at the curb, exhaust fumes puffing out of its idling engine.

"She's still there."

Shawn looked up from the computer monitor. "Which is a good thing."

Gus peered out at the car, then ducked back behind the curtain at a sign of movement inside the car. "We need to be out there investigating the impound guy's murder, but instead we're trapped in this office by a psychotic psychic groupie. How is that a good thing?"

"It proves that I'm not really sending her psychic orders, because if she had to do whatever I wanted, she'd be gone by now," Shawn said. "Did you know people actually write blogs about impound lots? Apparently, among connoisseurs the Santa Barbara lot is ranked one of the best, since it's also one of the region's largest wrecking yards."

"I wasn't really worried that she was under your super

mind control, because you're not really psychic," Gus said. "I don't suppose the blogger says anything useful, like confessing to murdering the attendant?"

"This guy spends his life writing about impound lots he dreams of wandering through. I wouldn't count on him being useful in any way," Shawn said. "And even if I'm not psychic, maybe Tara is. Did you ever think about that?"

"I don't plan to ever think about this crazy woman again." Gus peeked out the window. The car was still there. "If we can ever find a way to get rid of her, that is."

Shawn hadn't thought it would be difficult. He first realized what she was thinking while they were waiting in the hospital for news of Gus' condition. She was so attentive to all Shawn's needs, so considerate of his concern for his best friend, he assumed she was simply a kind woman who felt understandably worried about a man she'd seen leap off a cliff. But as the night wore on, Shawn began to realize she was actually too quick to respond to his desires, or what she believed were his desires. He gave her a simple test by making his stomach growl loudly—a skill he'd perfected in fifth grade. She jumped up and offered to get them food.

When she returned with BurgerZone burgers, Shawn asked her a few leading questions. She immediately admitted she was following his psychic orders.

Shawn knew he should try to get rid of her. The last thing he needed in his life was a mental patient obsessed with him. But she did seem genuinely concerned about Gus. It didn't seem right to cast her out before the doctors declared him out of danger. And, while Shawn would never admit this to Gus, it was good to have someone around to talk to in the hospital. A way to keep him from getting too frantic over his best friend.

Not that he let his guard down around her. Well intentioned or not, she was still nuts. But Shawn spent the next hours studying her, and couldn't find a hint of malice, cruelty, or danger in her.

He assumed that once Gus was awake, he'd simply command her to leave them alone. And while the need for a ride from the hospital postponed that plan a little, he still intended to send her away once they got back to the office.

Once they were back in her car leaving the crime scene, however, Shawn realized that the longer he let this drag out, the harder it would be to stop. He couldn't let it wait even the short time it would take to get back to the office. He had to let her down gently. "I am not sending you orders with my brain," Shawn said.

"I know," Tara said cheerfully as she accelerated through a crosswalk, cutting off two women pushing strollers. "I'm waiting for my next command."

Shawn turned back to look over the seat at Gus, who was listening helplessly. Gus shrugged, and Shawn turned back to Tara. "When exactly did I start sending you orders?" he said.

"It's hard to say."

"Really? If someone were pushing into my brain and telling what to do, I think I'd have a pretty good idea who it was."

"That's because you're a great psychic," she said. "I'm just a follower. So when I started hearing your voice in my mind, I didn't know where it was coming from. Can you imagine it? For a few weeks, I thought I was going crazy."

"That is hard to imagine," Shawn said.

"I can't tell you how many false leads I tracked down. And then one day I turned on my radio to listen to Artie Pine and heard your voice coming out of it. And I knew."

"I knew it!" Gus said. "I knew you should never have gone on Artie Pine's show."

"So why didn't you ever mention it, if you're so smart about everything?"

In fact, Gus had done more than simply tell Shawn not to go on with Artie Pine, whose late-night radio show was nationally syndicated to an enormous audience of shut-ins, paranoids, alien abductees, friends of Bigfoot, and fanatics who'd discovered that their friends and family had started to cross the street rather than hear the newest revelation that the ether had beamed into their brains. Gus had nagged. He had preached. He had urged. He did research on Pine's topics cross-referenced by frequency, starting with flying saucers and extending all the way to the inevitable conquest of the United States by citizens of Atlantis. Finally, with no other option, he even violated the airspace in the Echo by turning on the show while he was driving Shawn back from a midnight pizza crisis.

And after all that, Shawn couldn't understand why Gus didn't want him to do the show. So there were a bunch of fruitcakes who listened in every night? How could that hurt them? Especially since any one of those fruitcakes might have a case that needed solving, and a couple of extra bucks to spend unraveling some deep, dark mystery.

"Anyway, once I heard your voice on the radio, the one I heard in my head just kept getting louder and louder, telling me to come to Santa Barbara and follow your every order," Tara said, tipping the wheel slightly to the left to avoid clipping a bicyclist who'd been riding under the mistaken assumption that the thick white line separating his dedicated lane from the rest of traffic gave him some kind of permission to slow her down.

"And how did the orderlies feel about that?" Shawn said.

Tara laughed, and Shawn grabbed the wheel to keep her from steering into an oncoming UPS truck. "I always forget how funny you are in person," she said. "When I hear you in my head, you're much more stern."

"Well, it takes a lot of effort to project one's thoughts into the mind of another person," Shawn said.

Gus reached up and slapped the back of his head. "Maybe you should stop using so much energy and use your words to tell her what to do," Gus said. "As long as we're all together in the car like this."

"I suppose I could try," Shawn said. "Tara, are you ready to receive my order?"

"I'm always ready for your orders." She turned to him, her wide eyes boring directly into his. "Please, direct me. I am now under your complete control."

"Maybe you could direct her to look at the road!" Gus squeaked, folding himself into the crash position as he saw the back of a stopped Hummer rushing up to meet them.

"Yes, I think that would be a good idea," Shawn said. "Tara, I order you to look at the road."

Tara tore her eyes away from Shawn's face and stared out at traffic. The Hummer seemed to fill the entire windshield, and it kept getting bigger.

"Tara, stop!" Shawn screamed.

She slammed her foot down on the brake and the Mercedes fishtailed to a stop an inch away from the Hummer's "My Child Is an Honor Student at Some School You've Never Heard of" bumper sticker. Gus clawed at the door handle and threw himself out of the passenger's side, nearly slamming into the bicyclist they'd almost hit just moments before.

"You can do what you want, but I'm not letting that crazy woman drive me anywhere!" he shouted to Shawn.

Shawn's window glided down silently. "Don't you think that's a little discriminatory?" he said. "The mentally handicapped deserve our respect, too."

"And I deserve to live long enough for my muscles to stop hurting," Gus said.

"That brings up an important point," Shawn said. "So far, you haven't been seriously injured as long as you've been *inside* Tara's car."

Gus glared, but he couldn't find fault with the logic. He opened the door and bent back in. "I'm here, but I'm not happy about it," he said. "You have to do something."

"I'm going to, right now," Shawn said. He turned to Tara. "I am giving you an order. You will obey this order. Is that clear?"

"Yes."

"First of all, you're going to drive us back to our office," Shawn said.

"Safely," Gus prompted.

"You're going to drive us back to our office safely, obeying all the traffic laws. All the important ones, anyway. You don't have to worry about stopping at yellow lights. No one does that, anyway."

"Shawn!"

"And once you've dropped us off at our office, you don't have to obey me anymore." Shawn looked back at Gus. "Isn't this like throwing away a perfectly good toy?"

"Yes, if the toy happens to be insane and a potential threat to everyone you hold dear," Gus said.

"I always wanted one of those."

The rest of the drive was uneventful. Tara drove at exactly the speed limit, accelerating above it only when a light turned yellow as she approached the limit line. She pulled up outside the Psych offices and left the motor idling as Shawn and Gus got out.

As they walked up the short path to their front door, Shawn and Gus kept turning back, Shawn to give Tara one last wave goodbye, Gus to make sure she was really going. But every time they turned, the Mercedes was still idling by the curb.

Even once they had gotten inside and Gus had locked the door behind them, the Mercedes waited at the curb.

"She's still there," Gus said, checking the window after they'd been back long enough for Shawn to tear through the office fridge, searching for something to drink.

"And yet Coca-Cola Blāk is gone," Shawn said, settling for a regular red can. "Why is it that the truly momentous inventions are ignored by the public, while trifles like cell phones, the Internet, and artificial insulin are treated like miracles of science?"

"What do you think she's doing out there?" Gus said, staring at the car.

"Idling."

"That's what her car is doing. What's she doing?"

"I don't know, Gus. Why don't you ask her?"

"I want her to go away."

"So tell her."

"You tell her. She's your psychic slave."

"I'm afraid I gave up my power over her when I freed her from my control," Shawn said. "Because you insisted, by the way. So if anyone's going to give her an order, it's got to be you."

It wasn't until fifteen minutes later that Gus was nervous enough to take Shawn's advice. Opening the office door just wide enough for him to slip through without letting in any lurkers who might be waiting for exactly this chance, Gus squeezed out, slamming it behind him. He looked around. He was alone, and the Mercedes was still sitting at the curb, chugging away.

Maybe if I stand here and glare at her she'll drive away on her own, Gus thought. He remembered Old Man Maccoby and how one of his stern looks could chase even the toughest of the neighborhood kids right off his lawn. If only Gus could summon up that force of crankiness in his gaze. He narrowed his lids and felt his irises contract. He was radiating waves of sternness directly at the Mercedes' driver's seat.

Nothing happened.

Gus sighed. He didn't have Old Man Maccoby's gift. And of course, he didn't have generations of kids spreading rumors around the neighborhood that he had the dismembered parts of missing children hanging from chandeliers in every room, either. That might have helped with the intimidation. He was going to have to handle this up close.

Taking small steps—the only kind his still-stiff legs would allow—Gus walked as quickly as he could to the Mercedes. He stood outside the front passenger-side window and waited for her to roll it down. He could see her inside, sitting behind the wheel, staring straight ahead. Even after he knocked on the window, she didn't turn to acknowledge him. Wishing he were anywhere else in the world—well, maybe with the exception of the impound shack—Gus pulled open the car's door.

"I couldn't help but notice you're still here," Gus said to her unmoving profile.

"I'm waiting," she said.

"Waiting for what?"

"For Shawn's next order."

Gus let out a loud sigh of exasperation. "He's not sending you any more orders. He's freed you from psychic slavery. You're free to do whatever you want."

"And what I want is to wait for my next order," she said. "Shawn knows I'll always be there for him when he wants me."

Gus stifled a scream. "He doesn't want you. I don't want you. Nobody wants you."

"But when he does, I'll be here. Now would you mind closing the door? You're letting the air-conditioning out."

Gus gave up, going back into the office and only peering out to confirm she was still at the curb every ten seconds or so. "How long do you think she's going to stay out there?"

"I seem to recall her gas gauge was just about full when she dropped us off," Shawn said. "She can probably idle for another six hours or so. Then she'll have to go get gas."

"What if she doesn't? What if we go out there one day and find her mummified corpse sitting behind the wheel of her dead car?"

"Then we'll know she can't follow us anymore."

"We can't just keep waiting and hiding in here. We've got to do something proactive."

"As opposed to what? Anti-active?"

Gus marched over to the desk and swept Shawn's feet off the computer keyboard. "We don't know a thing about this woman."

"We know she's got great legs. Fabulous fashion sense. And she deserves her own show on Cinemax."

Gus typed furiously at the keyboard. "Maybe that's enough for you."

"I think it should be enough for any man."

"I want to know what we're dealing with. To start with, just how crazy is she?"

"Do you really need a computer to tell you that? And where are you planning to look? I don't think there's a Web site that lists every lunatic in the country by their dress size."

"No, just their license-plate numbers."

The computer let out a chime, and the screen filled with the uninspiring gray logo of the California Department of Vehicles. Gus went to the window and checked the Mercedes' plate, then typed the letters and numbers into the form. After a moment, the computer chimed again and a page of information filled the screen.

"So who is our mystery woman?" Shawn said.

Gus studied the monitor. "Apparently her name is

Enid Blalock, and she lives in Arcata. And according to this, she weighs three hundred forty-five pounds."

"Wow, she's really dropped a lot of weight," Shawn said. "Do you think she did that for me?"

Gus barely wasted a glance at him. "She also has green eyes and blond hair, and she was born in nineteen forty-eight."

"Don't see a lot of women over fifty who look that good."

"Shawn, she stole that car."

"For all we know, there's a perfectly good reason for her to be driving around Santa Barbara in a hundred-thousand-dollar car that belongs to some fat, divorced Realtor in Arcata."

"Give me—" Gus broke off. "Wait a minute. How do you know that Enid Blalock is divorced?"

"Easy," Shawn said. "Clearly she's let herself go physically—I mean, three hundred forty-five pounds is more than a second helping of turkey over the holidays. Hubby loses interest, starts looking into other options. Enid catches him, and he buys her the expensive car to keep her happy."

"So then she wouldn't be divorced," Gus said.

"The car's three years old," Shawn said. "You think hubby could keep it in his pants that long? So on strike two, she takes him to court."

"Okay, fine," Gus said. "So how do you know she's a Realtor?"

"This is California," Shawn said. "When was the last time you met a divorced woman who wasn't?"

Gus had to concede that point. "That doesn't change the fact that Tara is driving around in her car."

"Enid Blalock could be her mother," Shawn said. "Or maybe Tara works as a valet at Enid's club, and she's just looking for a really good place to park it. The point is, Tara is innocent until someone proves her guilty."

"Next thing you'll say is she's sane until someone proves her insane."

"I'm willing to stand up for this woman's constitutional rights, even if you're willing to throw them away."

"Because she looks hot in a minidress."

"That's not part of the Constitution?"

Gus gave Shawn's desk chair a shove and sent him rolling away from the desk. Then grabbed the phone.

"What are you doing?" Shawn said, scooting himself back toward the desk.

"I'm calling the police."

"What if she's innocent?"

"Then the police will make a couple of calls, find out the truth, and there won't be any problems. But if she's guilty and we don't call, it's going to look bad for us."

"You're right," Shawn said. "We should call the police. The only question is who exactly we call—the detective we humiliated in front of Veronica Mason's jury or the one we humiliated in front of her superior officer?"

"There are more than two people in the Santa Barbara Police Department," Gus said.

"I think two people with a reason to hate us are enough for now," Shawn said, "although historically it's a pretty low number."

"If we turn a car thief over to them, maybe they'll hate us a little less," Gus said.

"You mean the car thief who's been chauffeuring us around in her stolen car?" Shawn said. "The one who has told top members of the SBPD that she is controlled by my psychic orders?"

Gus was on the verge of coming up with the exact, perfect reply to that when his hand started ringing. He looked down and realized he was still holding the receiver.

"That's her," Gus said.

"It's not her," Shawn said. "Why would she use

the phone when she's got a direct psychic link to my brain?"

"Whatever," Gus said. "It's not going to be good news, whoever it is."

"One way to find out." Shawn tried to grab the phone again, but Gus hid the ringing receiver behind his back. Shawn sighed, then reached across the desk and hit the SPEAKER button on the base station. "Psych Investigations, Burton Guster speaking," he said.

"What did you do that for?" Gus whispered.

"I can't be absolutely certain it's good news," Shawn said.

"Mr. Guster, my name is Devon Shepler, and I've got good news for you and Mr. Shawn Spencer."

"Pretty certain, though," Shawn said.

"What can we do for you, Mr. Shepler?" Gus said.

"Before you answer that, you're not Mr. Shawn Spencer's psychic mind slave by any chance?" Shawn said.

The silence from the other end of the line stretched on for what seemed like minutes before Shepler's voice returned. When it did, it brimmed with superiority and condescension even through the tiny speaker. "No, I can't say that's the case."

"Just checking," Shawn said. "Can't be too careful these days."

"I'll keep that in mind," Shepler said. "Is Mr. Spencer there?"

Shawn nudged Gus. "I'm here," Gus said. "But it's Mr. Guster you want to talk to. He's the real brains behind the organization."

Shawn threw a pencil at him.

There was another silence from the other end; then Shepler's voice started again. "I represent Mr. Dallas Steele. Are you familiar with this name?"

"Dallas Steele." Shawn pronounced the words as if they were in some unfamiliar Eastern European language. "Dallas Steele. Was he the kid who got sent home in tears when he failed the shoe-tying test in kindergarten?"

By now Gus suspected he could count down the seconds that would elapse before Shepler's voice came over the speaker again. "I wouldn't know about that," he said. "I've only worked for the man since he became the third-most-successful venture capitalist in Wall Street history."

"Just third?" Shawn said. "That must hurt. I bet the first two get together and make fun of him behind his back."

Gus decided to put Shepler's predicted silence to work for him. "So, Mr. Shepler, what is the good news you're calling about?"

"I'm glad you asked, Mr. Spencer. As I mentioned, I work for Mr. Dallas Steele, and he has asked me to invite you to meet with him this afternoon to discuss a business proposition."

"He's free to drop by if he wants to," Shawn said. "I can't guarantee we'll be here, because we're working on a murder investigation, but there's a spray-on tan place next door if he wants to wait."

"Mr. Steele requests that you come to see him at Eagle's View," Shepler said after the by-now-traditional pause.

Gus could feel his mouth dropping open. During the brief period when he had wanted to be an architect, Eagle's View was the building that had inspired him most. Erected in the 1920s by shipping magnate Elias Adler, it sat in a private valley fifty miles into the hills outside Santa Barbara, and its opulence and decadence were legendary by the standards of the time. Or of any time. Even William Randolph Hearst reportedly found it "a bit too much," and after an overnight stay ordered his architect, Julia Morgan, to scale down certain aspects of his own castle for fear of looking as crazy as Adler. Over the decades the mansion had passed through a series of extremely wealthy and private hands. Very few people had actually been through the estate's massive gates in years, and Gus had never even met one of them. Now they were being invited in, and Shawn was refusing.

"We're happy with our view here," Shawn said. "Tell him no deal."

"No, wait!" Gus said, but Shawn had already disconnected the call. "What did you do that for?"

"Who does that jerk think he is?" Shawn said. "Summoning us to see him like he's some kind of king."

"Most kings couldn't afford Eagle's View," Gus said. "In the fifties, there was one who actually offered to trade his crown for the place."

"I'm not him, and I'm not giving away my crown for anything."

"You don't have a crown."

"No, but I have my dignity."

Gus didn't bother to argue. He just picked up the trophy Shawn had won in the Hollywood Tropicana Jell-O Wrestling Championship and pointed to the bottom, where the words "Dirtiest Fighter" were engraved.

"Okay, so I don't have dignity. But I'm not going to go crawling to Mr. Dallas Steele just because he's got some snooty secretary summoning us."

"I don't understand," Gus said. "Why do you hate this guy so much?"

"I don't understand why you don't," Shawn said. "He spent the entire senior prom making out with your date."

"No," Gus says, "that was you."

"Oh. Well, he asked to read your English essay, then turned it in as his own, so you got an F for copying him."

"No," Gus said, "that was you, too."

"Really?"

"Really."

"I don't just hate people for no reason," Shawn said. "And I definitely hated him. So there must have been something."

"Because even though he was incredibly handsome, hugely intelligent, and came from the richest family in town, he worked harder than anyone else in school and honestly earned everything he got," Gus said.

"Right," Shawn said. "I hate that guy."

The phone rang again. Shawn hit the SPEAKER button. "Psych," he said.

There was a familiar pause. "Mr. Guster."

"No, this is Mr. Spencer," Shawn said. "Can't you even tell our voices apart?"

"But I—"

"I told you before, we're not coming."

"I thought that was Mr. Guster."

"I'm Mr. Guster," Gus said. "I'm the one who isn't crazy."

"And I'm Mr. Spencer," Shawn said. "I'm the one who isn't a suck-up toady for any multibillionaire who happens to have his assistant call my office."

The silence on the other end of the line lasted twice as long as any of Shepler's previous pauses. "Mr. Steele expects to see you within the hour," he finally said.

"Then he's coming to our office?" Shawn said.

"He would," Shepler said. "But it seems there's a problem."

"I'm sure he can get someone to tie his shoes for him," Shawn said.

"The problem is not with Mr. Steele," Shepler said. "It's with your office. You see, since our last conversation Mr. Steele has bought your building, and if you're not here within the hour, he's going to demolish it and put a community garden on the lot. So you can spend the next hour driving out to Eagle's View or moving your possessions to another location. But I wouldn't bother with the spray-on tan parlor next door. Mr. Steele bought that building, too."

There was no pause before Shepler hung up his phone with a loud click.

"Now do you see why I hate that guy?" Shawn said.

"You don't get to be a multibillionaire by letting people say no to you," Gus said. "I wonder what he wants."

"Too bad we'll never find out." Shawn walked around the office making a mental catalog of the items stored on the shelves. "How long do you think it will take to pack all this stuff up?"

"Almost as long as it did to collect it all," Gus said. "You're not going to let him knock down our offices?"

"I don't see that we have a choice."

"Can't you just get over this bizarre high school fixation with the man?"

"Of course I can," Shawn said, "because I'm a professional. I can get over just about anything. Last year, didn't I get over the bird flu?"

"You didn't have bird flu. You got food poisoning after eating week-old chicken salad."

"But I got over it, all the same."

"What's your point?"

"There's one thing I can't get over."

"What's that?"

"The Santa Ynez Pass. At least, not without a car."

That did present a problem that hadn't occurred to Gus. To get to Eagle's View required a long and arduous journey up a winding road into the mountains above Santa Barbara. The route was so slow and twisty that even if they had the Echo, it would still be a fight to get there before the sixty-minute window had closed. On foot they wouldn't even make it to the base of the mountains, even if Gus could walk at his normal efficient pace.

"Maybe your father would let you borrow his truck," Gus said.

"He's off fishing."

"Again? Isn't he fishing an awful lot lately?"

"He's old. He's bored. He needs an excuse to wear that hideous hat."

"But the coast is closed for fishing right now. There was another sewage spill last week, and the fish have been marinating in human waste."

"Maybe he went to a lake."

"What lake?"

"Lake Why the Hell Are We Talking About This," Shawn snapped. "Can we get back to whatever we were talking about?"

"We were talking about how to get out to see Dallas Steele before he bulldozes our building," Gus said. "But now I'm curious about why you're so touchy."

"You're not going to let this drop, are you?" Shawn said.

"Would you?"

That was one argument Shawn couldn't counter. "Okay, he's not fishing. He's . . . he's . . ." Shawn's voice trailed off in disgust.

"He's what?"

"Scrapbooking."

From Shawn's tone of voice, Gus' first thought was that "scrapbooking" must be a new slang term for drug running. Or murder for hire. Or white slavery. "What do you mean scrapbooking?"

"Exactly what it sounds like," Shawn says. "Some old lady dumps a load of old photos, ticket stubs, used napkins, and all sorts of other garbage on him, and he sorts through it and pastes it all into a tastefully designed photo album."

"Why is he doing that?"

"I can only think of one reason," Shawn said. "To humiliate me and destroy any last vestiges of respect the world might have for his many years as a fine police detective."

"That's two reasons."

"It's two more than he's given me. In fact, he's so terrified of having to answer the question that every time I call, he hangs up before I can demand that he justify himself again."

"So no ride. Why don't we just call Shepler back and explain the problem? I'm sure they'd send a car."

"And let him know you're so poor you can't even afford to get your own car out of the impound lot?" Shawn scowled. "There has to be a better way. One that will allow us to arrive there in style. In elegance. In—"

Gus felt his heart sinking. "You can't be serious."

Shawn was. "In sane," he said.

Chapter Eight

"Stop!" Gus shouted.

Tara stomped on the brakes, and the Mercedes left rubber along a hundred yards of narrow mountain road before it came to a screeching halt. Shawn felt his appendix sliced neatly in two by the seat belt.

"What is it?" Shawn said, clutching at the belt release.

Gus was already out of the car. He walked the few feet to the top of the mountain's summit, then stopped, gazing down at the valley below him. It was like an enormous cereal bowl carved out of granite, deep, almost perfectly round, with enormous boulders protruding from the walls like stray Lucky Charms stranded after the milk was gone. A one-lane road spiraled around the bowl, taking three full revolutions before it finally reached the bottom of the valley and straightened out into the mansion's long driveway.

And exactly in the center of the circle, Eagle's View sprawled majestically, an artistic testament to attention-deficit disorder. Elias Adler was a man of great and sudden passions who could fall in love with an architectural style as quickly as a chorus girl, and dump it just as easily. When Adler first commissioned this house, he had just come back from a month in Italy, and the entrance was designed to look like a Roman villa's. But before construction could be completed, Adler took a trip to Germany, where he fell in love with Ludwig's Bavarian castle. So behind the villa's atrium there rose three stone towers, each one topped with crenellated watchtowers. Apparently, however, Adler's attention drifted away again during this construction, because the rearmost third of the house seemed to be modeled on a Japanese palace.

Even from half a mile away, the house was everything Gus had ever dreamed it would be. He was so totally engrossed in studying it, he didn't notice Shawn come up behind him.

"That has got to be the ugliest house in the world," Shawn said. "It's like an aerial view of Disneyland, if each different land was a building and they were all crammed up against one another."

"Spectacular, isn't it?" Gus agreed.

"If you're a lunatic."

A car door slammed and Tara tottered up to them on her spike heels. She was about to say something when she saw the landscape spread out in front of them.

"What a beautiful house," she cooed.

"There you go," Shawn said.

To be fair, Tara hadn't acted particularly crazy on the long trip. Even her driving was shockingly sane on the road's tight turns, although Gus supposed she was still acting under Shawn's earlier instruction to drive safely and obey almost all traffic laws.

Even that wasn't enough to keep him from spending the first half hour of the ride ducking under the window every time they passed a police cruiser. A stolen car was a stolen car, no matter how considerately driven. Finally Gus decided he needed to tackle the question head-on. Or at least slightly to the left of head-on.

"Say, Shawn," Gus said as insouciantly as he could with his head lying on the armrest, "how's that other case going? You know, the one in *Arcata*?"

"I don't know, Gus," Shawn said. "Why don't you tell me? After all, you're the one who insists there's a case in the first place."

Gus studied Tara closely to see how she'd react to the mention of the scene of her crime. She didn't seem to notice at all. At least, the small lock of her hair Gus could see poking around the headrest didn't. From his position, he couldn't see the rest of her. After a quick check for police vehicles, Gus sat up and tried again.

"You remember what I'm talking about, don't you, Shawn? The *Enid Blalock* case?"

As soon as the words were out of his mouth, Gus realized he'd made a terrible mistake. If Tara was as crazy as he feared, what was there to stop her from driving them right off the edge of this twisty road, sending them all plummeting down to a fiery death? Gus didn't know the odds against surviving two cliff plunges within a twenty-four-hour period, but he didn't want to test them.

"I'm sorry, Gus. I couldn't hear you over the all the subtlety flying around in the car," Shawn said. "What was that name again?"

"Enid Blalock."

"Not *the* Enid Blalock," Shawn said.

"It's hard to imagine there could be more than one," Gus said.

"I wonder if Tara has an opinion on the subject," Shawn said.

Gus realized he didn't know what he was expecting from Tara. A stern denial, possibly, or a look of fake incomprehension. Or worse, a look of real incomprehension, which would suggest pretty strongly that she'd never learned the name of the woman whose car she had stolen. And of course, that long shot in the back of his mind: the terrifying plunge off the cliff after she deliberately missed a turn.

The one thing he definitely didn't expect was what he saw—one tear running down her cheek.

"What's wrong?" Shawn asked.

"That name," Tara said. "It reminds me of my own aunt Enid."

"Aunt Enid?" Shawn shot a chiding look back at Gus.

"She was so kind to me." Tara sniffed. "When I needed a place to live, she helped me find an apartment, even though she specialized in houses."

"So she's a Realtor?" Shawn said, barely trying to hide the victory in his voice.

"She was," Tara said. "She got her license after the divorce."

"That is something new and different," Shawn said. "Where is she now?"

"I hope she's in Heaven," Tara said. "I mean, I know they say gluttony is a sin, but do you really think someone would get sent to Hell just because she could polish off a pound of See's Soft Centers for breakfast?"

"We try to leave those heavy theological questions for the experts," Gus said. "Are you saying that Aunt Enid is dead?"

Tara sniffed back a tear. "I was with her until the very end. I think she was finally at peace."

"I'm sure she'd be happy to know you were driving her car." Shawn's face was alight with triumph. "Almost as happy as Gus."

"That's very kind of you, Gus," she said, sniffling. "She would have liked you a lot."

Gus didn't know what to say. Again, he was feeling

that same guilt at having misjudged another person. And it wasn't fair. There was every reason to believe Tara had stolen this car. Just like there was every reason to make fun of Bobby Fleckstein's glasses—they were thick black horn-rims, and they had made him look like a 'tard. Just once, Gus wanted the freedom to think terrible thoughts about other people and not feel bad about it afterward. The woman had hit him with her car, after all. She was a dangerous, delusional psychotic. And even so, Gus was nearly overwhelmed with the urge to sit in the nearest corner.

Apart from the guilt, the revelation about Tara's aunt freed Gus from his fear of riding in a stolen car driven by a remorseless psychopath, and as the road wound its way toward the top of the mountain, he began to enjoy the trip. He was finally going to see Eagle's View. And for all of Shawn's complaining, there was something particularly exciting about being summoned by one of America's most brilliant investors. Maybe he'd give them some tips. Maybe he'd even give them some money. At the very least he was giving Gus something to think about besides the prospect of being arrested for murder.

Gus spent the rest of the ride to the summit happily switching between thoughts of Eagle's View and dreams of actually being paid enough to cover all the bills. Until he saw the gates flanking the road ahead of them and ordered Tara to stop the car.

"It's easy to call the house ugly," Gus explained to Shawn and Tara as they looked down on the valley. "But that's just the first, visceral reaction. Once you get past the initial impression, you can begin to appreciate just how momentous an architectural accomplishment it is."

"So when I call it ugly now, that's ignorance," Shawn said. "But if I go to architecture school and spend years studying it—"

"You can call it ugly and really know what you're talking about," Gus said.

"Then let's get our education started," Shawn said. "You know how much I hate an uninformed opinion."

Although they were no more than half a mile from the house, it took them another twenty minutes before the Mercedes pulled up in the circular drive outside the villa's front door. There was no straight road from the summit to the valley floor; instead, the drive hugged the side of the bowl, running slowly down in three concentric rings.

When Shawn and Gus stepped out onto the flagstone driveway, the house's mammoth front door yawned open and a small man in a precisely tailored gray pin-striped suit stepped out, checking his watch. His razor-cut hair seemed to have been combed with tweezers, each strand placed exactly in the right location. When he walked over to them, he placed his feet so deliberately Gus found himself looking for the marks he appeared to be hitting.

"You're thirteen minutes late," the man said. "The bulldozers were on their way."

"No point in wasting them," Shawn said. "Maybe they could knock down this monstrosity while they're on the clock."

"I am Devon Shepler," the man said. "You must be Mr. Spencer."

"Or what?"

Gus had gotten used to Shepler's pauses on the phone, but to see one in person was unexpected. It was as if Shepler existed only on a DVD, and someone had pressed the PAUSE button. His muscles froze; his breathing stopped. Gus couldn't be sure, but it looked like the breeze even stopped rustling through his hair as he decided on the appropriate response. Then, after a few seconds, Shepler came back to life.

"Mr. Steele is waiting for you," he said. "Come this way."

Shepler turned and marched toward the front door without checking to see if they were following him.

"If Steele asks us to invest in his robot factory, we are so in," Shawn said. "That thing is amazing."

Shawn and Gus followed Shepler through the door into a wide-open atrium flanked with ancient columns that reached up to the sky. A shallow still pool glowed blue in the sunlight.

"This is based on the Villa Uffizi, the most famous house in Rome," Gus whispered as if they were walking through a museum and a guard was glaring at them.

"I guess they spent all their money on the pool, so they couldn't afford a roof," Shawn said. "And would it have killed them to dig the swimming pool a little deeper? I like to get in above my ankles."

At the end of the atrium, Shepler was holding another door open for them. They passed through into a wide corridor, its walls covered with elaborate tapestries. Their footsteps rang out on the gleaming marble floor.

"This place would be a lot less noisy if they put some of those carpets on the floor where they belong," Shawn said.

Shepler stopped outside a stained oak door and rapped sharply on it with his knuckles, then swung it open. "Mr. Spencer and Mr. Guster are here," he said, then moved out of the way to let them through.

The room was the size of the international terminal at a major airport. All four walls appeared to be lined with antique books, but they were too far away for Gus to be sure.

"Shawn! Gus! Great to see you!" The voice seemed to be coming from right next to them. Gus jumped, then turned in all directions. He didn't see anyone.

"You didn't tell me Steele was a ghost," Shawn said to Shepler.

"It's the acoustics," the disembodied voice said cheerfully. "Amazing, isn't it? The design was based on the fortress citadel of Golconda, the famous sixteenth-century Indian palace built by Ibrahim Quli Qutb Shah Wali. They said you could clap your hands at the main gate and they'd hear it at the top of the citadel."

"That's a really useful invention," Shawn said. "I mean, it would be if no one had ever invented the doorbell."

Gus squinted his eyes, and in the far distance, he was able to see the outlines of an enormous desk. There seemed to be a person behind it, waving at them.

Shawn and Gus crossed the great expanse of office, finally reaching a mahogany desk the size of the *Hindenburg*. By the time they got there, Dallas Steele was coming from behind it, his hand outstretched in welcome.

"Shawn! Gus!" Steele's pearly teeth flashed in a warm smile. Gus could hardly believe what he saw. The years hadn't just been kind to Steele—they'd been his best friend in the world. Somehow he'd become even more handsome now than he had been as quarterback and homecoming king in high school. "It's so good to see you!"

"Why?" Shawn said. "Need someone to tie your shoes?"

Gus slapped Shawn's arm. But Steele just let out another booming laugh. "Devon told me how you remembered that nursery school thing. What a memory you have! I'd forgotten all about it—but you were right. I cried my eyes out for a week after that humiliation."

"Some people would be bitter about things like that," Gus said. "Some people can't ever seem to get over what happened to them in school."

"Got to move on, right?" Steele said.

"Possibly," Shawn said.

"Besides, there were no hard feelings. Especially not after I bought the company that made those shoes, drove it into the ground, and sent the CEO to prison on trumped-up embezzlement charges."

Shawn and Gus stared at Steele, who burst out laughing again. "I'm joking," he said. "Not all businessmen are evil, any more than all psychics are frauds."

"Who's a fraud?" Shawn said.

"No one, no one," Steele said. "That's why you're here, because I believe you're the real deal. But let's not stand around my crummy old office. Let's go somewhere we can be comfortable."

"Is it far?" Shawn said. "Because I forgot my hiking boots."

Gus hit Shawn again. "That sounds great, Mr. Steele."

"It's Dallas. But to you, it's Dal. Just like the old days."

Steele led them back across the office toward the door.

"What old days?" Shawn whispered. "We don't have any old days with this guy."

"Sure, back in high school—"

"When he was the king of all he surveyed, and we were nothing. In four years of high school, did you ever once call him 'Dal'?"

"I don't think anyone called him 'Dal.' The teachers used to call him 'sir.' "

"Exactly," Shawn said. "He's up to something."

Gus took one last look around the office as they stepped back into the corridor, trying to calculate just how much bigger it was than every place he'd ever lived put together.

"Yeah, he's up to about four billion dollars as far as I can tell."

"And how do you think he got all that money?"

"His official biography says he took his inheritance and invested it in—"

Shawn raised a hand to cut him off. "Does the phrase 'massive criminal conspiracy that reaches into the highest echelons of Santa Barbara society' mean anything to you?"

"No."

"Yes, it does," Shawn said. "I saw it on your face. Isn't it suspicious that a day after we stumble across the Impound Lot Massacre—"

"What massacre?"

"Fine, the day after a refugee from a chain gang tries to kill us for revealing his identity at the impound lot and ends up murdered," Shawn said. "Although I think Impound Lot Massacre is a lot punchier. Anyway, one day after that, Dallas Steele drags us up here for a chat. Doesn't that strike you as odd?"

"Not necessarily," Gus said. "It could be a complete coincidence."

"Exactly!"

"Exactly what?"

"Exactly what Auric Goldfinger said: First time it's happenstance. Second time it's coincidence. Third time is enemy action."

Gus tried to follow the logic. "Then this isn't even a coincidence. We're still on happenstance. You know, I was prepared to share your prejudices and suspicions about this man, but I think he's pretty clearly proved you wrong. He's been nothing but friendly and welcoming since we got here."

"If you ignore the fact that we only did get here because he threatened to tear down our office."

"You can't stand this guy because he's one man who isn't going to let you manipulate him. You can't take advantage of Dallas Steele, so you have to find some way to say he's a bad guy."

"I do not take advantage of people."

"Then why is there a delusional woman sitting in the driveway, spending her afternoon waiting to drive us back to Santa Barbara?"

"Because it makes her happy," Shawn said. "Just like it makes you happy to believe that this Dallas Steele is a great guy. And because I want you to be happy, I'm going to put everything I know on hold and treat him the way you would. I'll give him every benefit of every doubt. And at the end of the day, we'll see who's right."

Steele stopped outside another door. "I thought we'd be more comfortable in the game room."

"Sure," Shawn said. "If you need to relive those few moments of adolescent glory when you still played football, I guess a room dedicated to childish games is the place to hang."

Steele swung open the door and led them into the middle of a nighttime forest. At least, that was what it seemed like at first. It took Gus a moment to realize that the close-growing stands of firs were actually a mural painted on the walls of another huge room. The moon and stars that shone down were artfully designed electric lights, and the pine needles that crackled underfoot were woven into the carpet.

"So which moments of adolescent glory do you think he relives in here?" Gus whispered to Shawn.

"I'm not sure, but if he suggests we join him in a hunt, we'd better make sure he's not using us as his target," Shawn said. "There's a long tradition in this country of rich people hunting the less well-to-do."

"That tradition only exists in Jean-Claude Van Damme movies," Gus said.

"Right, and the army isn't resurrecting dead soldiers as zombie warriors, either," Shawn said.

Somewhere in the forest, Dallas must have flipped a

light switch. The moon and stars winked out, replaced by a blazing sun of a chandelier.

"Elias Adler, who built this house, loved to hunt," Dallas said as emerged from behind the door and led them to a rectangle of four leather sofas in the middle of the room. "But he realized once he'd moved in that there was no game in this valley, aside from the occasional skunk or coyote."

"Or hobo," Shawn muttered to Gus, who slapped his arm again.

"So he commissioned this room, where he'd sit for hours, dreaming about the hunt. If you look hard, you can still see patch marks in the murals from when Adler forgot he was only dreaming and pulled out his rifle. I'm not much of a hunter myself, but I do like to sit in here and meditate."

Gus settled into a wicker chair the size of the Great Pyramid at Giza.

"Comfy, isn't it?" Steele said, dropping down onto a large leather sofa.

The jungle door opened, and a waiter came in carrying a sliver tray laden with an ornate coffee service that probably cost more than Shawn and Gus had ever made in their lives. He placed the tray on the table, then stepped back and stood absolutely still.

Steele reached for the coffeepot, then stopped himself. "I'm sorry. I should have asked if there's anything other than coffee you'd like."

"Coffee's great," Gus said.

"I guess it will do," Shawn said. He paced around the room like he was looking for booby traps. "I mean, if it's good enough for you, why would anyone want anything else, right?"

"Whatever you want," Dallas said. "We've got it."

"I'd love a Coca-Cola Blāk," Shawn said. "But that's probably something that never even crossed your radar, what with your being a multibillionaire and all. I mean, you can't be expected to keep up with the popular culture when you're sitting all the way up here in your eagle's nest."

"Mr. Spencer would like a Coca-Cola Blāk," Steele told the waiter.

Gus heard a polite throat clearing behind him and turned to see that Shepler had materialized there. "Would you prefer the American version or the European? As I'm sure you're aware, the American formula is sweetened with high-fructose corn syrup, aspartame, and acesulfame potassium, while the one made in France and sold mostly in Slovenia uses sugar and is said to be less sweet, but with a more pronounced coffee flavor."

"Why don't we give him my special blend?" Steele said.

Shepler signaled to the waiter, who disappeared without a sound.

"I like to mix the two in a sixty-forty American-to-European ratio, which gives it the stronger coffee flavor while still providing the jolt of sweetness we all love in this country," Steele said. "And then I top it off with a twist of Pepsi Tarik, a rival cola-coffee blend that's all the rage in Malaysia. I think you're really going to like it."

"I'm sure I will, Dal. I'm an easy man to please. I like to travel light, move fast, and keep myself from being burdened by too many possessions." Shawn paced around the room as if demonstrating his freedom.

"I envy you, Shawn," Steele said. "People read about me in the press, and they assume my life is easy. And I'm not complaining. I know that I've got what most people can only dream of. But there are times when I'd throw it all away to live simply and peacefully again."

Shawn stopped. His hands gripped his temples. His eyes squeezed shut, then flashed open. "That's why you called us," Shawn said. "I see it all. You've planned your escape already. You're going to fake your death and assume a fictional identity you've created. But you're not completely sure you've covered all the angles, so you need us to investigate the fake you and make sure there are no holes in the story."

"That's a very intriguing idea, Shawn, but I have to say no," Steele said.

For a moment, Shawn looked like he was going to argue the point. Gus shot him a look, and he reconsidered. "Of course not," Shawn said. "Because a man as famous as you can't escape just by changing his name. You'll always be Dallas Steele. The only escape for you is death. And one night, when the pressure was too much to take, you picked up that phone and dialed the number you'd been carrying in your wallet for months. The untraceable number. You let the phone ring three times, then hung up and dialed again. This time a man answered. You said no more than a dozen words, and it was all done."

"What was?" Steele said.

"Yeah, what was?" Gus said.

"He was in motion," Shawn said.

"Who?"

"That's the question, isn't it?" Shawn said. "Because part of the deal is you don't know his name. You've never seen his face. You'll never even know he exists until the moment he steps up behind you. Until then you live knowing he could be anyone. Even Gus."

"Who could I be?" Gus said.

"The hit man, Gus," Shawn said. "The one Dal put in motion, but can never stop. The money's been wired into his account, and now he's going to be coming after you relentlessly. That's why you called us. Because we're the only ones who can track down his identity and stop him before it's too late."

"If I had hired someone like that, it's good to know that you'd be able to call him off," Steele said. "But when I bring a new person into my work family, I like to meet them face-to-face first. Talk over the parameters of the job, get a good feel for how the other guy thinks. And let him know that while I do appreciate individual initiative, I also need to know that if I want an employee to make a major course correction—such as, for instance, not carrying out a hit on me—he'll be responsive."

"That's good management," Gus said.

"Bad plotting, though," Shawn said. "How would Barnaby Jones ever have made it through a single season if people didn't hire hit men they couldn't call off?"

Before anyone could come up with an answer, the waiter came back into the room, this time carrying a junior version of the original silver tray. On it was a crystal highball glass, filled to the brim with sparkling black liquid. "Your beverage, sir," the waiter said as he handed the drink to Shawn.

"You might want to think twice before you drink that," Steele said with a smile. "I've got to warn you, it can be pretty addictive."

"I'll take my chances," Shawn said, and took a large gulp of the drink. As soon as the tiny bubbles started popping on his tongue, he knew that he'd be lying awake night after night craving another taste. "Not bad."

"And, Gus, how's your coffee?"

Gus took a sip and swirled it over his tongue. "Intriguing," he said. "My first thought was Sulawesi, but there's an undercurrent I can't place." He took another sip. "Wait a minute—this isn't Kopi Luwak?"

"I'm impressed," Steele said. "It is. Have you had it before?"

"Only in my dreams," Gus said.

"Since when do you dream about coffee?" Shawn asked. "Especially coffee with such a stupid name?"

"Since that time I studied to be a professional nose," Gus said.

"Professional brown nose, more like it."

"Kopi Luwak is the rarest coffee in the world," Gus said. "And the most expensive. There are at most a thousand pounds of it available for sale every year."

"And this is actually a little rarer than that," Dallas said.

Gus gaped. "You mean this is Vietnamese weasel coffee?"

"In a way. I find the Vietnamese weasel produces a more sophisticated product than the Asian palm civet, which they use in Indonesia. But I'm not wild about the actual Vietnamese coffee, so I ship Sulawesi beans to my own private weasel ranch outside Saigon."

Shawn was looking from Gus to Dallas and back to Gus again, trying to make sense of the conversation. "Wait a minute. They grind up weasels and put them in the coffee?"

Gus and Dallas shared a knowing laugh. "You've got that backward, I'm afraid," Dallas said. "The coffee berries are fed to the weasels."

"So how do they get them— Oh," Shawn said.

"The animals eat the berries, but the beans inside don't get digested," Gus said. "The enzymes in the weasels' stomachs break down the proteins that make coffee bitter."

"So you're drinking coffee that comes out of a weasel's butt," Shawn said.

"Not directly," Gus said.

"I realize the butler isn't down in the kitchen pumping some rodent's tail to dispense the coffee, but what you are drinking is made from beans that were crapped out of a weasel."

"First of all," Gus said, "the beans are cleaned extremely well. And second, you're drinking a beverage that's forty percent made by French people, and their women don't even shave under their arms."

"Does that make sense to anyone here?" Shawn said. "I only ask because I had a spicy garlic shrimp burrito before bed last night, and I think I might still be dreaming."

Gus took a loud sip of his coffee and turned to Dallas. "So what is it we can do for you? I mean, unless Shawn wants to ask the spirits again."

"Yes, as much as I'm enjoying catching up on old times, I guess we should get down to business. This is really about my bride—"

"You're married?" Gus was surprised.

"Very recently."

"I didn't see anything about it in the papers."

"My bride is very shy about publicity," Steele said. "The wife of a billionaire is subjected to a lot of pressure, and we'd rather enjoy our honeymoon privately for as long as possible. I can count on your discretion, can't I?"

"Absolutely," Gus said. He looked over at Shawn for confirmation. Shawn was bent over double, his fingers curled around his skull. "Shawn agrees, too."

"Is he all right?" Steele said. He motioned to Shepler, who started across the room to check. Before he could get close, Shawn bolted upright, his eyes blazing.

"A man of your wealth is prey to any number of parasites—and the worst kind of parasite is the woman who latches on to a man's fortune and proceeds to suck him dry," Shawn said. "You love your bride, but you need to be absolutely certain that she loves the real you, and not just your money."

"No."

"Of course not," Shawn said without hesitation. "In your business you can see through people and know their real intentions. So you know she loves you for who you really are. But lately, as you've been planning the wedding, a cloud has come between you. She lapses into silence, and when you ask what's wrong, she doesn't have an answer. You've come to suspect that before she met you, your new wife was in a long, complex romance with a man of great beauty but little wealth. An artist. It was a torrid, passionate relationship, and she had to break it off for fear that she was losing her very selfhood in it. But break away she did, and when she ran off to some exotic resort to forget about Reynaldo—"

"Reynaldo?" Gus said.

"They're always named Reynaldo," Shawn said. "It's like a law. Anyway, she went off to this resort, and there she met you, and ever since, she's been happy. But on a recent trip back into Santa Barbara, she ran into Reynaldo again. He's working as a landscaper, but he's trying to put together a new show, the one that will make him famous throughout the art world. And he wants her by his side when he does. Now she's torn between the rich, kind man who makes her feel safe and warm and the poverty-stricken artist who treats her badly but raises her passions to a level she's never felt before."

"Wow," Dallas said. "That's really incredible."

"You mean he's right?" Gus said.

"There is a reason we call the agency Psych, you know," Shawn said.

"Actually, nothing you said had any relation to anything that's ever happened in my life, but it's such an incredibly detailed story, for a moment I felt I was actually living it," Dallas said.

Gus cleared his throat loudly. Shawn ignored him. He glared at Shawn. Shawn refused to meet his gaze. He drummed his fingers as loud as he could on the arm of his chair, but the noise was swallowed up by the padding. Finally he stood up, grabbed Shawn by the collar, and pulled him to his feet. "Excuse us for a moment," he said to Steele. "Sometimes Shawn's psychic batteries need a kick start."

"You mean a jump start?" Steele said.

"We may try a jump, but a kick is coming soon." Gus dragged Shawn into the depths of the forest. "What do you think you're doing?"

"Astonishing him with my psychic prowess," Shawn said.

"He doesn't look very astonished to me," Gus said. "And you're not even trying."

"I'm giving him exactly as much effort as he ever gave me," Shawn said.

"You're dredging up clichés from seventies detective shows."

"That's okay. He never watched TV," Shawn said. "He studied, practiced, and worked instead. I remember how he used to brag about it." He shuddered in revulsion at the memory.

"And this is helping you how?" Gus said. "You're making us look like idiots. You didn't even know he was married."

"I could have known if I'd wanted to," Shawn said, casting a glance over his shoulder at Steele, who waved at him cheerily. "He's got the beginnings of a tan line on his wedding finger, and he's touched it a couple of times as if he's trying to decide whether he likes it better with the ring on or off."

"That's good," Gus said. "A little late, but good. What else?"

"Aside from the fact that he's a phony?"

"Yes, aside from that. Because even if he's phony, he's rich, and he owns our building."

Shawn sighed and cast another quick glance back at Steele. And then he *saw*. Saw the sole gray root on his temple that had somehow outgrown the last application of dye. Saw the tiny scar under his left ear. Saw the custom-made clothes designed to hug and show off every toned muscle in his body.

Shawn bent over as if in pain. "It can't be," he wailed.

"Of course it can," Gus said. "Shepler called and told us—"

He broke off as he saw Dallas staring at Shawn.

"What can't be?" Steele said.

"All this beauty, all this wealth, all this success," Shawn moaned. "You've worked so hard for so long to reach this reward, and soon it will all be gone. Worse, it will still be here—but you will be gone. Age is catching up with you, and while you still have decades to live, you know they will pass like minutes. And then what happens? Is it all just gone?"

Gus looked over at Dallas and saw he was staring at Shawn as if his innermost soul had been torn out and tossed on the table in front of them.

"I need to know," Steele said.

"You called me up here to see if I actually had a connection to the world of spirits," Shawn said.

"To find out if that world exists," Dallas agreed. "I have to know." Dallas had risen from his seat, almost physically reaching for the answer.

"If I said yes, it wouldn't help you at all," Shawn said.

"Maybe a little," Gus said. "Maybe enough to get our building back."

Shawn ignored him. "You thought it would be enough for you to believe, but it's not. That's why I was spinning you all those ridiculous plots from seventies detective shows. It was a test."

"Is that what they were?" Steele said. "I never watch TV. I'd rather read or work."

Shawn worked to suppress his shudder.

"If belief was enough, you would have seized on one," Shawn said. "But you didn't become a billionaire by believing what people told you. You did your own research, found your own truths. You need to prove it for yourself."

"That's exactly right," Steele said. "Funny thing is, I didn't even realize it until you said it out loud. I need proof that there's a life after this one."

"You need to test me in a way I can't possibly cheat. No looking at cards or bending spoons. You will test me in a field you understand and I don't."

"That doesn't narrow it down much," Gus said.

"Investments," Dallas said. "It's what I do. I want to take a small pool of capital and put it at your disposal. If you're really psychic, you'll pick winners."

"See?" Gus whispered into Shawn's ear. "You put in a little effort, you get something back."

"The spirits don't respond to money," Shawn said.

"Some of them do," Gus said.

"I don't mean to insult them or you with the offer," Steele said. "We could arrange to give all the results to charity."

"Spirits aren't so crazy about charity, either," Shawn said quickly.

"Then let's just do it this way," Steele said. "I'll give you a pool of money to invest. Anything you earn over that initial nut, you do with whatever you feel will please the spirits best."

"I don't need anything, but I think the spirits would be pretty happy if my friend Gus could raise about six thousand dollars about now."

"I was thinking of a slightly larger pool."

"How slightly?" Shawn asked.

"How does a hundred million dollars sound to you?"

Chapter Nine

"Who'd ever think it would be so hard to spend a hundred million dollars?" Gus looked up wearily from his desk, which was littered with brochures, prospectuses, and press releases. "Haven't we bought enough companies already?"

In the weeks since they'd agreed to consult for Dallas Steele, Shepler had inundated them with paper. Apparently every request Dallas got for venture capital was being shipped directly over to the Psych offices. And as Gus was discovering, there were a lot of people in the world who wanted a multibillionaire to make their dreams come true.

At first Gus and Shawn hadn't intended to spend so much time on the consulting job. After Tara had brought them back from Eagle's View, their first priority was to solve the murder of the impound lot attendant. It was the one way they could be certain they wouldn't be blamed for the death.

Shawn was sure it wouldn't be all that hard. After all, they knew that the attendant wasn't who he claimed to be. He'd served time on a chain gang, and even if he had finished his sentence rather than escaping, the city of Santa Barbara didn't hire ex-cons to work in jobs where they'd be handling money. So first up was to figure out who the dead man really was. From there it would be easy to see who might have had a grudge against him. Probably someone he'd served time with or an old criminal associate. Couple of days to put it all together tops.

But even as Shawn walked into the Psych office, the taste of that amazing Coca Cola Blāk mixture still dancing on his tongue, the fax was already whirring a stack of financial documents into its in tray. Before the day was out, the FedEx and messenger deliveries started to arrive.

Even so, they might have shoved all the papers into the corner and focused on the murder. But their visit to Eagle's View had changed them in ways they didn't realize. They'd had a tiny taste of the life available only to the superrich, and they liked it. Shawn had never cared much about money, and if you asked him, he'd say he hadn't changed. But the ability to have absolutely whatever you wanted whenever you wanted it—even if you didn't want it all that badly—was a more powerful idea than he'd ever imagined. Every time he tried to concentrate on the dead impound lot attendant, he found his mind wandering to that sixty/forty blend of European and American Blāk. And though they never discussed it, Shawn was sure that Gus was dreaming of coffee emitted from weasel butts every time he sipped his Starbucks.

As much fun as Shawn and Gus found solving murders, it was never going to make them rich. True, they were living comfortably, but they were hardly amassing huge savings. And even after Shawn offered the contents of his own bank accounts, Gus was still almost three thousand dollars shy of the cash he needed to ransom his company car. Steele had promised them ten percent of whatever profits were generated by the companies they chose to invest in. After the cash started rolling in, they could go back to detective work, and this time they'd do it in style.

"It's only hard because you make it hard." Shawn was standing in the center of the office, a stack of prospectuses in his hand.

"When you say 'make it hard,' you mean we actually do our due diligence and make sure we're investing the money wisely," Gus said.

"Exactly."

"You have a better plan?"

"Of course." Shawn screwed his eyes closed and let the dossiers fly. Once they'd all flapped to the ground, he grabbed one up. "This is it. The big moneymaker."

"And you know that how?"

"Look where it landed."

Gus got up to see the floor was covered with DVD boxes. Shawn pointed at a spot directly to his right.

"The prospectus landed on top of *Wall Street*, so you think it's a good investment?"

"Greed is good, right?" Shawn flipped the file open.

Gus stared down at the boxes on the floor. "All this time, this is how you've been designing our investment strategy?"

"Of course not," Shawn said, kicking through the files scattered around his feet. "At first I was doing it your way."

"Studying the financial documents, checking the potential upside against the risk involved, trying to understand the underlying technology and whether it means a real step forward?"

"Really? Is that what you do?" Shawn said. He shuddered. "I just pick the companies with names I like."

"You do *what*?"

"If Dallas wanted to make investments based on sound judgment, market experience, and financial wisdom, he could make them himself," Shawn said. "That's not why he came to me. He wants that something extra."

"Bankruptcy?"

Gus knew that wasn't fair. Despite the appalling method Shawn claimed he was using to discover them, he had come across a lot of businesses that seemed extremely promising. Some of them were predictably Shawn, like the Chinese company that made a line of toy boats that transformed into killer robots. But together Shawn and Gus had steered investments into alternative-energy firms, futuristic transportation designers, and others that looked like they could be as profitable as they were boring. Gus suspected that Shawn was doing a lot more work than he'd ever admit.

If only those profits would start rolling in soon. Their deal with Dallas granted them ten percent of all the profits their investments netted, but not a penny of cash up front. After a long and strenuous negotiation, Gus had persuaded the billionaire to guarantee the lease on their offices for the next five years, but that was the only concession he'd been able to add to Steele's initial offer.

"Don't even think that word," Shawn said. "Between this and the media bonanza from the Veronica Mason trial, the money's going to start pouring in faster than we can count it."

"I don't need to count it. I need to spend it," Gus said. "Every day that car sits in the impound lot they add another two hundred dollars to my bill."

"In a few days that will seem like nothing," Shawn said. "We're expecting a big payday from Veronica Mason, remember?"

"Of course I remember," Gus said. "But remembering her isn't doing us a whole lot of good—she needs to remember us."

Despite the fact that they'd saved her from a lifetime in prison, it did seem that Veronica Mason had forgotten all about Shawn and Gus. They hadn't heard a word from her since the day of her acquittal. No matter how many messages they left at her various houses, she never got back to them.

"I have to admit, that one really puzzles me," Shawn said. "After the trial, she seemed so grateful. I thought it was going to be the beginning of something special."

"You mean you thought she was going to show you all her birthmarks."

"That, too," Shawn said. "But more important, after all that time investigating every tiny corner of her life, I really began to feel that we were close. Connected."

"But that was a completely one-way relationship, Shawn. You were spending all your time thinking and learning about her—that didn't mean she was thinking about you. You fooled yourself into thinking it was mutual."

"I can't believe that," Shawn said. "What existed between us was real. It's just not possible for one person to feel so connected to another human being and not have that feeling reflected in some way."

"Are you sure about that?"

Shawn was about to answer when he noticed the look on Gus' face. "This is a trick, isn't it?"

"Is it?"

"Don't you dare go Yoda on me," Shawn said. "I'm not going to go into the swamps and battle a hideous creature only to discover it's my own dark side. I see what you're up to."

"And what is that?"

Shawn thought. "I have no idea."

"Maybe you should think a little harder about the people you take advantage of."

"Gus, I do not take advantage of you. I treasure your

friendship and your partnership. You know it's true. Everything I do I do it for you."

"I'm not talking about me," Gus said. "And I've told you never to quote Bryan Adams at me. I'm talking about Tara."

"Where is she, anyway?" Shawn said. "We sent her out for lunch ages ago."

"That's exactly what I'm talking about," Gus said.

"You think that I'm taking advantage of her?"

Gus did. And he'd been saying so for days. After she had driven them back from Eagle's View, Shawn once again told her that he was freeing her from all psychic control. But instead of leaving, she just kept idling in front of their office. When the owner of the tanning parlor next door complained about the exhaust fumes, Shawn invited Tara into their office and tried again to send her away. Again, she seemed incapable of understanding. Short of calling the police and having her hauled away, there seemed to be no way to get rid of her. So Shawn started assigning her errands that would keep her out of the office. At first, it was only to give Gus and him privacy to talk about their cases and their investment strategy. But as the days went on, Shawn started to discover how convenient it was to have someone whose only desire in life was to do all the things he didn't want to do.

"Last week she did your laundry, cleaned your office, and brought you four meals every day."

"The woman has a void where her life goals are supposed to be. She's decided to fill that gaping black hole by anticipating and fulfilling my every need. It's not that I really want her to do all these things for me. In fact, I find it extremely draining. But it's what she needs, so I'm willing to sacrifice my own desires for her health and well-being. It's like Major Nelson and Jeannie, except Jeannie's outfits weren't quite as revealing." Shawn looked down at his watch. "How long does it take to get a medium-rare cheeseburger?"

"Since you sent her to Oxnard to get it—"

"There you go again. I didn't send her. She instinctively knew that I preferred the Oxnard BurgerZone to any of the closer branches."

"And the fact that you mentioned this to me in front of her didn't have anything to do with her intuition?"

Shawn sighed heavily. "She thinks she's taking psychic orders from me. If she gets them wrong, she's going to start doubting the very fabric of her existence."

"Yes," Gus said. "She might even start to act on her own initiative, instead of waiting to figure out the smallest thing you might want."

"So you're saying that if I were to leave these prospectuses and DVDs scattered all over the floor, knowing that as soon as she comes in with our lunch she'll pick them up, that would be taking advantage of her?"

"Of course it would."

Shawn stared down at the mess on the floor.

"And that would be wrong?"

"Obviously."

"So if there's something I'd like her to do for me and she'd like to do for me, if I let her do it for me, that's wrong."

"You're not going to pick up this mess, are you?" Gus said.

"I'm still working on the morality of the issue."

"I knew it." Gus bent down and started to pile all the prospectuses together.

Shawn watched him curiously. "Okay, here's my question: If I let you pick this stuff up before she has a chance to, am I taking advantage of you? Or am I still taking advantage of her, because you're only doing this to protect her from my evil ways?"

Gus dumped the files back in the box and jammed the

top over it. "All I'm saying is that Tara is a sweet, sad, delusional girl who's just lost her beloved aunt Enid and is looking for some purpose in her life. And she's never going to find it as long as she can convince herself that taking the pickles off your cheeseburgers is what she was put on Earth to do."

"She wouldn't have to if you could ever get a burger without them," Shawn said. "Even if you ask specially, it's like they're incapable of hearing it."

Gus was back on his knees, gathering the DVDs into stacks. "This isn't about pickles."

"You'd be surprised how much turns out to be, in the end, about pickles."

"Shawn!"

Shawn picked up one of the stacks of discs and carried it over to a shelf. There were several empty slots where the DVDs had come from. Gus had spent two full days organizing their collection. Shawn glanced back to make sure Gus wasn't looking, then pushed the discs together and slid the new stack in at the end.

"I guess you're right," Shawn said, "even if I don't understand how giving her what she wants is wrong. But what can I do about it?"

"To start with, you can put those discs back in the right order," Gus said. "And then you can have a nice, quiet conversation with her in which you graciously thank her for everything she's done for you and explain it's time for her to leave."

"Haven't I done that about fifty times?"

"And then tell her you're going to have her arrested if you ever see her again."

"That sounds kind of cruel."

"Of course it's cruel," Gus said. "You're going to have to break her heart. But it's for her good and it's for our good. And I think we both know that nothing else is going to work."

The bell over the door rang, and Tara came in carrying white take-out bags. She was dressed in red, as always, but she'd traded the minidress for a pair of tiny shorts and a T-shirt so tight that Gus could see the order in which the cells of her lungs gave up their allotment of oxygen.

"Sorry it took so long," Tara said. "That guy did the pickle thing again, and I figured it was worth a little extra time to make sure he didn't do it again."

"That was thoughtful of you," Shawn said, "although it's hard to believe you'd have to say anything twice to any man who saw you in that outfit."

She blushed happily at the compliment. "I don't think that's going to be a problem in the future," she said.

Gus cleared his throat. "Did you hear that?" he said significantly to Shawn. "Tara says it's not going to be a problem in the *future*."

"Are you expecting that she should somehow do something about the problem in the past? Because that would risk bringing up the whole time-travel paradox thing. We start out trying to change the pickle count on a cheeseburger, and before we know it, I've killed my own grandfather, the Nazis won World War II, and there's a dinosaur in the White House."

"You know what I'm talking about."

If Shawn was hoping for a reprieve from Gus' judgment, he wasn't going to get it. "I do," he said.

"Are the cheeseburgers okay?" Tara asked. "Because I'm feeling like my orders have changed."

"Just a little bit," Shawn said. "Maybe we should talk outside for a moment." She dropped the three white bags on the desk and headed brightly for the door.

Gus waited until Shawn was outside, then moved over to the window and drew the curtain aside so he could watch what was happening. Tara was leaning happily against the Mercedes as Shawn went up to her. But as Gus watched, whatever Shawn was saying to her seemed to be bringing her mood down to earth. At first, she just looked confused, as if Shawn's words were in direct conflict with the psychic orders she was receiving from him. As he kept talking, her face began to darken and she started trying to object. Gus had to give Shawn credit—it seemed like he wasn't letting her get out more than a syllable before he was able to talk over her objection. Even from this distance, Gus could see her protests getting weaker and weaker.

Just as Tara's anger was beginning to fade away into tears, the phone rang behind Gus. He knew he should answer it. It might be Shepler, asking if they'd decided which firms they were putting their funds into. It could be Veronica Mason, apologizing for her long absence and offering to messenger over a check right now. It could even be a new client with a hot case who'd be willing to give them a big cash retainer in advance. But for the moment, none of that was as intriguing as the scene that was going on outside this window. Nothing would keep Gus from watching Shawn finally send Tara away for good.

Nothing, that is, except for the voice that came over the machine.

"I know you're there, Spencer. This is Carlton Lassiter of the Santa Barbara Police department, and you have exactly ten seconds to pick up this phone."

Immediately Gus forgot what he'd been so engrossed in just seconds before. He sprinted for the phone and snatched up the receiver before half the allowed time had passed. "Psych Investigations. Burton Guster speaking," he said.

"If I were interested in talking to a sidekick, I'd have called Ed McMahon," Lassiter growled.

Normally Gus might have given in to his instinctive desire to defend Ed McMahon's underrated acting career. He certainly would have bristled at being called a sidekick. But there was something in Lassiter's voice that strongly suggested this wasn't the time for repartee. "Whatever you have to say to Shawn, you can say to me."

"You sure about that?"

"Absolutely."

Lassiter did.

And Gus tried to figure out why he had been so insistent that Lassiter tell him personally.

When the bell over the door chimed and Shawn came back in, Gus was still staring down at the receiver in his hand.

"That was tough," Shawn said. "And I don't mean 'figuring out your taxes' tough. This was more like 'Babe finding out his mother had been ground up for hamburger' tough."

Gus didn't even look up at him. He just kept staring at the phone.

"Don't tell me you don't want details, Gus," Shawn said. "Or that you're not dying to tell my that Babe's mother was a pig and they make hamburger out of cow. Let me have it."

Shawn waited for Gus to take the bait. But Gus didn't even seem to hear him. "Lassiter called."

"Speaking of Babe. Which, to protect me from charges of cliché-mongering, you may apply to the lovely Juliet O'Hara, not to the oft-drawn comparisons between police officers and our oinking friends. So what did he want?"

"Us," Gus said. "There's a warrant for our arrest."

Chapter Ten

Walking through the bright yellow corridors of the police station, Gus was certain everyone was staring at him. He'd been here so many times before, but always as a consultant helping out on a case. While there were usually a few suspicious glares from members of the force, there were also people who were glad to see him. And even the ones who resented him knew that there was a small chance that he'd help clear a case off their board and make their averages look better.

But this time Gus had come in the backseat of a squad car. He was here as a suspect, and the mood was completely different. Harsh stares came from every corner of the precinct. If Gus had been cuffed, chained, and manacled, the reception couldn't have been any colder.

Why hadn't they simply told the truth when they had been called down to the impound office? Gus vaguely remembered being afraid that he'd be accused of the murder. It could have made for a couple of unpleasant days. But now they'd lied to the police and obstructed justice. When Lassiter accused him of killing the impound clerk now, what could he say that would convince anyone of his innocence?

"Hey, guys!" It was Officer McNab, whose usual cheery smile had been replaced by an ominous baring of his teeth.

"Don't let him get me alone in my cell," Gus whispered to Shawn.

"What are you talking about?" Somehow, Shawn seemed to be oblivious to the hostility radiating out at them.

"Officer McNab," Gus said. "He's got some new interrogation technique he's learned from the feds, and he's itching to take it out on me. I saw it in his eyes."

"The only thing in those eyes was the adoring friendliness of a well-fed puppy," Shawn said. "Officer Friendly thinks McNab is too soft."

"That's a technique," Gus said, "because he knows we're suspects. He wants to soften us up."

"How much softer could you get? You've already passed Jell-O on the wiggle test."

"Lassiter said he wanted to talk to us about a violent, ugly criminal act," Gus said. "And he made it sound like he wanted to perform one on us."

Shawn clapped Gus on the back. "There's nothing to worry about, Gus. We haven't committed any violent, ugly crimes. Unless you count the sweater you're wearing."

Lassiter stepped out in front of them. "Chief Vick's office. Now."

He turned and headed into Vick's office. Shawn gave Gus a reassuring smile. "See, it's just the same as always. Nothing to worry about."

Living in Santa Barbara, Gus had never had much experience with snow. But one winter his parents took him up to the mountains to go cross-country skiing. He had started out happily, but ten minutes after he left the trailhead, he'd gotten hopelessly lost in the woods. He wandered around in the snow for hours before he was finally discovered by a troop of Boy Scouts. He had never felt so cold again until he stepped into Vick's office.

The chief was sitting behind her desk and didn't even make an effort to rise as they came in. That worried Gus, because she was unfailingly polite and professional. Aside from a brief period during her pregnancy, he'd always known her to be cool and steady at all times. She was exactly the kind of leader he'd dreamed of being when he imagined himself as president. But now she was looking at him like something she wished she hadn't stepped in.

Lassiter had taken a place on one side of her. That he was scowling at Shawn and him was no surprise. But Detective Juliet O'Hara was on the other side of the desk, and even her usually friendly face was set in a hard glare.

"Hey, Chief." Apparently Shawn hadn't noticed the frost in the room. He greeted the police as if they'd just jumped out to wish him a surprise happy birthday. "Jules, Lassie, what's the story?"

"It seems that you are, Mr. Spencer," Vick said. "I wish it were a happier one."

"Can't tell if a story is happy until you get to the ending," Shawn said. "Take *Of Mice and Men*, for instance. If you never bothered to read the last few pages, it could be the delightful tale of two carefree young men making their dreams come true."

"Only if you're an idiot," Lassiter said.

"Oddly, that's exactly what our eighth-grade English teacher said. She was quite harsh on poor Gus."

"You're the one who lost the book before I could finish it."

"Perhaps we could turn our attention to the matter at hand," Vick said.

"The very serious matter at hand," Lassiter said.

"Are we all grumpy today?" Shawn said. "Even you, Jules?"

"It's Detective O'Hara." The air seemed to freeze as it came out of her mouth. "And while we all appreciate your concern about our mood, we have more important issues to deal with."

Gus could feel his blood pressure rising. His heart pounded; his palms were covered in sweat.

"We're dealing with a serious allegation here, gentlemen," Chief Vick said. "I appreciate the work you've done for this department, and would like to give you the benefit of the doubt. But there's a great deal of evidence, and I need some explanations."

It was too late for that, Gus knew. If they'd talked at the impound lot, everything would be fine. But there was nothing he could say now that wouldn't get them both into bigger trouble. There was really only one choice now, and that was to lawyer up. If they were going to treat him like a criminal, he was going to act like one.

Gus was preparing to declare his rights when he realized someone was talking in a voice that sounded remarkably like his.

"We went to pick up my car the day of the murder," the voice was saying. "The attendant pulled the shotgun and tried to kill us."

Gus looked around to see who was imitating his voice. No one was speaking. There were all staring at him.

"Before you go any further, you might want to consult a lawyer, Mr. Guster," Vick said.

"Or at least with me," Shawn said.

Apparently whoever was mimicking Gus was doing it from inside his body. Gus decided to give up and let the impostor take over. "He pulled out a shotgun and tried to kill us, just because we were trying to get my car back.

I knocked the gun out of the way on his first shot. That's why there were holes in the shack's wall."

"At least there's something to thank you for," O'Hara said.

"Then we ducked below the counter, and I grabbed the barrel of his gun to keep him from aiming it at us. When I released it, he flew backward and the gun went off again, blowing that big hole in the ceiling. Before he could get up, we ran out of there. He might have gunned us down in flight if Tara hadn't showed up right then."

"So Tara Larison was on the scene as well," Lassiter said thoughtfully.

"Please go on, Mr. Guster," Vick said.

"That's really all there was to it. Except that when we went to the crime scene, we were concerned because our fingerprints were on the barrel of the gun. And Lassiter had a theory of the crime that fit exactly with everything we'd done, except we didn't kill the guy."

"Why didn't you just explain all this to the detectives?" Vick said.

Gus started to answer, but then stopped. He hadn't thought of a single good reason all morning, and one wasn't coming to him now. "Shawn?"

"Yes, Gus?"

"Why didn't we just explain all this to the detectives?"

"Because the spirits were calling out for us to solve the case ourselves," Shawn said. "Because he'd tried to kill us. This time it was personal."

"And did you?" the chief asked coolly.

"It's on our list," Shawn said. "All the spirits seem to be working on this project for Dallas Steele right now. Amazing what kind of service a couple billion dollars brings you."

"Maybe that's the reason," Lassiter said. "Or maybe

it's because you assume the police are stupid and lazy. That we care less about solving crimes and catching criminals than we do settling petty personal scores against people who make us look bad. So you figured that after you humiliated me at the Veronica Mason trial, I'd be thrilled at the chance of accusing you of murder and seeing you put to death."

"You did have Gus' car towed," Shawn said.

"And that makes you think I would ignore a real murderer, possibly leaving the general public at great risk, simply to satisfy my own hurt feelings. Let me say I'm shocked at the assumption."

"After all the times we've worked together, Mr. Guster," Vick said, "do you really think so little of us?"

Gus' head was spinning. Somehow in the space of seconds he'd found himself transformed from the victim of coincidence and a possible police conspiracy into a heartless maligner of his closest friends. The temperature in the office seemed to drop another ten degrees.

"What about you, Shawn?" It was O'Hara, and she looked personally injured. "Do you share your partner's despicable view of us?"

Shawn studied the question carefully, searching for an answer that wouldn't make the situation worse in one way or another. Then he started to tremble. His fingers twitched, and the spasms seemed to move up his arms.

"What's he doing?" Vick said.

"Looks like the Watusi," O'Hara said, stifling a yawn. "I hope we don't have to sit through forty years of dance crazes before he answers a question."

"It's so hot," Shawn moaned, clutching his head. "The sun blazes down on me. Oh, why won't they let me have some water? Why can't I sit down for just one second?"

"What is it, Shawn?" Gus asked theatrically, thrilled that he was at the very least doing something.

"The rocks, the rocks, I have to break the rocks."

Shawn scanned the room and found an umbrella stand in the corner. He snatched an umbrella out and raised it over his head. "Have to break the rocks."

Shawn brought the umbrella down sharply on the desk. He was raising it for a second blow when Lassiter reached over and pulled it out of his hands. "Use your words, Spencer," he said.

Shawn grabbed his forehead and staggered a couple of steps. "The vision was so clear, like it was beaming directly out of the past into my head. I was a prisoner on a chain gang, breaking rocks in the blazing sun."

"We wish," Juliet muttered.

"Really, Jules, you, too?" Shawn said. Her frosty look answered for her. "I'm trying to make sense of this vision, because it must be some kind of metaphor. It was telling me that the man who was killed at the impound yard was a prisoner on a chain gang, but that's not possible, because there haven't been chain gangs in decades."

"Hold on for a second, Shawn," Gus said. "I seem to recall reading that they were using them again for particularly vicious criminals in Arizona."

"That's true," Vick said.

"Then that must be what I was seeing," Shawn said. "The victim was an escapee from a chain gang. Which means he'd need an assumed identity to work for a lot that was licensed to the city."

Gus looked from face to face, hoping to find any sign of warming. They stared back, just as icy.

"That's a very good insight, Mr. Spencer," Vick said. "It's the kind of thing we might never have figured out without your unique talent."

"Unless we happened to run the vic's prints," O'Hara said.

"Which we did," Lassiter said.

"John Marichal was indeed an escapee from an Arizona chain gang," Vick said. "A second-generation criminal who'd done time for armed robberies all over Florida, just like his daddy before him. He moved to Arizona and started a new life. Apparently the new life wasn't much different from the old one, and he got himself arrested for what's believed to be his second liquor store holdup. He got twenty years on the chain gang, escaped six months ago and fled to Santa Barbara."

"Where he managed to snag a hot job right off the bat," Shawn said. "Got to give props to our local economy."

"He didn't exactly apply for the job," Vick said.

"The employee of record was one Albert Jones. Apparently Mr. Marichal killed Mr. Jones and simply started showing up in his place."

"And nobody noticed?" Gus said.

"Who would?" Vick said.

"And even if they did, they'd assume that Jones had quit and Marichal was the new guy," Lassiter said. "In some ways it was the perfect crime."

"Perfect, yes," Shawn said. "Except that instead of winning him a million dollars in cash and bonds, he ended up with a job so crummy even a dead guy could do it. So what's the point?"

"We're still trying to figure that out," Vick said.

"If I get a vibe, I'll let you know," Shawn said. "So, anyway, glad we could help, and I guess we could use a ride back to our office."

He started toward the door.

"Not so fast, Spencer," Lassiter growled.

"That's my normal walking pace," Shawn said. "If you're having trouble keeping up, you might want to look into a Lark. If you qualify, Medicare will make all your payments."

"We didn't bring you here to ask you about the impound lot murder," Vick said. "Because we had no reason to connect you with it. Whoever killed Mr. Marichal wiped all the prints off that shotgun—including, apparently, Mr. Guster's."

Those were exactly the words Gus had been longing to hear. They were off the hook. They were free. So why was he still paralyzed by stress? There was something his subconscious had figured out that it wasn't sharing with the rest of him.

"Tell me, Mr. Spencer. What do you think about pickles on a burger?"

Gus could practically hear his subconscious laughing at him. What was about to happen was so much worse than what he'd originally feared, and his conscious mind still had no idea what it could be.

"Are you ordering lunch? Because we just ate," Shawn said.

"Answer the question, Spencer," Lassiter growled.

"They're an abomination," Shawn said. "You unwrap the paper, and you get that first rich, meaty smell mingling with the yeasty goodness of the bun. Maybe just a hint of toasted sesame. Then you take a bite and the juices flow out onto your tongue, beef fat mingling with the sour-sweet attack of the secret sauce. It's a perfect flavor combination—and then it's ruined by the acid tang of decayed cucumber. But no matter how many times you ask, can you ever have your burger made without pickles? No. Because it's just assumed that even if you beg for a dill-free experience, you couldn't possibly mean it."

"You sound pretty worked up about the issue," O'Hara said.

"I've considered running for office on the platform," Shawn said. "But aside from that, it's not really something that takes up a lot of my time."

Vick pulled a file off her desk and handed it to Gus. Inside was a photo of a young man in a white Burger-Zone uniform. At least, it used to be white. Now great areas of it were stained red, and Gus was pretty sure it wasn't with ketchup. His face was barely recognizable under the cuts and bruises.

"That happened at roughly twelve forty-two this afternoon," Lassiter said.

Shawn peered over Gus' shoulder at the picture. "He fall under a Zamboni?"

"Apparently he made one small mistake," Lassiter said. "He was working the grill at the Oxnard Burger-Zone and got a take-out order for three burgers with no pickles. Do you know what happened next?"

"I'm going to guess pickles," Gus said.

"Oh, yes," O'Hara said. "Pickles."

"The customer wasn't happy," Lassiter said. "Harsh words were spoken. And then the customer asked the victim to step out back to discuss the issue."

"Why would he agree?" Gus asked, ignoring the terrible feeling that he already knew the answer to his question.

"Turn the page, Mr. Guster," Vick suggested.

The photo felt like lead in Gus' hand as he struggled to flip it over, desperately not wanting to see what he knew was waiting for him on the next page.

"Imagine you were a twenty-three-year-old part-time student working a minimum-wage job in order to finish a degree in accounting so you can go on to live a long, boring, lower-middle-class existence in the Valley," Lassiter said. "Is there anything you wouldn't do if she asked you?"

Gus and Shawn stared down at a police artist's sketch of a beautiful young woman in a tight T-shirt and tiny shorts. Even though the sketch was in pencil, Gus could practically feel the redness coming out of it.

"We didn't bring you down here to discuss the murder at the impound lot," Lassiter said.

"Although we do appreciate your belated honesty on the subject," Vick said.

"We brought you here because we need to answer a very important question," Lassiter continued.

"Is it about pickles?" Shawn said.

"In a way."

"Any particular way?"

"We know you asked Tara Larison to bring you back lunch from BurgerZone. She mentioned your name several times at the pickup window. And we know that you specifically asked for your burger without pickles. Our question is, did you tell Ms. Larison to beat this man half to death if he got your order wrong, or did she just assume that you'd want her to?"

"Is there another way to put that?" Shawn said.

"Certainly, Mr. Spencer," Vick said. "We need to know if you're merely harboring a deranged psychopath, or if she's acting under your direct orders."

Chapter Eleven

Evidence. It was always about the evidence. Before he retired from the Santa Barbara Police Department, Henry Spencer would spend hours poring over every shred of paper, every scrap of fiber, every drop of ooze until he could piece them together to tell a story. Then he'd tear it all apart to see if he could put it together in another way that would tell a different story. If he could, then he knew he had to keep searching for other clues that could be added to the puzzle until there was only one possible solution.

But the stack of evidence piled in front of Henry now made those challenges pale by comparison. To start, there was far more here than he'd ever had on any case with the SBPD. An entire shoe box of photos going back sixty-seven years, and an additional eight carousels full of slides. Plane tickets. Wedding invitations—the subjects' own, and dozens more for their scores of relatives and friends. A paper napkin with a lipstick kiss fading after many years. Swizzle sticks from restaurants long gone. A sequence of drivers' licenses dating back to the days when they were photoless cards, and two expired passports with stamps from countries that had long been wiped off the map. And that was only from the file boxes that Henry had already been through. There were three more stacked beside his dining room table.

The huge amount of evidence was only part of Henry's problem. Even after he'd been through it all once, categorized it and cataloged it and sorted the useful pieces from the trash, he'd still have to confront the real challenge. What was the story these clues were trying to tell him? How could he put together these tiny scraps in a way that would turn them into a coherent narrative?

At least in a murder investigation, half the story was predetermined. He knew the basic parameters going in. Someone had been killed. Someone else did it. Henry had to figure out who that was. Difficult certainly, but at least he knew the beginning and the end of the tale going in.

This story had no predetermined structure. If it could be said to have a beginning, it was only that the subject had been born many years ago. There was no ending, and there would be none until the subject passed away. And in between there were only random artifacts of the moments that make up any life. It was completely up to Henry to decide which incidents defined a life and which ones were simply trivia.

He'd never intended to start scrapbooking. In fact, if someone had mentioned the idea to him only a month ago, it would have meant nothing more to him than the minor irritant of seeing one more noun recklessly turned into a verb.

That was before Betty Walinski, the still-attractive widow who ran her late husband's tackle shop, complained over a tray of bait that her fading eyesight was making it hard to sort her old photos into an album for her new granddaughter. She dropped several broad hints about how nice it would be to have some help. Henry suspected that she was less interested in preserving her legacy for future generations than in a chance to demonstrate what an excellent cook and companion she could be to a lonely divorcé, but he didn't object. He had an ulterior motive, too.

When Herman Walinski was still alive, he was legendary for his handcrafted fishing lures. A few of those he put up for sale, but the entire Santa Barbara fishing community still buzzed with legends of the lures he'd kept for himself. Especially his masterpiece, the one he called YTBL3. It was rumored that the very presence of the YTBL3 in any body of water would draw fish all the way from the Atlantic. Henry knew that if he could just get inside Betty's door, he could sweet-talk her into letting him get his hands on that collection.

When he got to Betty's tidy bungalow on the inland side of the hills, Henry's first thought was to make a bit of small talk, eat whatever she might put in front of him, promise to spend as much time as she wanted going through her photos, then subtly change the topic of conversation to her late husband's lure collection. It was something he'd learned long ago while interviewing suspects—people rarely notice that you're trying to get something out of them when they think they're getting something out of you.

That was before Betty placed the shoe boxes full of snapshots in front of him. Out of politeness, and a desire to look like he was helping, Henry leafed through a couple of the yellow mailing envelopes, each containing the product of one roll of genuine Kodak film. At first he barely glanced at the pictures, but when he opened the third envelope he saw something that grabbed his attention—Herman Walinski in a police uniform. Henry stopped in at the tackle store at least once a week for twenty years before Herman's death, and in all that time, the owner had never mentioned he'd been a cop.

The normal response to a discovery like this might have been to ask Herman's widow about it. After all, she was standing right over him, asking if he'd like another piece of seed cake crammed with enough poppy to make the entire US Olympic team test positive for opiates. But Henry had known Betty almost as long as he had her husband, and she had never mentioned his law enforcement history, either. It wasn't a general prohibition on talking about the past, because they'd both told stories about the years he spent driving a tow truck when he originally arrived in Santa Barbara. Forgetting about the lures for the first time since Betty had asked him over to the house, Henry invented a series of reasons why he had to return home immediately—he'd left the water running or the stove burning or the water running onto the burning stove—and asked if he could take the photos home with him to start organizing them.

If Betty's quick assent gave Henry a reason to reconsider her motives for inviting him over, he didn't spend too much time mourning the loss of the possible relationship. Instead he loaded up his truck with boxes of her old photos and got away before she could change her mind.

That was when the detective work started. Using the photo of Herman as his starting point, Henry began to build a time line of his life stretching out in both directions from that moment. He worked slowly and methodically, organizing the photos not only chronologically but also thematically, so he would have parallel histories of Herman's career, his vacations, his children, and the various weddings, funerals, bar mitzvahs, fishing derbies, anniversaries, and holidays that made up his life in pictures.

The story that began to emerge out of the photos was

one that bore almost no relation to the Herman Henry
had thought he'd known. The man behind the counter
at the tackle shop had been a jovial backslapper, apparently uninterested in anything that couldn't be used to
persuade a fish to swallow a hook. The private Herman,
the prefishing Herman, was a much more complex soul.
Starting with the pictures and concluding with a long
bout of Googling, Henry met a young police officer on
the Miami force who'd started out with great promise,
and then had been teamed up with a corrupt partner.
As far as Henry could piece together, Herman had ini-
tially tried to switch partners, and then for reasons that
weren't apparent in the photographs, he had decided
instead to help Internal Affairs clean out the department. He worked undercover long enough to learn that
his partner and several officers were tied to the thieves
who pulled off a daring daytime robbery of the Calder
Race Course. The officers and the criminals were all believed to be captured, even though the money was never
recovered. A few months after the picture that sparked
Henry's interest had been taken, Herman testified to a
grand jury about corruption in the Miami PD.

There was one picture of Herman shaking the hand of
someone who must have been the chief, while a graying
man, most likely the mayor, smiled down on them, but
that was the last image of Herman in uniform. In fact,
that was the last image of Herman of any kind for the
next six months of his life. The next time he showed up
in one of the yellow envelopes, he was smiling cheerfully
from a hospital bed, his arms and legs in traction.

That was a story Henry could figure out without additional information. Herman had informed on his fellow officers, and the rest of the force had frozen him
out. Henry couldn't say for sure how he'd ended up in
that hospital bed, but it was easy to assume that Herman
had called for backup on a dangerous assignment, and

none of his brother officers had bothered to show up. That was the most positive version Henry could come up with.

After that, a sequence of photos showed Herman's slow recovery, the sale of a house in Florida, a trip across Europe—Henry assumed he'd reached some kind of cash settlement with the Miami PD—and the businesses he ran in Santa Barbara, starting out as the owner-operator of a one-truck towing company until he became the dominant player in the area, then cashing out and buying the tackle store.

It took Henry almost two full weeks to put the whole story together in an album, complete with subplots about the couple's friends, their siblings' children, and all the other people who drift in and out of a life.

When he was done, Henry drove the album over the hill and presented it to Betty. She was thrilled. She was just leaving for a week to visit an old friend in Montana, but she promised that when she got back, she'd have something very special for him.

Henry could almost taste the fish Herman's lures were going to catch for him. But it turned out that what he considered special and what Betty did were two very different things. What she wanted to give him was a recommendation.

It turned out that all of Betty's friends wanted books just like hers. She was willing to set him up in business. She even had a name for him—the Memory Detective.

Henry tried to decline politely. He told her he had time-management issues. That he was concerned a paycheck might interfere with his police pension. Finally he came flat out and told her he'd rather die.

That was when the first lure came out. And what it caught wasn't a fish—it was a retired Santa Barbara police detective. Betty understood that he didn't want to do this anymore, but she had promised her best friends, the Perths, that Henry would do a scrapbook for them. She couldn't let them down. So she was willing to make a deal—if he did her this small favor, he could choose three of Herman's lures. Any three—even the YTBL3.

He had no choice once that lure was dangled in front of him, any more than the shovelnose guitarfish Herman caught off the pier with it had. Henry had to bite.

Now that he was hooked, he was about as happy as one of those guitarfish. Rod and Elaine Perth had lived contentedly together since their wedding in 1962. They were as devoted to each other today as they had been on the first day they met. They'd spent just about every minute of the last forty-seven years together, and they'd documented it all in loving detail. And somehow, in those entire forty-seven years, they had managed to do absolutely nothing that was of any interest to anyone.

Henry surveyed the endless landscape of photo mailers and keepsake boxes littering his living room. He'd been through them all twice, and he couldn't find anything that even looked like a story. Apparently the Perths had spent the last five decades sitting happily on their living room couch drinking tea—or, when they were in a mood for a wild time, coffee. Occasionally Elaine ventured out into the garden to pull a weed or two; apparently Rod did his work as an accountant at a desk in the den while Elaine knitted next to him. Even when they traveled overseas, all they seemed to do was sit on foreign couches. The only things that changed in all the pictures were the gray hairs on their heads and the wrinkles on their faces. These people didn't need a scrapbook to document their lives together; any one picture grabbed at random would have told the story just as well.

Henry pushed his chair back from the table irritably. He'd spent enough time on this project. He should just slap in a handful of random pictures, put a ribbon around the album, and call it done.

But the Perths wouldn't let it be done. Every day since he'd taken on Rod and Elain's lives, they'd dug up another box of identical photos they wanted him to go through. Every afternoon there'd been a knock at the door, and when Henry opened it, he'd find the Perths' unbelievably unmemorable grandson standing on his porch with another delivery. The first few times Henry was excited, hoping that the new arrival would bring something of interest. But he'd been disappointed so many times that he'd come to dread the young man's knock.

Which was why he almost chose to hide in the kitchen when there was a firm rapping on the door this time. Maybe if he didn't answer, the kid would leave the box on the porch, and Henry could claim it had been stolen before he got home.

He was halfway to the kitchen when the rapping came again. He stopped at the sound. The Perths' grandson's knock was as uninteresting as anything else about him. It was more like the kid was brushing his knuckles across the wood, as if an actual blow was too assertive for him. But this series of raps was firm, assertive, urgent. Either the kid had stopped on the way over here to get a spine, or this was someone else. If Henry was really lucky, it was an ex-con he'd put away years ago who'd come to kill him and put him out of his Perth-induced misery.

Henry crossed the living room quickly and pulled the door open. The woman standing there smiled up at him shyly.

"Can I help you?" Henry said. "Miss . . . ?"

"You are Henry Spencer, aren't you?"

"Yes," Henry said. "And you are?"

"So excited to meet you." She held out a hand.

Henry lived his life by a few simple rules. Number seventeen was this: If you ask a stranger for his name twice and he still doesn't answer, he's hiding something. Henry knew he should slam the door in this woman's face and, if she didn't leave on her own, have the cops cruise by and check her out.

Somehow the door didn't seem to slam. Henry's left hand remained frozen on it. Like any man who finds himself violating lifelong beliefs when confronted by a beautiful woman, he could come up with dozens of reasons why he should let her in. Maybe she was lost. Maybe she had car trouble. And anyway, it was hard to imagine that she could be hiding anything. Her bright red T-shirt and shorts were so tight she couldn't conceal a dollar bill without his being able to read the serial numbers.

Henry extended his right hand and took hers in it. He felt a tingle running up his arm as if she'd given him a minor electric shock.

"I can see the resemblance," the woman said, peering intently into his eyes.

Henry felt a slight tang of disappointment as he realized that she was here looking for Shawn. Probably some girl he'd met in a bar and never bothered to call back. Although blowing off a woman this beautiful didn't seem to fit Shawn's standard operating procedures.

"Shawn's not here." Henry tried to withdraw his hand, but she wouldn't let go.

"I know." Her voice was like a seduction. "He sent me."

"I see." Now Henry was getting annoyed. It was one thing for Shawn to call the health department and report a toxic plume coming from Henry's house that time he had tried to brew his own beer. That was funny—at least after Henry had retaliated by reminding the head librarian at the Santa Barbara Library that Shawn still hadn't returned the copy of *Harriet the Spy* he'd checked out in 1984 and that he owed fines running into the thousands of dollars. But sending a hooker to Henry's house went far beyond the realm of the prank. This was a crime, and he wanted no part of it. "I think you'd better run along now."

"But I have a message from Shawn." She still didn't let go of Henry's hand. Despite his irritation, he found the electric tickle from her touch was still running up his arm, and that made him even more annoyed.

"What's that? He's embarrassed to see me dating women my own age and thinks I should be going out with children?"

"He doesn't like you doing the scrapbooks. He thinks it makes you look like an old lady."

The tingling in Henry's arm got stronger, and he realized it wasn't sexual attraction at all. It was electricity. Before he could pull away, she tightened her grip on his hand and sent eight hundred thousand volts through his body.

Chapter Twelve

Over the days since John Marichal's melting body had been scooped up and taken out, the stench in the tin impound shack had begun to dissipate. But the room was still stiflingly hot, and every atom of oxygen seemed to carry a small piece of decayed flesh with it.

As soon as Shawn had sliced through the yellow crime scene tape and pushed open the shack's door, he passed quickly through toward the rear exit. But before he could get out into the lot, Gus had stopped to peer around the small office.

"What are you doing?" Shawn said.

"Looking for evidence," Gus said. "Isn't that why we're here?"

Actually, it wasn't. The real reason they'd come here after their long session in Chief Vick's office was because they needed to find Tara. They had to turn her over to the police so they wouldn't get blamed for any other assaults she might commit. But, as Shawn pointed out, Tara had a car and they didn't, which meant that any attempt to find her was really just hoping for a lucky break. That they could do anywhere. Shawn's first choice was an air-conditioned movie theater, preferably the revival house currently running a Jessica Alba film festival. Second choice was Eagle's View, where Shawn and Gus could chill with Dallas Steele over a frosty Coca-Cola Blāk. When Gus ruled out that option on several grounds, starting with the impossibility of getting there, the impound lot made a pretty good runner-up. Not because they actually expected to run into Tara there. But they had as good a chance of finding her here as anywhere, and this way they might also uncover clues to the murder of John Marichal. Solving that crime might buy them some goodwill with the department. At the very least, it would remove them from the list of suspects.

Gus ducked under the counter and swore under his breath. "The laptop's gone."

"We knew that," Shawn said. "Lassiter said it was missing. And if it had been here, the cops would have taken it. Now can we get out of here?"

Shawn pushed open the back door and stepped out into the bright sunshine. He took a deep breath of clean, corpse-free air and looked out over the lot. It stretched out as far as he could see, acres of abandoned cars slowly rusting away in the salty air. In the center, the gigantic crane stood idle, iron jaws hanging open like a drooping flower.

"And what exactly do you think we're going to find out here?" Gus said as he stepped up next to Shawn.

"For one thing, air." Shawn took a deep breath and let it out slowly. "For another, the answer."

"What's the question?"

"That is a question."

"What?"

"That's another question. And where did it get us? Nowhere. Whereas I actually have an answer."

"Fine," Gus said. "Congratulations."

"Don't you want to know what it is?"

"I think you already know the answer to that one, too."

"I can't help but notice a small tone of hostility in your voice ever since we left the police station," Shawn said.

"Why would I be hostile?" Gus said. "Just because you've gotten us mixed up with a psychotic stalker?"

"Gus, I don't think anyone could have anticipated that Tara would turn out to be crazy."

"I could have," Gus said. "And you know how I know that? Because I did. And I warned you. But it was convenient for you to ignore the fact that she was a raging psycho because she was doing your laundry."

"And doing a good job, too." Shawn rubbed the fabric of his shirt. "She really managed to get my clothes soft."

"Maybe they'll let her launder our prison uniforms," Gus said.

"We're not going to prison, because I've found the answer," Shawn said. "Look."

He pointed out at the crane in the distance.

"That's not an answer—that's a crane."

"It's both," Shawn said. "It's the reason John Marichal was killed."

Gus stared at the crane. It stood on thin legs and had a yellow metal operator's cab between the base and the jib. He tried to imagine it in action, the great jaws falling on a car, crunching through the windows as they lifted it through the air and dropped it into the crushing mechanism. He'd never seen one working in real life before, but he knew he'd seen one in a movie. It came to him in a flash: *Goldfinger*. Bad guys put another bad guy in the trunk of a car and sent it to the crusher. That was where Shawn had found his answer.

"There's no way that fat creep was planning to rob

Fort Knox," Gus said. "And why is it that movie keeps coming up?"

"It's a coincidence," Shawn said. "Or maybe it's enemy action. Anyway, you don't need to jump all the way to the denouement to figure out what's going on here. Stop at the 'bad guy in the trunk' moment. Imagine that as an ongoing business concern."

"How many agents of the British Secret Service do you think there are out here?" Gus said. There just didn't seem to be much of a market for such a service.

"He was disposing of bodies," Shawn said, trying to keep the irritation out of his voice. "Let's say you're a killer. You knock off your victim, and you're looking for a way to get rid of the evidence. You bring it down to Marichal, he sticks it into the trunk of an abandoned car, and crash, crunch, it's part of a metal cube heading for the smelter."

Gus had to admit, it sounded like a plan. But there were too many loose ends. How would you market a scheme like that? It was true, according to Chief Vick, that Marichal's father was a crook, too, so there might be some old family friends in the business. But that was all the way across the country. Marichal had only been here a few months. It wasn't like he'd had time to build up a large social network.

Still, as Shawn said, it was an answer. Maybe it would do for now. He looked over at the crane again, and his heart sank.

"Nope," Gus said.

"What do you mean nope?" Shawn said. "I give you a perfectly worked-out theory, and all you give me is 'nope'?"

"Yup."

"I refuse to accept that," Shawn said.

"Then maybe you should accept this." Gus took off across the lot, leading Shawn through a maze of autos,

first the recently impounded vehicles the police had
towed in for repeated parking violations, then generations of dead cars, killed by head-ons, rollovers, and
plain neglect. As they walked, shapes changed from soft
curves to sharp corners and back to curves again. Colors
came and went as fashions changed. It was like an open-
air museum of automotive styling, as long as you could
look past all the crumpled metal.

Finally they reached the area directly under the crane.
Nothing here seemed to have been made after Richard
Nixon's second inaugural.

"Look at this," Shawn said, peering at the license
plates. "New Mexico, Utah, Florida, Minnesota, Dela-
ware. It's like cars from all across the country came out
here to die."

"More like to rest in peace," Gus said. "And that's exactly what they've been doing for decades." He pointed
at the tires on a few of the cars. They'd decayed away
until they were barely shreds hanging off the wheels.
"They're not doing a lot of car crushing here."

Shawn looked so deflated, Gus almost felt guilty for
bringing him out here. Shawn's theory was good. The
only real problem with it was that it wasn't true. Not
that that was going to stop Shawn.

"Maybe Marichal was planning to go into the body-
disposal business," Shawn said. "And a rival wanted to
stop him before he got started."

"Or maybe we should look for a new theory," Gus
said.

Something whistled past Gus' ear. Metal popped
behind him. At first, he thought Shawn had chucked a
headlight at him. But Shawn was looking around for the
source of the sound, too. He pointed at the trunk of a
sixty-nine Ford Fairlane.

"Was that hole there before?" Shawn said.

Gus bent down to peer at the small round hole in

the trunk just as the rear windshield shattered over his head.

"Duck!" Shawn grabbed Gus and pulled him down to the concrete behind a yellow sixty-five Thunderbird with Florida plates.

"Someone's shooting at us!"

Three more holes blossomed in the cars around them. Shawn poked his head above the hood, then dived to the ground as the rearview mirror shattered.

"Who is it?" Gus said. "Could you see anything?"

Shawn shook his head. "He must be behind one of these cars. We've got to find a way to sneak up on him."

"How can you sneak up on a guy when you don't know where he is?"

Shawn thought that through for a moment. "One of us needs to stand up to draw his fire. The other one can see where the shot comes from."

"Go ahead," Gus said. "Stand."

"I would," Shawn said. "But he's already shot at me once. He probably wants a new target."

"That is the lamest excuse I've ever heard."

"Really?" Shawn said. "I thought it showed some 'outside the box' thinking."

" 'Outside the box' is where we need to be," Gus said. "We've just got to figure out where that box is."

Shawn was about to answer when they heard the faint sound of a cell phone ringing across the lot. "That's him!"

The phone rang again. Shawn pointed across the lot at the place it seemed to be coming from. Then he pointed to Gus and swept his arm around to the west. Gus would creep up on the assassin's left flank. Shawn thumbed his own chest and indicated he'd go around the other way. They gave each other a grave thumbs-up, and each duck-walked in his chosen direction, making sure to keep his head below the level of the cars.

Gus crept forward, his knees screaming at the strain, using the sound of the cell as his homing beacon. As he squeezed through the gap between two rotting Cressidas, the phone stopped ringing. He froze. Now what? He was about to lift his head above the trunk line in hopes of catching a glimpse of the shooter when the phone started ringing again.

Gus started toward the noise. Now another question began to gnaw at him. Why didn't the killer answer his phone? Or if he wasn't going to pick up, why not just turn it off? Why did he let it keep ringing like this? For one triumphant moment, Gus realized they must have taken him out. But then he remembered that they had never returned a shot, and in fact didn't even have a gun. It seemed extremely unlikely they'd scored any kind of hit, let alone a kill shot. Could it be a trap?

Gus poked his head between a rusted-out Accord and a newer Sonata. He was almost back to the shack. The ring now was loud and clear, but there was no one around. Gus crawled forward and froze. Now he realized where the ringing was coming from.

Gus reached up into the open window of his own beloved blue Echo and flipped open the glove compartment. He pulled out Shawn's ringing cell phone and flipped it open.

"Shawn!" Henry Spencer's voice nearly took Gus' head off.

Gus glanced up to see that Shawn had made it over to the Echo. He handed him the phone.

"It's for you," Gus said.

Chapter Thirteen

"She tased me! And then she did this."

Henry pushed Shawn through the front door into his house. Gus followed, stunned at the damage. The table and floor were covered with the charred, soaked remains of hundreds of photographs. A thick coating of ashy soup covered the hardwood; ashes clung to every surface. The smell of burning chemicals hung in the air.

Shawn studied the scene carefully. "She burned all your pictures?"

"They're not my pictures," Henry said. "They belonged to a client."

"Really, a client?" Shawn said. "Is that what you call the old folks you do your little hobby for?"

Henry leveled an accusing finger at this son. "Aha!"

" 'Aha'?" Shawn said. "I don't see an 'aha' here. Gus, do you see an 'aha'?"

"I see a big mess," Gus said. "I'm not getting much in the way of 'aha'."

Henry's accusatory finger didn't move. "She said

you were embarrassed by my scrapbooking. That you thought it made me look like an old lady."

"Look, I said she's crazy. I didn't say she was stupid."

Henry grabbed Shawn and dragged him over to the wreckage on the table. "This is really funny to you, isn't it?"

Gus couldn't look at Shawn. If he did, he knew they'd both burst into giggles. Not because they didn't take this seriously. When Henry had picked them up outside the impound lot, his muscles still twitching slightly from the electric shock, his skin pale, and his eyes red, they were both terrified that something awful had happened. And when he demanded they come with him without saying anything except "your friend stopped by," they jumped into the truck without a question. Gus knew how guilty Shawn must feel about Tara's assault on his father; he felt guilty himself, even though he couldn't figure out any way in which he was more than fractionally responsible.

But Gus and Shawn had been getting called on the carpet together for decades now, and the pattern was always the same. It didn't matter how seriously they took their scolding or how much they feared their punishment. If they looked at each other, they'd start laughing. And while they could sometimes manage to hold off the giggling fit until the lecture was done, as soon as anyone told them that the situation wasn't funny, they were lost.

"Of course not, Dad," Shawn said. "Not the part about her shooting you with a stun gun, anyway. I hate to think how much that must have hurt."

That was a small lie, Gus knew. They both welcomed the thought of Henry's pain, since it was the only thing that was keeping them from bursting into inappropriate and unintended laughter.

"If we'd ever thought she'd come to see you, we would have called with a warning," Gus said.

"She did this because you wanted her to."

"No!"

"So you didn't want me to stop scrapbooking?"

"Well, I wouldn't go that far," Shawn said. "I'd like to see you maintain some dignity."

"Like when I was lying helpless on the floor, my muscles twitching uncontrollably?"

"Maybe a little more dignity than that," Shawn conceded.

"I don't know what's more disturbing," Henry said. "The fact that there's a lunatic out there acting out your deepest desires, or that you have so little respect for me that you don't trust me to live my own life."

"It's a tough call, but I'm going to go with the lunatic," Shawn said. "Gus?"

"Lunatic, definitely," Gus said.

"A lunatic you just happened to tell what an embarrassment your old man is."

"I never did that," Shawn said.

"Then how did she know?" Henry demanded. "She read your mind?"

"You know, there's a really funny thing about that," Shawn said. "She thinks she did."

"Tara believes that Shawn is beaming her orders psychically," Gus said.

Henry stared at Shawn, his anger momentarily eclipsed by disbelief. "She what?"

"It's true," Shawn said. "I thought it made her happy to help out. You know, the way some people claim to like picking up litter or helping the homeless or standing outside supermarkets trying to get me to sign petitions. Anyway, it turns out that Tara thinks she's my psychic mind slave."

"Oh, Shawn." Henry thought wistfully back on the days when he could lift his son over his knee and paddle some sense into him. "I told you this psychic nonsense would bring nothing but trouble."

"It's brought me a lot besides trouble," Shawn said. "This time it just happened to drop a little trouble along the way."

"And the second she told you this, what did you do?" Henry said. "Did you take her to a doctor? Bring her to the police so they could hold her for psychiatric evaluation? Try to ease her out of her delusion?"

"Well—"

Henry's hands were twitching again. Gus wasn't sure if it was the aftereffects of the stun gun or sheer rage.

"No, let me guess. You took advantage of her mental illness and used her as a servant. Just like you take advantage of everybody."

"I don't take advantage of people," Shawn said. "Do I, Gus?"

"Yes, Gus, go ahead and tell him."

Gus stared down at the ground. It was a trick he'd been trying since he was three—ignore the problem and wait for it to go away. It hadn't worked yet, but Gus was hoping this time might be the charm.

"He can't do it, Shawn. Because he knows the truth— you've been taking advantage of him for years."

Shawn looked shocked at the accusation. "I don't take advantage of Gus."

"It just always works out that you get whatever you want no matter what it costs him."

"Yeah, it works out that way," Shawn said. "No, wait. It doesn't always work that way. I do lots of things for Gus."

"Name one."

"I kept him from going to Guatemala with the chess club, because I knew his delicate system couldn't handle all those Latin American germs."

"And because you didn't want to be alone for two weeks."

"So it was a win-win," Shawn said. He turned to Gus. "Come on, Gus, tell him he's crazy."

It's amazing how much detail you can see in the plainest of wood floors if you really look, Gus thought. The pattern of the grain was so interesting he couldn't bear to lift his eyes from it.

"Gus?" Shawn was pleading now.

Henry fixed Shawn with a piercing stare. "You use people, Shawn. You manipulate them, and you take advantage of them. Most people don't mind too much, because you're a fun guy to be around. But this time you've used a terribly sick person, and it's got consequences."

For a moment, it looked like Shawn was going to argue. But before the first words were out of his mouth, he saw the look on his father's face and reconsidered.

"I don't think I treat people all that badly," Shawn said. "But I'll concede I might have made a mistake with Tara. What I took to be an adorable eccentricity turned out to be a psychotic compulsion, and if I had realized that earlier, I probably could have saved us all a lot of trouble."

"Us all?"

"Well, you more than me," Shawn admitted.

"That's a beginning." Henry patted Shawn on the shoulder, then picked up one of the less charred file boxes from the floor and handed it to him. "This is a better one."

Shawn stared at the soggy mass of charred cardboard. "That's a box."

"More precisely, it's an empty box. At least it is until you get busy cleaning this mess into it. Then it will be a full box."

"I've got to find Tara," Shawn said.

"Yes, you do," Henry said. "But first you need to re-store my house to the way it was before she showed up here."

"Couldn't we just burn the rest of it down? It'll be faster."

Henry picked up another box and handed it to Gus. "He's going to get you to do most of the work anyway. You might as well start now."

Gus didn't bother to argue. He took the box and started dumping sodden photos into it.

"And while we're cleaning up your house, what are you going to do?" Shawn said.

"I'm going to sit in my chair and watch you work," Henry said. "And when I'm done enjoying that, I'm going to try to figure out what I can tell the Perths."

Shawn picked up a stack of prints, each one of the happy couple sitting on their living room couch and staring straight into the camera.

"Maybe you can tell them that something interesting finally happened to them."

Henry scowled at his son, then headed for the arm-chair in a far corner. But just as he settled in, there was a knock at the door. All three men froze.

"She's back," Gus said.

"What do we do?" Shawn said.

Henry pulled himself out of the chair. "I don't know what you two brave souls are going to do, but I'm going to answer the door."

"What if it's Tara?" Shawn whispered.

"Then you can send her a psychic order to commit herself to the nearest nut hatch." Henry walked to the door and threw it open.

His first thought was that someone had left a man-nequin on his porch as a joke. The man was frozen ab-solutely still, one hand outstretched in retreat from the door it had just knocked on. After a brief moment, the man seemed to come to life, the hand retreating mechanically to his side.

Henry glanced back over his shoulder. "Shawn," he said, "this has got to be for you."

Chapter Fourteen

The ride through the mountains to Eagle's View seemed even longer than it had before. The first time Gus had spent most of the drive terrified at the probability that he was being chauffeured by a psychopath. Looking back, that seemed like such a small problem, on a level with being caught reading under the covers with a flashlight or attracting the attention of the mean kids from first grade or all the other things that used to send him into a panic when he was six.

Now Gus realized that there was a great advantage to having a psychotic stalker as your driver: You didn't have to worry about where she was or what she might be doing.

As Shepler piloted the car mechanically through the hairpin curves, Gus tried to keep his mind on the possibility that Steele's assistant might slip into one of his mind-freeze moments just as they rounded a switchback, and send them plummeting hundreds of feet to a fiery death. But as with most of Gus' attempts to keep a cheery thought in the face of imminent disaster, the appealing notion of dying kept being replaced by the more troubling image of what Tara might be doing now.

It was an issue he'd tried to raise with Shawn when Shepler first showed up at Henry Spencer's door. Shawn, not surprisingly, had seen his arrival as a reprieve from the onerous task of cleaning up his father's house. Of course he tried to hide that fact from Henry by insisting he was motivated only by his fiduciary duty to a man who'd entrusted him with an investment fund of one hundred million dollars. And that started an entirely different argument.

"Please tell me that this is another attempt to cheat your way to the world Monopoly championship," Henry said.

"First of all, that wasn't cheating," Shawn said, jumping back into an argument that had reached an armistice fourteen years ago as if they'd been in the middle of it when Shepler knocked on the door. "I was going to bring the concept of monopolization to Monopoly itself. If I'd been successful, it would have changed the game forever."

"Whatever," Henry said. "It's a silly game for silly children, and nothing a grown man should be wasting his time on."

"As opposed to say, cutting out pictures and gluing them into albums?" Shawn said.

"I'm preserving my clients' precious memories, and if you think that's a waste of time, I feel sorry for you," Henry said.

"And I'm being paid to invest Dallas Steele's money," Shawn said. "Maybe you can feel sorry for me about that, too."

"Technically speaking, we're not getting paid," Gus said. "Not until we show a profit."

"If I wanted to speak technically, I would have chosen a profession that required some actual knowledge," Shawn said.

"Maybe that might have paid some actual money," Gus said.

There was a discreet throat clearing from the front door. Shepler stood at the doorstep like a vampire waiting for an invitation into the house. "Mr. Steele has a small window available and would very much like to speak with the two of you."

"I'd think in that monstrosity of a house he'd have every size window you could think of," Shawn said. "How did you find us here anyway?"

"Is that how you talk to a man who entrusts you with one hundred million dollars?" Henry said.

"This isn't that man," Shawn said. "And how would you talk to someone who gave me a hundred million dollars?"

"First I'd make sure his straitjacket was on securely," Henry said.

"Oh, well, as long as we're speaking respectfully," Shawn said.

Gus glanced at his watch. He figured that Shawn and Henry could keep going at each other for at least another three minutes, which was fine with him. He needed the time to figure out what they should do.

The first choice was easy—they could go with Shepler. After all, Steele had entrusted them with a huge responsibility, and if he wanted to meet, it seemed ungenerous to refuse. It was disconcerting to have Shepler simply arrive with a summons, Gus had to admit, but he'd never met a multibillionaire before. Maybe that was how they did things.

Still, Gus didn't like to think that Steele could send his minion for them whenever he wanted, and they'd be expected to jump. Even ignoring the question of just how Shepler had tracked them down to Henry's house, there was the issue of the precedent this would set. If they agreed to come now, would that say that they'd be available for Steele no matter what they were doing? What if they were in the middle of a case? What if they were undercover? What if they were tracking a dangerous suspect?

And that was what was really troubling Gus. They weren't tracking a dangerous suspect, and they should be. Tara was somewhere out there planning to enforce some twisted version of Shawn's desires, which was a truly terrifying thought once you considered how twisted Shawn's own version of Shawn's desires could be. She was a monster they had helped to create, and it was their responsibility to track her down and put her back in a cage. Beyond that, someone had taken half a dozen shots at them, and that seemed like something that could use some investigating.

Unfortunately, by the time he'd come to this realization, Shawn was already halfway to Shepler's car and Henry was yelling after him, "This mess is going to be here when you get back!"

Gus gave Henry an apologetic smile along with the half-filled box of charred photos and ran after Shawn.

As soon as Henry's house had disappeared from the Bentley's rear window, Gus tried to make Shawn share his urgency. "We have got to make this meeting short," he said. "We've got to find Tara."

"What's the hurry?" Shawn said. "Odds are she'll find us sooner or later."

"The hurry is what she might do in that time between sooner and later."

"She's only doing what she thinks I want, right?" Shawn said. "It's not like she's going to kill anybody."

"Are you sure?"

Shawn thought about that. "I think I'd remember if I sent her psychic orders to commit murder."

"You mean you did order her to tase your dad?"

"Not exactly," Shawn said. "But I'm pretty sure I was complaining about his ridiculous scrapbook hobby at least one time she was driving us around."

"And who else were you complaining about?" Gus said. "What are we going to do to protect all those people?"

Shawn glanced out the rear window as the car began the long slow ascent up the mountains. "For the moment, nothing."

Gus couldn't believe what he was hearing. "She's already beaten one guy into the hospital."

"If you can call him a guy," Shawn said. "What kind of man is going to be taken out by a girl?"

"And she set your father's house on fire."

"For which the neighborhood-improvement committee will probably give her a medal."

"Do you think this is funny?"

"Not *Monty Python* funny, but maybe *Brady Bunch* funny. You know, no big laughs, but a wry smile, a warm chuckle, and that nod of recognition that we're all riders in the same cockeyed caravan of life."

Shawn glanced out the back window again. Gus wanted to grab his face and force Shawn to look at him. Pretending it was all a joke wasn't going to make this any less serious.

"Then let's not think about her innocent victims for a minute," Gus said, forcing his voice to stay calm. "Let's think about us. The police know she beat up that BurgerZone kid, and if they don't know what she did to your father, they will soon. If she acts again now that we know what she's doing, they will come after us."

Shawn glanced out the rear window again. "So that's what you're so worried about? That Tara's going to do something awful before we can stop her?"

Gus wanted to scream. "Yes!"

"Then I don't think there's anything to worry about."

"Why not?"

"Look."

Shawn pointed out the rear window. The road stretched out for a hundred yards behind them, then disappeared around a hairpin curve.

"I don't see anything," Gus said.

"Keep looking."

Gus did. All he saw was the roadway, the sheer drop next to it, and a pair of hawks circling slowly over a road sign. "I still don't see—"

Just before the car twisted around another switchback, there was a flash of metallic red emerging from around the last twist.

"That's why," Shawn said.

For the rest of the ride up, Gus kept his eyes on the rear window, just to make sure Tara was still following them. There were long stretches when there wasn't a hint of red, and he feared that she'd come just far enough to make sure where they were going, then turned back to Santa Barbara. But every time he came close to panic, he'd catch a glimpse of her creeping around a turn.

When they crested the last rise before the descent into the cereal bowl, Gus couldn't help craning his head for another long look at the famous house. The last time they were here, the sun was shining and the sky was brilliant blue. Now there were storm clouds hiding the sun and painting the entire valley a dismal gray. To Gus' delight, Eagle's View was even more magnificently ugly in the gloom.

A thick wet drop splashed on the windshield. Shepler flicked on the windshield wipers before it could even start to trail away toward the roof.

"So what happens if it rains a long time up here, Shepler?" Shawn said, peering out at the clouds. "Does the whole bowl fill up? Or is there a drain somewhere you just have to pull the plug on?"

Shepler ignored Shawn, focusing all his attention on the spiraling road ahead.

"That was actually a major concern of the original landscape architects who designed the property." Gus was happy to have history take his mind off the present. "There was much debate about how quickly natural runoff would occur, and what the risks of flooding were. They ended up carving out a series of drain tunnels that would channel . . ."

Gus spent the rest of the ride explaining the landscape architecture of the Eagle's View grounds. Shawn spent the rest of the ride pretending to listen. Every so often Gus glanced out the rear window to see if there was a red Mercedes behind them. But Tara must have decided the concentric rings into the cereal bowl would be too exposed for her to follow surreptitiously. Gus hoped that she was waiting at the top of the pass.

When the car finally pulled into the driveway, Steele was there to meet it. He marched up before Shepler put on the parking brake and flung open Shawn's door, a champagne bottle in one hand and three flutes in the other.

"Welcome back to Eagle's View," Steele said. Gus was practically blinded by the brilliant white of his teeth against the gray sky. "I guess you don't need to be psychic to know why I brought you here."

Shawn and Gus scrambled out of the car as the cork exploded out of the champagne bottle.

"I'm getting a celebratory vibe," Shawn said. "It seems like someone's happy about something."

"Try ecstatic." Steele threw his arms around Shawn and Gus, and led them into the house. Shepler started the car and steered it toward the entrance to the underground garage.

"So I guess we're doing okay on the investments?" Gus said as Steele led them through the atrium. This time they passed both Steele's massive office and the game room.

"Let's just say that it seems particularly appropriate that we meet in the celebration room," Steele said.

Gus gasped with excitement.

"Why do I get the feeling I'm about to get another history lesson?" Shawn said.

"The celebration room was famous in its day," Gus said. "They had huge parties where the rich and famous could do whatever they wanted, because there was no chance anyone would ever find out. There were rumors of drugs, orgies, you name it."

"That's really exciting," Shawn said. "But we could also meet in the 'pay your consultants a ton of money room' if that's convenient."

Steele let out a booming laugh and turned them down a wide, dark corridor that dead-ended at an enormous bronze door. As Gus got closer, he could see it was covered in a frieze of couples engaged in various sexual activities. Sometimes trios.

"Are they doing what it looks like they're doing?" Shawn said.

"Oh, yeah," Gus said.

"Wow," Shawn said, studying the images. "Try to bring this into the bathroom with you. No wonder they invented magazines."

After giving Shawn and Gus a few moments to study the images on the door, Steele reached past them and pushed on it. Despite the door's massive size and weight, it glided open silently at a touch of Steele's finger.

Gus squeezed his eyes shut as the door swung open, wanting to get the full impact of the reveal. When he opened them, he found himself staring into a small black box of a room, barely more than a closet. A rough wooden floor ran for no more than six feet before hitting a plain stone wall. A couple of folding chairs leaned in one corner; a tray of rat poison lay open in another.

Steele reached up and pulled the chain that switched on the lone bare bulb. "Gentlemen," he said, his smile even wider now, if that was possible, "welcome to the celebration room."

"Must have been some rocking parties here," Shawn said. "You could fit at least four people in this room."

"I don't understand," Gus said. "There are supposed to be rotating beds. And where's the obscene Maxfield Parrish mural?"

"Where did you hear about those?"

"I studied this house in school," Gus said, surreptitiously rapping his knuckles against a wall to see if it would slide aside to reveal the real room. It didn't. "I read accounts of the parties."

"And who wrote those accounts?" Steele said.

"People who talked to people who'd been at them, I guess," Gus said.

"But never a firsthand account, right?" Steele said.

Gus tried to think back on his texts. "I guess," he said.

"Because there were no firsthand accounts," Steele said.

"Right." Gus was putting it together now. "Because the parties were so private and the behavior so scandalous that no one would ever dare talk about them for fear that they'd be exposed."

"Because there were no parties. Elias Adler hated people. Despised being in their presence. And yet he wanted them to worship him. So he had his architects leak false information about an enormous, decadent room that would be dedicated to elaborate celebrations. He had this door imported from Padua and let one reporter sneak a photograph of it. Just a hint of all the terrible things that were going to happen behind it."

"And then no one would admit they'd been to the parties for fear they'd be accused of perversion," Gus said.

"Adler never even invited anyone," Steele said. "He just had his paid flacks spread rumors of all the movie stars and politicians that had showed up for his parties. At first, they tried to deny it. But no one believed any of the denials, because who wouldn't deny being in such a place? After a while the parties had such a cachet that people hoped no one would believe their denials. Adler became the most famous host in the United States, and he never let a guest cross his threshold."

"Must have saved him a fortune on catering bills," Shawn said.

"It reminds me what a genius that man was," Steele said. "He understood that if you simply say something with enough confidence, people will believe you. You've got the same kind of genius, Shawn. That's what we're here to toast."

Steele raised the bottle and refilled their glasses, then knocked his back in one gulp. Gus glanced over at Shawn and saw that he was beaming under the praise. Gus wasn't so sure this was a time to be celebrating. There was something in Steele's tone that suggested there might be more than a few thorns hidden among the roses.

"So why exactly did you bring us up here, Dal?" Gus said.

"As I said, for a celebration," Dallas said. "I'm very impressed with the work you've done for me."

"So the investments are just as good as you expected?" Shawn said.

"Every bit."

Again, Gus had the sensation of a thorn biting through his thumb.

"What do we do now?" Shawn said. "Can we start dividing up the profits yet? Because my friend here could certainly use six thousand dollars. And I hope you notice that I'm acting entirely in his interests here, and that I'm putting my own desires second. Because that's what friends do for each other."

Gus aimed a kick at Shawn's ankle, but Shawn stepped neatly out of the way.

"You'll certainly be getting a large share of the profits," Steele said. "But that's just money. I want to let the world know all about your astonishing accomplishment. That's why we're having the press conference tomorrow."

Gus wasn't sure why he was feeling so uncomfortable with the direction this conversation was taking. He was even less sure why Shawn wasn't. "Press conference?"

"I've invited the local media," Steele said. "And some of the more important figures in the community: mayor, city council president, police chief, heads of various charitable organizations. All groups that stand to profit from our investments in the local business community. I'm sure they'll all want to express their gratitude to you for your hard work."

Gus glanced over at Shawn again. Was it possible that he was actually blushing?

"I don't know what to say," Shawn said.

"Just say you'll be here."

"Of course we will," Shawn said.

Steele pressed an intercom button on the wall. Before he lifted his finger from the buzzer, Shepler had already arrived. "Yes, Mr. Steele?"

"Are the rooms ready yet?"

"Of course. I thought we'd put them in the north tower."

"Terrific," Steele said, then turned his dazzling smile on Shawn and Gus. "The press conference is going to start at eight in the morning to make sure we maximize the news cycle. I thought it would be much more convenient for you guys to stay here overnight instead of schlepping down and back up the mountain."

What had been a nagging feeling in the back of Gus' head was now spreading throughout his brain and trickling down into his body. He couldn't remember which fairy tale he'd read as a kid that had a scenario frighteningly like this one, but he was sure that it had one hell of an ugly ending. And even if Gus managed to convince himself that the invitation was entirely for their own benefit, he couldn't stop thinking about Tara. It was possible that she was still waiting for them at the pass. But would she stay there all night? Or would she realize that they were tucked safely away and go off to do some of Shawn's psychic bidding?

"That sounds great, Dal," Shawn said.

Gus tugged at Shawn's sleeve. "Yes, Dal, great," he said trying to put as much a significance into his voice as he could. "But we promised Shawn's dad we'd help him clean up a little mess in his house. You remember what happened at your dad's place, don't you, Shawn?"

"That's the place Shepler picked you up today? The bungalow by the shore?" Steele asked.

"Hasn't moved in decades," Shawn said. "He's kind of like a fungus that way."

"How did you know where Shawn's dad lives?" Gus said. "And how did you know we were there?"

"Can't hire a consultant without performing my due diligence," Steele said, then turned to Shepler. "Get a full cleaning crew to that address this afternoon. Oh, and have the painters tag along, see if any of the rooms need freshening."

"Oh, they do," Shawn said.

"Great," Steele said. "Send the whole crew: painters, plasterers, plumbers, electricians. Tell them to improve everything in the house, and not to stop until I tell them to personally."

Shepler turned away and spoke quietly into his cell phone as Steele gestured for Shawn and Gus to follow him back the way they'd come.

"That's incredibly generous of you," Shawn said.

"Got to keep my crew busy somehow," Steele said. "You're going to love the north tower. You'll feel like kings of the world."

"Hear that, Gus?" Shawn said. "You always wanted to be like Leonardo DiCaprio in *Titanic*."

"Yes, because it worked out so well for him," Gus said. "Don't you think if we're going to be speaking at a press conference tomorrow we should at the very least go home and change our clothes?"

"What's wrong with what we're wearing?" Shawn asked.

In Shawn's case it was a plaid flannel shirt over a white T, blue jeans, and white sneakers. At least that was how his clothes had started out this morning. Now they were all various shades of gray and black, smeared with the ashy remains of the Perths' less-than-memorable lives. Although Gus had tried to be careful when cleaning up the mess, his baby blue button-down and khakis were spotted with old oil from the chase through the auto-wrecking lot.

"Nothing," Gus said, "if the press conference is to launch a new laundry powder, and we're the 'before' picture. You know, 'I just spent the day rolling in oil from a thousand rotting cars. How can I ever get the spots out?' Otherwise, I think we should go back home so we can get some clean clothes."

Shawn turned to Steele and gave him an apologetic shrug. "Some people just don't understand how rich people live."

"It does take some adjustment," Steele said.

"Gus, I'm sure if we stay here, Shepler can have our

clothes cleaned before eight o'clock tomorrow," Shawn said. "Isn't that right, Shep?"

Gus hadn't noticed that sometime in the conversation Shepler had caught up with them.

"Of course my staff will have your clothes cleaned," Steele said. "You'll find robes in the rooms. Just put your stuff in a bag outside the door, and you'll have everything back cleaned and pressed in plenty of time."

"Excellent," Shawn said.

"But—"

"I won't hear any buts, Gus," Shepler said. "If there's anything at all you need, we can provide it for you."

"What if we have tickets to a ball game tonight?" Gus snatched at one last straw. "Remember, you were going to take *Tara*?"

"Dude, when have we ever had tickets to a ball game?"

"When have the Pumas ever had an unbroken win streak?"

"The Pumas? Really?" Shawn said. "The Santa Barbara Middle School Pumas?"

"I like to support our alma mater," Gus said. "And with the new coach and their winning season, Puma softball is the hottest ticket in Santa Barbara."

"They don't even have tickets," Shawn said. "They ripped out the bleachers after Vice Principal Provenza found out Mary Lombardi was selling peeks at her bra for fifty cents under them."

"Lawn seating is extremely competitive," Gus said. "You have to line up early to get a good spot."

A crack of thunder boomed somewhere above them. At the end of the corridor, sheets of rain pounded down into the open atrium, turning the tranquil surface of the reflecting pond into the kind of surf that capsized lobster boats.

"I don't think the championship is going to be settled tonight," Steele said. "And now I really have to insist that you stay. You don't want to ask Shepler to drive down and up the mountain in this kind of weather, do you?"

Gus wanted to say that he didn't care what Shepler had to do. He was getting the creeps here, and he wanted to get away from this place. But it didn't look like that was going to happen easily, and the goofy grin on Shawn's face suggested that he wasn't going to help Gus out.

"Of course not," Gus said. "Besides, who could resist the north tower?"

After they'd been walking for what felt like an hour, the slick marble of the walls gave way to rough, unfinished stone blocks. The floor, too, was paved with uneven flagstones.

Gus pulled Shawn aside and whispered in his ear, "Something's wrong here."

"I agree," Shawn said. "We seem to be going back in time. But Roman is actually older than German. So which way is the Wayback Machine going?"

"Not with the house, with Steele," Gus said. "I think he's setting us up for something."

"Of course he is," Shawn said. "Didn't it ever occur to you that this whole thing was too good to be true?"

For a moment, Gus was speechless. In his entire life he'd never been able to accept a gift without wondering about the motivation behind it. But he had welcomed Steele's attention without question, lunged at the opportunity he offered with no qualms. Because he wanted it so badly. "You've known all along?"

"I figured he must be up to something," Shawn said.

"Then why did you let us go along with it?"

"Couldn't think of a better way to find out what it was," Shawn said.

"So what is it?"

"No idea," Shawn said. "But I figure we'll find out in the morning. So we might as well have a good time at Steele's expense tonight."

Steele stopped in front of a massive wooden door. "These are the stairs to the north tower. I wish I could provide you with an elevator, but I'm afraid Mr. Adler was a stickler for authenticity, and if King Ludwig didn't have an elevator in his tower, then Eagle's View wouldn't either."

"How did King Ludwig feel about cable?" Shawn said.

Steele laughed again. "If there's anything you need, just let Shepler know." He glanced at his watch. "I was hoping to join you two for dinner, but I've got an international conference call that's going to go late, so if you wouldn't mind eating in the dining room up there, I'll make sure you're well taken care of."

"Sweet," Shawn said.

Dallas lifted a wrought-iron hoop the size of a hubcap and used it to pull open the door. In the gloom beyond, a tight spiral of stairs loomed upward roughly to eternity.

"Well, I guess I'll see you in the morning," Steele said. "Shepler will bring you down to the auditorium for the press conference."

Shepler stepped through the doorway and started up the spiral staircase, and Shawn was right behind him. Gus wasn't quite ready to follow.

"Dal?"

Steele was already halfway through dialing a call on his BlackBerry, but he slipped it back into his pocket at the sound of Gus' voice. "I was just going to make sure that the Pumas game really was canceled. Sometimes we get a storm up here, and by the time it gets down to the coast, it's just a little drizzle."

"That's okay," Gus said. "I just have a question about something you said before."

"What's that?"

Gus knew he could stop now. Let Dallas go without answering and try to enjoy the night ahead like Shawn. But Gus wasn't like Shawn, and he knew he could never enjoy the night. He'd spend it lying awake, worrying about what would come tomorrow.

"When we first got here you took us to the celebration room," Gus said. "You said it seemed appropriate."

"I did say that." Something in Steele's voice suggested that he was happy Gus had asked the question.

"Because we were celebrating," Shawn said. He and Shepler were standing on the steps just before they curved out of sight. "Let's go. Those stairs aren't going to climb themselves, you know."

"But there were never actually celebrations in the celebration room," Gus said. "As you pointed out, the whole thing was a fraud. Even the room itself was a fraud, just a big door hanging in front of a broom closet."

"That's true."

"So why was it appropriate that we celebrate there?" Gus said.

Steele's laugh boomed past Gus' ear on its way up to Shawn. "Whatever you do, Shawn, never lose this guy. He's one of the sharpest minds I've ever met."

The dark fears in Gus' mind suddenly grew large enough to split off into separate camps. One of them immediately set out and established a colony in his stomach. "So what is the answer?" he said, increasingly certain that he might never be as happy again as he was right now.

"I was going to let that be a surprise," Dallas said, mulling it over. "Hold this little thing back and spring it on you at the press conference. Let the whole world see your faces when you found out what any sentient beings would have known before they came up here."

Having completely conquered his stomach, the suspicions opened a new frontier in Gus' knees, leaving him reaching for the wall to steady himself. "Umm, Shawn, I think you want to come down for this," Gus called up the stairs.

"I'm already five stairs up," Shawn said. "Why don't you come here?"

"Shawn!" Gus didn't glance back over his shoulder to see if Shawn was coming, but the heavy sighs and heavier footsteps told him the story. "There's something Dallas wants to tell us before the press conference."

"I promise I won't bring up the whole shoelace thing, if that's what this is about," Shawn said.

"It's not," Gus said.

"Gus was asking why I thought it was appropriate to announce my intentions to you in a room that was designed as a complete fraud," Steele said. "The reason for that is as simple as it is obvious. Because you are complete frauds. And tomorrow the whole world will know."

Chapter Fifteen

Gus watched the line of light creep across the eastern lip of the cereal bowl. After six hours of staring into the darkness, the newly revealed view of the valley should have been a refreshing change. But all it did was make Gus realize that the press conference was going to start in a couple of hours, and they still had no plan for what they were going to do.

At least Gus didn't have a plan. Shawn seemed to have come up with one on his own. The light snoring from the adjoining room suggested that he had put it into action.

Gus knew that he should be the one sleeping peacefully. Shawn should have spent the entire night staring hopelessly out the window. After all, it wasn't Gus who had a reputation as a psychic to protect. It wasn't Gus who'd be singled out for the greatest ridicule.

But there was going to be plenty of ridicule to go around, and even a fraction of it would be enough to cover Gus with a veneer of shame he'd never be able to scrape off. Everyone they'd ever met, everyone they were ever going to meet, everyone in the whole world they'd never meet would think of them as phonies. His name would be a punch line on the late-night shows. He thought back on all the ways the kids in middle school had twisted "Guster" into obscene variations, and shuddered to contemplate what highly paid comedy writers could do with it. He'd finally managed to convince his parents that his work with Shawn was a real career, not a distraction from his conventional job pushing pharmaceuticals; there was no way they'd take Psych seriously now. If he ever wanted to have another civil conversation with them he'd have to go back to pharmaceutical sales full-time—if his company didn't fire him first. He wasn't sure about the exact wording, but he was pretty sure that there was a clause in his contract that said being exposed on national television as a fraud was grounds for termination.

The scale of their losses was that huge. In a matter of weeks, they had not only lost the entire hundred million dollars Dallas gave them to invest—they were now actually thirteen million dollars in the red.

Shawn and Gus' first disastrous investment was an electric car that could run six hundred miles on a single charge. Gus thought it had the potential to change the world, and it might have—but only as long as no one ever drove above seven miles an hour. It turned out that once the cars hit the eight-mph mark, their batteries burst into flame. Except that "burst" didn't adequately capture the true quality of the explosion that ensued. Two late-night janitors had decided to drag race through the factory in a couple of test models, and investigators were still trying to figure out exactly how deep the crater was.

At least that damage was confined to an abandoned corner of New Mexico. Shawn and Gus had also invested Steele's money in a company called Urban Petrolcum that planned to use their new low-footprint technology to drill for oil where no one had ever been able to drill for oil before. Their first well, a demonstration project, was set up inside a vacant storefront on Fifth Avenue in Manhattan, right across from Rockefeller Center. That way, when oil started gushing the *Today* show wouldn't have to go far to cover them. Unfortunately all they discovered was that there was a subway tunnel right under their drill, along with the main water, sewer, and electric lines serving all of Midtown. The only gusher they hit was a gusher of lawsuits.

And then there was the Transformatrons, the Chinese toy boats that turned into battling robots. At first they were every bit as successful as Shawn had predicted. They might have taken over the entire toy business if only some of the consumers hadn't insisted on immersing their toy boats in water. It seemed that the Chinese manufacturer had used a special glue, which, when wet, dissolved into a substance chemically identical to a powerful hallucinogenic drug.

The rest of the investments failed less spectacularly, but not one of them had earned a nickel yet. Still, the huge financial disaster wasn't the worst part. That was the joy Dallas Steele took in the loss. As Dal laid out the scope of their failure, his smile only got broader.

"How can you be so happy?" Gus had finally managed to choke out after Dallas finished listing their disasters. "You just sat by and let us blow a hundred million of your dollars?"

"He wasn't sitting by," Shawn said. "He was actively involved. Weren't you, Dal?"

Steele gave him an ironic bow. "I did preview some of the files before I asked Shepler to send them over."

"Preview and edit, I'd say," Shawn said. "Removing key information that would keep any intelligent investor away."

"Oh, much more than that," Steele said. "I took out information that would have scared off even you two. But you'll be happy to know I've restored it all now, so if you try to claim you were framed, there's plenty of evidence to prove you're lying."

"But why?" Gus said. "It cost you a fortune."

"It would be worth three times that," Steele said.

"If all you wanted was to humiliate us, you could have just written us a check for fifty mil, and we would have done it ourselves," Shawn said.

Steele turned his blinding smile on Shawn. "As I told you, my wife was quite impressed with your work at the Veronica Mason trial. She thinks you're some kind of miracle man. And I hated the idea of my beloved bride actually believing in nonsense like psychic powers."

Gus tried to make sense of what he was hearing. "You spent a hundred million dollars, you destroyed half of Midtown Manhattan, you blew a hole in Arizona—all to win an argument with your wife? That doesn't make any sense."

"As Shawn said, you don't understand how rich people live," Steele said.

As the line of sunlight crept down the bowl, Gus tried to catch any glimpse of metallic red. His last sighting of Tara's car had come hours ago when they were still driving up to the pass. It seemed almost impossible that she'd stayed up in the mountains waiting for them. And yet that impossibility was his only hope for any benefit to come out of their trip up here. It sure wasn't coming from the press conference.

The next two hours passed with the same mixture of tedium and anxiety as a death row prisoner's final moments. There was the last meal of Gus' favorite breakfast foods, which he could barely bring himself to nibble at. There were the hearty words of encouragement that it was all going to be over soon, and he'd be in a better place. Gus suspected that such sentiments would be no more convincing coming from a prison chaplain than they were from his oldest friend, even assuming that the priest wouldn't keep interrupting his homilies to ask, "Are you going to eat that?" And then there was the heavy jangling of keys outside the cell door—or in this case, the trilling of Shepler's cell phone as he fielded calls from reporters who'd gotten lost on the way to the press conference—followed by the long, slow walk down the last mile. In this case, the last mile was actually that, since they had to make their way down the twisting stairs, then through endless corridors until they finally arrived at Eagle View's private theater, where the spectators were waiting for Steele to flip the switch on Shawn and Gus.

During the entire endless march, Gus and Shawn hadn't said a word to each other. Gus had barely looked up from his feet, while Shawn was lost in what some might have assumed was worry but what Gus knew was actually just his usual prenoon haze. Now that they were finally standing right outside the chamber, it seemed that they should have some kind of significant last words. Gus couldn't find any. It was up to Shawn to say what they both felt.

"Shep tells me there's a bowling alley in this place," he said. "After we're done with the press conference, what do you say we do a couple frames?"

Before Gus could answer, Shepler pulled open the great doors and ushered them through. "Enjoy the press conference, gentlemen," he said. "I have to run the sound and the lights, so I can't be with you. But I will be watching from the booth."

That there was no explosion of sound as the doors closed behind them was merely the failure of the world to live up to what was going on inside Gus' mind.

Gus always loved the idea of having an actual theater

in a home. Not a wide TV with a popcorn machine next
to it, but an actual auditorium with curtains and reclin-
ing chairs and lots of velvet. But he never dreamed of
anything as grand as the room they found themselves
in now. There was barely an inch that wasn't covered in
gold or silver; the gilded jaguars leaping out of the doorway seemed to have gemstones for eyes. The walls were
covered with a golden frieze telling the story of God's
creation of Earth, His raising of Man from the muck,
and His guidance through the great cultures of history.
While some might have quibbled over minor theological issues—it's not generally accepted that the Egyp-
tians built the pyramids with help from a UFO-driving
divinity—what would have upset many more believers
was the notion that God was created entirely in Elias
Adler's image.

Even through his fog of despair, Gus marveled at the
theater. If only he had more time to study it, to examine
carefully every gold-slopped inch of it, he'd devote his
life to understanding this temple to one man's ego. He
might even be willing to convert to the Church of Elias
Adler.

Anything, as long as it would put off walking down
the scarlet carpet to the front of the auditorium.

Because the first three rows of seats in front of the
slightly raised stage and grand gold curtain were filled
with people who had turned to stare at him and Shawn.
Gus recognized most of the faces, and a couple of them
belonged to people he hoped he could still consider
friendly despite the events of the last few days—Chief
Vick was in the front row with the mayor who'd ap-
pointed her; Detective Juliet O'Hara was a row back
with Lassiter.

But most of the faces showed no sympathy at all. The
assembled reporters, many of whom had been so eager
for a quote after the Veronica Mason verdict they prac-

tically licked Gus' hand, now gazed at them with the hungry stare of a diner making sure his waiter grabbed the meatiest lobster from the tank.

It was the smiling faces that bothered Gus the most. He didn't know what Steele had said when he'd invited these people to the press conference, but he must have suggested it wasn't going to be a particularly pleasant experience for Shawn and Gus. Because the happiest smiles in the room belonged to people who spent a lot of time wishing them a hideous, drooling death.

It wasn't just Carlton Lassiter who looked like he was about to receive the pony Santa had never brought him. Three seats down from him was Ernie Farrago, a crime reporter for the *Santa Barbara Times* Shawn had embarrassed on a half dozen occasions. There were other happy faces Gus couldn't quite place, but he was pretty sure that Shawn had done something to all of them that would leave them eager to see him publicly humiliated. And then there was the biggest grin of all, plastered across the face of District Attorney Bert Coules.

For one moment, Gus considered bolting from the room and disappearing into the bowels of Eagle's View. It wouldn't stop the press conference; even if he wasn't there Steele would insist on having his revenge. But at least he could put off the humiliation until he got home. And who said he ever had to go home? Maybe he could stay in Eagle's View forever. He'd haunt the place like the Phantom of the Opera.

Gus was in the middle of designing his unique haunting costume when he glanced over and noticed that Shawn was already halfway down the aisle. Gus walked quickly until he'd caught up with him.

"What's our plan here?" Gus whispered.

"It's a little thing I call Operation Improv."

"Improv? *Improv?*" Gus had to fight to keep his voice from rising to a shriek. "You have no idea what you're going to do."

"Really?" Shawn said. "We've had all night to come up with a plan, and you think I'm going to get up on that stage and wing it?"

"Are you?"

"Of course," Shawn said. "But it will go much better if you can pretend we know what we're going. These reporters are like bears—they can smell fear."

"Then they're getting a noseful already," Gus said.

"Yeah, and it's not just from you," Shawn said. "Where's our old pal Dal?"

"I assume he's preparing some kind of grand entrance," Gus said. "It takes a long time to get a cauldron of oil to boil."

"Well, these people are expecting a grand entrance from somebody," Shawn said. "Let's give them one."

Shawn strode cheerfully down the aisle, stopping only to slap the occasional back or smile for the cameras that swung up to meet him. He stepped up in front of the heavy golden curtain and smiled out at the audience as Gus joined him.

"Glad you could all make it this morning," Shawn said. "I'm sure you're all wondering why Dallas Steele asked you here so early."

"No, we're not." Bert Coules seemed to have sharpened his military buzz cut into blades for the occasion. "Steele said he was going to crucify you."

"Uh-huh," Shawn said. "That sounds like old Dal. But I bet he didn't tell you what he really meant by that."

A short man wearing a toupee that seemed to be fashioned from dog hair stood up in front. "He said he was going to expose you as a complete fraud, and then demonstrate the harm that your scam has caused the entire population of Santa Barbara County. After that there was going to be a light lunch."

"You fell for that?" Shawn looked incredulous. "And you call yourself a reporter."

"I don't call myself a reporter," the man said. "I'm Arno Galen, the owner of the Seaside Vacation Kennel. Or I was until you claimed that we were renting out the pets people boarded with us to an underground dog-fighting ring. Now I spend my days in court fighting frivolous lawsuits."

Shawn looked out at the man under the toupee, and he *saw*. Saw the strands of the pet hair clinging to his slacks. Saw the scrap of duct tape stuck to his blazer pocket. Saw the scratches on both hands and the splint on his left where the little finger had been broken.

"And where do you spend your nights?" Shawn said.

"That's none of your—" Galen started, but Shawn held up a hand to cut him off.

"Not you," Shawn said, casting his gaze heavenward. "I want to hear from Fluffy." Shawn batted the air with his hand, then drew it across his face, licking it, then using it to slick back his hair.

"What's this?" called a voice from the audience.

"A kitten," Gus said. "I'm guessing it's Fluffy."

Shawn batted at the air again, then shrunk back in horror. "What's that you say, Fluffy?" Shawn listened so intently the audience could practically see the sound waves entering his ears. *"Meow meow meow. Mew mew. Meow. Raoar?"*

Shawn staggered backward, as if released by the spirit that had momentarily taken control of him.

"This is ridiculous," Galen said. "Do we really have to wait for Steele to expose this phony?"

"I think you need to translate for these people," Gus said. "They don't seem to speak kitten."

"Isn't there one educated person out there?" Shawn

peered at the audience. No one volunteered. "Fine. What Fluffy told me was a tale that started with domestic bliss but ended in a fate worse than death. Actually, not worse than death so much as death, which is pretty bad on its own. He was always a happy kitten, content to while away his hours playing with a bit of string or cuddling up in his mistress' lap. Then one day he slipped through an open door to see what the world outside was like. At first, it seemed like paradise, filled with—"

"Even if we believed you could talk to dead cats, which we don't, this is still moronic," Galen shouted, pushing his way through the sea of knees to march down the aisle to the stage. "He said four *meows*, two *mews*, and a *raaor*. You can't possibly get all this out of that."

"The cat language is very complex," Shawn said. "If a cat had written the Harry Potter books, he could have gotten through the whole thing in fifteen pages, tops. And he would still have found the space to mention that Dumbledore was gay, if that's what he meant."

"Perhaps you could take an example from your feline friends and minimize your word count now, Mr. Spencer." Chief Vick looked like she hadn't warmed up to them much since their last visit to her office. "If you have a point, this would be the time to make it."

Shawn gave her a cheery wave and turned back to Galen. "Once Fluffy got out, he was snatched off the street and stuffed into a cage. No matter how much he fought and clawed, he couldn't get away. The kidnapper wrapped his mouth and paws in duct tape so he couldn't bite or scratch, then threw him into a ring with a pit bull. He didn't understand the concept, but he was being used as a bait animal to train the dogs to fight."

"That's terrible," cried a woman in the audience. "My poodle Baxter disappeared last month. Is it possible that he was . . . ?" She couldn't bring herself to finish the thought.

Shawn looked up again, then let his tongue drop out of his mouth. He panted.

"You're wasting our time," Galen shouted. "No one wants to hear this."

"Sure they do," Gus said. "It's just you who doesn't. Why is that, do you think?"

Shawn snapped out of his doggie trance. "Baxter tells much the same story. Although since he's talking in dog, there are a few more digressions. Apparently dogs don't really care if their snacks taste like bacon or not. The point is, he was stolen off the street and used to train fighting dogs. Who also didn't care if he tasted like bacon or not."

The woman collapsed into her seat. "Poor Baxter."

"Now you've upset that poor woman," Galen said. "I demand you apologize to her right now."

"Fluffy and Baxter think you're the one who should apologize," Shawn said.

"Me!"

"Your kennel was closed down, but that didn't mean the dog fighters were willing to let you out of your contract," Shawn said. "You had promised to supply them with a steady stream of bait animals, and they didn't care where you got them from. I'll give you credit—you tried to refuse."

Gus noticed Galen reflexively cradle his splinted fingers in his free hand. Score one for Shawn.

"But they made it clear you were going to deliver on your promises, or they were going to use you as their next bait animal. So now you haunt the streets of Santa Barbara by night, stealing the innocent pets who are naive and loving enough to let you get close to them."

Arno Galen's eyes had been getting wider through

Shawn's entire explanation, and now they looked like they were planning to set out and find a new home for themselves. He backed away up the aisle.

"You've got no proof of that," he shouted.

"Except the testimony of two eyewitnesses," Shawn said. "Fluffy and Baxter."

Galen turned and ran up the aisle, disappearing through the heavy doors as if they were lace curtains. "Somebody stop that man," Gus shouted.

"I don't think so," Lassiter said.

"He killed my Baxter," sniffed the woman in the audience.

"All we have to support that is the word of these frauds," Coules said. "Why don't we wait until they've been exposed and disgraced, and then we can see what we think of their evidence?"

Baxter's owner started to object, but Chief Vick turned and spoke soothingly to her. "I pulled in right after that man, and I believe my car is blocking him. So unless he wants to walk back to town, he's not going anywhere until the press conference is over."

"I'd say it's over," Shawn said. "Wouldn't you, Gus?"

"I can't imagine what's left to prove," Gus said.

For the first time all morning, Gus was feeling optimistic about the future. The people sitting on the aisles were already gathering up their belongings and putting on their coats. If one or two of them actually walked up to the door, that would be it for the press conference.

Gus didn't notice that behind them the golden curtain began to rise slowly.

"Thank you all for coming, and please remember to drive safely on your way back home," Gus said.

There was a massive, unified gasp of shock from the crowd. One elderly woman in the crowd rose to her feet, then collapsed back into her chair. And now Lassiter was pushing through the seated spectators in his aisle, with Vick and O'Hara close behind. Shawn shot a puzzled glance at Gus before turning back to the crowd.

"People, people, people," Shawn said, "is it really that big a deal?"

Lassie pointed behind them. Gus knew he should turn around. Knew he should see what everyone in the audience had already witnessed. All he wanted to do, though, was curl into a ball underneath one of the theater seats and hope that everybody else would go away.

Since that didn't look like it was going to happen anytime soon, Gus turned to see what the crowd was staring at.

Dallas Steele was tied to a chair, his normally bronze complexion drained to an ashy white. A large knife stuck out of his heart. Tara stood over him, her hand still grasping the knife.

Gus screwed his eyes closed, praying that when he opened them again, this would turn out to be a terrible dream. That worked as well as it always did. Tara was still standing frozen before Steele's corpse.

For a moment nobody moved. And then a shriek pierced the stunned silence.

"Mr. Steele!" It was Shepler, who leaned out of the window in the projection booth. "She killed him!"

Lassiter and O'Hara pushed past Shawn and Gus to grab Tara. She barely seemed to notice as they spun her around and slapped the cuffs on her wrists and pulled her toward the exit.

Tara seemed to be completely unaware of her surroundings, or even that she was being arrested. The only thing she noticed as the police pulled her down from the stage was Shawn.

"That's the way you wanted it, right?" she said. "Please tell me you're happy."

Lassiter yanked her away from Shawn and dragged

her up the aisle. People scattered to get out of her way as she left red footprints up to the door.

"I haven't heard your answer yet, Mr. Spencer." Chief Vick was standing in front of them. "Is this the way you wanted it?"

Chapter Sixteen

The interrogation room's walls were the same bright, happy yellow as the rest of the police station, as if the SBPD's decorator had decided that the best way to make a suspect talk was to let him think he was back in kindergarten.

Shawn and Gus had been in the room for two hours now, and there wasn't a hint of milk and cookies. In fact, there hadn't been any sign of human life. Every so often Shawn would pop up from the table to make faces in the two-way mirror, just to see if he could get a reaction. If there were people watching, they seemed to be peculiarly immune to the insult of the outstretched tongue.

"I don't think they're paying attention," Gus said as Shawn tried out a new set of expressions in the mirror.

"Oh, they're paying attention," Shawn said. "They're in there studying every move we make, listening to every word we say. Searching for a way to break us down and make us talk."

"Maybe they could just ask," Gus said. "I'm ready to talk anytime."

"So they've broken you already," Shawn said. "I thought you were made out of sterner stuff."

"I'm ready to talk because I don't have anything to hide," Gus said.

Shawn rushed over to him and whispered in his ear, "That's good, very convincing. Stick with that."

"I don't have to stick with it." Gus pushed away from the table and walked to the mirror. He rapped on it sharply. "It's the truth."

After a moment, the door swung open, and Lassiter marched in with a bottle of Windex and a roll of paper towels. He took Gus by the shoulders, steered him back to his seat at the table, then sprayed window cleaner on the mirror.

"Good to see you finally got that promotion you wanted," Shawn said.

Lassiter swept away the last of the ammonia streaks with a paper towel. "If you had any idea how much one of these mirrors costs, you might treat it with a little more respect."

"Maybe if you treated us with a little more respect, we might treat your toys with a little more respect," Shawn said.

Lassiter crumpled the towel and tossed it toward the wastebasket. It bounced off the rim, then dropped straight in. "Let me see," he said. "You're drawing a comparison between yourself and this mirror. You're both shallow. I can see right through both of you. And both of you will crack under the slightest pressure. So yes, I think that does work."

Shawn turned to Gus, amazed. "He didn't just do that."

"He did," Gus said. "He turned your flip comment around and landed it right on you."

"Lassie, that's a first for you," Shawn said. "And as a fair man, I give you my congratulations."

Shawn held out his hand to be shaken. Lassiter gave it a quick glance, but didn't take it. "Actually, Spencer, I should apologize. It's one thing for me to crack wise when you're trying to horn in on my cases and hog all the credit. But you're in serious trouble now. The district attorney has been in Chief Vick's office for an hour now trying to determine what he can charge you with."

"But we didn't do anything," Gus said.

"That will be determined in a full and fair investigation," Lassiter said. "I want to assure you right now that if we have reason to believe that you're actually innocent, then whatever our personal feelings for one another might be, I will work ceaselessly to make sure you go free. And if we find evidence suggesting that you're guilty, then my own personal feelings will have no impact either way on a full, fair, impartial investigation."

Now he did reach out and take Shawn's hand, which had been stranded in the space between them, and gave it a hearty shake. "Somebody will be back in to see you shortly."

He walked out, and the door locked behind him with the loudest click Gus had ever heard.

"What was that?" Shawn said. "It sounded like Lassie was treating us with respect."

"It sure did."

Shawn sank down on the table. "How bad is this?"

Gus couldn't believe Shawn had to ask. "If they believe Tara, they can charge us as accessories or conspirators. Or just plain murderers. Only it's not just plain murder, because if it looks like we commissioned Tara to kill Dal, then they're going to call it special circumstances."

To Gus' horror, Shawn actually seemed to like the sound of that. "I'd hope they'd see the circumstances as special," he said. "It's not every day we get accused of murdering someone."

" 'Special circumstances' is what they call it when the crime is so heinous they can ask for the death penalty," Gus said.

"They won't do that," Shawn said. "They know us. They know we'd never commit murder."

"It doesn't matter if they know us," Gus said. "Their job is to investigate crimes and judge the evidence, not follow their own prejudices."

"Have you ever considered that that's the reason our solve rate is so much higher than theirs?" Shawn said. "Because I never let the evidence confuse me when I've made up my mind for reasons that are completely petty and personal."

Gus slumped in his chair, trying not to think of his execution day. Of course the attempt itself sent death row images flooding through his head. He saw his mother weeping behind the glass, his father stubbornly refusing to look at him. Uncle Pete was there, clutching his Bible in his manicured fingers, and little adopted second cousin Daisy, no longer the cross-eyed child with braces he used to tease, but now a long, lanky beautiful reporter for CNN. She'd have written him once while he was on death row, saying how much she had loved him as a child and how she'd never stopped, and how she now regretted all the time they'd wasted without ever getting together. And next to her, weeping softly into a lace handkerchief, was Mariah Carey, expressing her grief by wearing a black peignoir over a matching bra and panty set. Oddly, while Gus' execution was set some time in the future, she seemed to have stepped right out of the "Vision of Love" video.

"First of all," Shawn said, drumming his fingers impatiently on the table, "we are not going to be executed, because we're not guilty. And more important, if we do get the death penalty, Mariah Carey is not coming to see you die."

"You don't know that," Gus said. "And I have no idea what you're talking about anyway. Who said anything about Mariah Carey?"

"You didn't have to say anything," Shawn said. "You were clutching your heart and mouthing the lyrics to 'Emotions.' "

"I wouldn't even be thinking about the needle if you had acted responsibly in the beginning," Gus said. "I begged you to get rid of Tara."

"So you're saying this is my fault," Shawn said. "Because if you are, I sure hope you're enunciating well for all the nice people who are sitting behind that mirror and recording every word."

Gus looked back up at the mirror guiltily. "Oh my God," he said. "We're turning on each other, just like they want us to."

"Technically, it's just you turning on me at this point," Shawn said.

"I'm so sorry. I panicked," Gus said.

"It happens," Shawn said. "Just keep reminding yourself that they can't touch us, because we haven't done anything. In America, our justice system doesn't convict innocent people. In fact, in California our justice system doesn't even convict guilty ones, as long as they've had their faces in the paper a couple of times before they pick up the meat cleaver."

The door swung open, and Bert Coules came in, scowling. "That's very amusing, Mr. Spencer," he said. "And I'm afraid all too true. OJ. Robert Blake. And of course your own personal favorite, Veronica Mason."

"She really was innocent," Shawn said.

"Right, because you said so."

"Me and the real killer," Shawn said. "I do seem to recall something like a dramatic courtroom confession."

"From a delusional hysteric who fantasized an entire romantic life with the victim," Coules said, "and who might well have confessed to his murder simply to bring some drama to her pathetic, lonely life."

"Veronica Mason is every bit as innocent as we are," Shawn said.

"For once we agree on something, Mr. Spencer," Coules said. His lips stretched across his teeth in a tight approximation of a smile. "Maybe if we talked, we might find a few other areas of agreement. Let's start with your friend Tara Larison."

Coules reached into his briefcase and pulled out a sheaf of papers. He fanned them out across the table like a winning poker hand. "I have sworn depositions from people who work at three fast-food restaurants, one coffeehouse, a video store, and several other businesses who sold goods or services to Tara Larison. They all say she told them she was doing your bidding."

Gus grabbed the documents and leafed through them. They all confirmed what Coules was telling them.

"She liked doing errands."

Coules piled the documents together and slipped them back into his briefcase. "She liked doing errands for you—isn't that right?"

"Yes," Shawn said. "What's your point?"

"Why are you asking what his point is?" Gus whispered. "You know what his point it. He's trying to prove you mentally ordered Tara to kill Dallas Steele."

"Right, and you hear how stupid that sounds when you say it out loud?" Shawn whispered back. "Let's make him say it."

"I'm happy to," Coules said. "I'm trying to prove that Tara Larison was acting under your orders when she committed murder."

"That's not fair," Shawn said. "We were whispering. Isn't there some kind of privilege here?"

Coules snapped his briefcase shut and went toward the door.

"Wait a minute," Gus said. "How is this even possible? Dallas Steele has only been dead for a couple of hours. How could you gather all these depositions in that time?"

"I didn't collect these depos in relation to the murder of Tara Larison," Coules said. "I was investigating the murder of John Marichal."

Gus knew he'd heard that name somewhere before, but he couldn't place it.

Shawn's memory was sharper. "The guy from the impound yard?"

"She snapped his neck," Coules said. "Nearly twisted his head off. And all because he wouldn't give you back that piece of crap car."

"Don't talk about the Echo that way," Shawn said. "Gus gets very emotional."

Coules just smiled that tight smile again.

"I don't think you're helping," Gus said to Shawn.

"I believe that, Mr. Spencer," Coules said. "I believe you both got emotional. So emotional that Tara killed John Marichal."

"He was a violent escaped convict," Gus said. "How could a scrawny little thing like Tara break his neck?"

"The same way she put a BurgerZone fry cook in the hospital," Coules said. "In a way, she did us all two great favors with Marichal—she took a wanted criminal off the streets, and she's going to send you away for a long time."

The door swung open, and Chief Vick came in, looking stern. "I'm not convinced about that yet, Mr. Coules."

Gus felt his heart lightening. Maybe they weren't completely alone in the world. Maybe they had one friend.

"Which part?"

"We have sufficient evidence to hold Tara Larison on suspicion of murder in the death of Dallas Steele," she said. "But we have no hard evidence tying her to Marichal's death yet."

"Except her prints at the scene."

"Two of my detectives were with her there long after the murder," Vick said.

"Because these two were trying to corrupt the crime scene."

"If we killed John Marichal, why did someone try to kill us when we went back to the impound lot to investigate?" Shawn said.

"This is the first I've heard of that," Chief Vick said.

"We meant to report it, but we got a little busy," Shawn said.

"What he means is they didn't have any reason to make it up before," Coules said.

"If you think we're making it up, go check it out for yourself," Gus said. "Look for bullet holes and broken glass in a bunch of cars from the sixties."

"Right," Coules said. "Kids never use wrecked cars for target practice. So any evidence we find of gunshots is proof someone was shooting at you."

They turned to Chief Vick for help. She shrugged apologetically. "I'm afraid he's right. If you had come to us right after it happened, maybe we could have done something."

"Next time don't wait so long to manufacture your alibis," Coules said.

Chief Vick turned back to the district attorney. "The only thing you have tying Tara to Marichal's murder is your belief that Mr. Spencer and Mr. Guster were angry at him," she said. "And your belief that she was psychically compelled to do his bidding."

"*Her* belief, not mine," Coules said. "I refuse to endorse the ridiculous notion that this man is actually psychic."

"In which case, you need to prove conspiracy," Vick said. "You'll need to demonstrate that Mr. Spencer made it known to Miss Larison that he wanted these victims dead."

"That's going to be easy with Steele," Coules said. "He'd called a press conference to expose Spencer as a fraud. When I worked in Florida, I put away an entire drug cartel with less evidence than this."

"That is troubling," Vick said. She turned to Shawn and Gus. "I guess there's no way out of this for you, is there?"

"You say that like you think we should be able to come up with an answer," Shawn said.

"Only if you're innocent," Vick said. "Otherwise I'm going to have to put you under arrest and let Mr. Coules hold you until trial. If only you could find a flaw in his otherwise excellent logic."

Gus' mind spun. Chief Vick was trying to throw them a lifeline. But as far as he could see, the rope was still hanging just out of reach.

The realization hit Shawn and Gus at the same time.

"I guess there's no way out for us," Shawn said.

"None at all," Gus agreed.

"You've got us," Shawn said to Coules. "We wanted Steele dead, and Tara acted on that desire, just like she did on all the others."

"I wonder how she knew so well what you wanted all the time," Gus said.

"Like she said, she took my psychic orders."

"But that can't be," Gus said. "Coules refuses to endorse the ridiculous notion that you're actually psychic."

"Good point," Shawn said. "Then we must have told her we wanted Steele dead before the press conference started."

"Of course," Gus said. "I can't remember—how did we do that again? Because we were locked in the North Tower all night. She didn't come up there, did she?"

Chief Vick shook her head. "We've been studying the house's security logs for that night. It turns out that most of the doors and windows are monitored. Thanks to that, we believe that Tara broke in through the underground garage and went straight to the auditorium. As far as we know, the door to the north tower didn't open between the time Shepler took you up there and the time he brought you down."

"That would certainly clinch our innocence," Shawn said, "if only it weren't for modern technology."

"That's right," Gus said, his spirits rising. "We could have plotted the entire thing out on our cell phones."

"Except there's no reception anywhere within five miles of Eagle's View," Vick said.

Coules' glare shifted from Vick to his two prime suspects. "I don't know what kind of game you're playing—"

"We're not playing. We're trying to help you," Shawn said. "Where were we again?"

"You were explaining how you conspired with Tara Larison to kill Dallas Steele," Vick said.

"Right," Gus said. "All we need is to pinpoint the moment when we gave her the order to commit the murder, and we're going down."

"I've been working through the time line, and I can't see any point where we could have communicated to Tara after we got to Eagle's View," Shawn said.

"That's easy," Gus said. "Clearly we gave her the order after Shepler picked us up."

"That could work," Shawn said. "Does make us look pretty stupid, though."

"Why is that, gentlemen?" Vick said.

"Well, when Shepler came for us, we thought Dal wanted to see us because we had made him a fortune," Shawn said.

"And we were going to share in that fortune," Gus said. "Ten percent of all profits were supposed to go to us."

"There were no profits," Coules growled. "That's one of the reasons you hated him."

"Yes, definitely," Shawn said. "After he told us that, we certainly were miffed."

"If only he'd told us before we went up to see him, this all would have been so much easier to arrange," Gus said.

"I guess it's possible that we hated Dal so much that we arranged to kill him before we collected our vast profits, even though his death would probably mean we'd never see a nickel," Shawn said.

"So we told Tara she should follow us everywhere we went, just in case we popped up to Eagle's View, so she could murder Dallas Steele in the exact time and place that would put the biggest burden of guilt on us," Gus said.

"That must have been what we did," Shawn said. "Except that it's not only incredibly stupid—it doesn't make any sense at all."

"I'm sure it will to a jury," Gus said.

"As long as the jury is made up completely of idiots," Shawn said. "Think they can arrange that?"

Coules was breathing heavily, and his hands were shaking. Chief Vick pulled him aside gently.

"I don't think you're ready to charge them yet," she said.

"They're guilty, and everyone in this room knows it," Coules said through gritted teeth.

"If you want to charge them, I can't stop you," Chief Vick said. "But in two minutes they've been able to poke huge holes in your case. Wouldn't it make more sense to release them now and rearrest them when you've got everything lined up?"

"By which time they'll be in Argentina."

Shawn managed to put on a look of shock. "This is our home," he said. "We didn't move here after spending most of our lives across the country like some people. We grew up here—and we're not going anywhere."

"What Shawn is trying to say is, we have deep roots in the community," Gus said.

Gus could practically see the neurons bouncing around in Coules' head as he tried to find a way to hold on to his case.

"Fine," Coules said finally. "Let them go for now."

Shawn and Gus exchanged a high five, a low five, a medium five, and a couple other fives that didn't have precise definitions.

"But you'd better enjoy your celebration now," Coules said, "because I am going to put you away for multiple murders."

Coules turned and walked out of the interrogation room.

"That man needs to slow down and enjoy life a little more," Shawn said.

"Don't be fooled by the red face and shaking hands," Chief Vick said. "Bert Coules loves his job. There's nothing that gives him more pleasure than putting a criminal behind bars."

"Except in this case," Shawn said, "I think he'd prefer to put us there."

"There's one thing you need to understand, Mr. Spencer," Chief Vick said. "I didn't believe he had the evidence to charge you today, and I wanted to spare you and Mr. Guster a great deal of unpleasantness and Mr. Coules a great deal of humiliation. But if we find evidence against you, I'll be working with him."

She opened the door and ushered them out to the corridor, where two state marshals were leading a manacled woman in an orange prison jumpsuit toward the door. As soon as she saw them, she started screaming.

"Shawn! Help me!"

It took Gus a second to recognize the woman, if only

because he'd never seen her in anything that wasn't tight and red before. Now, stuffed into the baggy jumpsuit, her hair still wet and stringy after the blood had been washed out of it, eye shadow running down her face like tears, she didn't look like the dangerously hot daughter of Satan. She looked like a little girl. A psychotic, delusional, murderous little girl, true, but even so, Gus felt his first twinge of pity for her.

"Shawn," Tara cried again, "I only did what you wanted me to!"

All traces of pity vanished from Gus' heart. Regan MacNeil was only a little girl, too, and she could make her head spin all the way around. There was no reason to think that this one couldn't have made Marichal's head do the same thing, let alone plunge a knife into Dallas Steele.

The deputies pulled Tara out of the room. Before the massive oak doors closed behind her, Gus got a glimpse of the short gray bus that would take her to the state prison for women near Chowchilla.

"Poor girl," Shawn said. "We've got to help her."

"We can testify in her defense, I guess," Gus said. "Try to explain to a jury how crazy she really is."

"We could do that," Shawn said. "Or we can do something really useful."

"What's that?" Gus asked with a sinking heart.

"We can figure out who the real killer is."

Chapter Seventeen

"The real killer," Gus said.

"You've said that about six thousand times," Shawn said.

"I keep hoping if I say it one more time the words will actually make sense."

Chief Vick had arranged for a squad car to take them back to the Psych office. During the ride, Shawn had refused to let Gus discuss the case on the assumption that the officer behind the wheel would report back every word they'd said. Which Gus hoped fervently wouldn't turn out to be the case, since Shawn had spent the entire trip talking about how much more alluring Chief Vick had become since they'd removed the Interim from her title.

The mindless conversation did allow Gus to think through what Shawn had said at the station. But by the time the squad car pulled up outside their bungalow, he still couldn't find a way to see it as anything but wishful thinking. They'd seen Tara standing over Steele's body, the knife in her hand. How could anyone disprove that?

"Think about it," Shawn said. "What do we really know about Tara?"

"She's crazy, for one thing," Gus said.

"Let's not use technical terms," Shawn said. "What else?"

"She's slavishly devoted to you, and she has a propensity toward violence."

Shawn started writing a list on a yellow legal pad. "That's good."

"No, it's not."

"I meant as a list," Shawn said. "What else do we know about her?"

"She likes to wear red," Gus said. "She never apologized for nearly running me over and sending me off a cliff. And— Hey!" Gus had a sudden flash of memory, followed by a spasm of muscle pain as his body joined in the remembering. "I don't know about Dallas Steele, but there's no way Tara could have killed John Marichal."

"That's good," Shawn said, writing furiously. "Why not?"

"You said it yourself," Gus said. "When I was in the hospital, she was with you every second of the night."

"That's good," Shawn said. "Except . . ."

"Except what?"

"Is that whole perjury thing still illegal?" Shawn said. "Because that might have some bearing on my testimony."

"You told me she was with you the whole time."

"Whole, part—that's just quibbling," Shawn said. "Didn't it ever occur to you to wonder exactly when Tara first learned my feelings on the pickle-burger conundrum?"

"Never."

"Really? Because that turns out to be such a major part of this whole situation, and I'd think that someone as smart as you might have put some thought into it. As my dad says, when you can't find a clue, follow the time line. And the time line here would—"

"Shawn!"

"While we were waiting at the Community General Hospital waiting room, she might have stepped out for a moment to grab a couple of burgers."

"She might have or she did?"

Shawn was too busy writing on the pad to hear the question. Gus tore it out of his hands. "Hey, that's work product," Shawn said.

Gus glanced at the writing. Shawn's work product was one sentence repeated all the way down the page. " 'All work and no play makes Gus a dull boy'? That's not even original."

"I changed the name," Shawn said.

Gus tossed the pad back at him. "So what you're saying is that Tara could have killed Marichal."

"It's not what *I'm* saying," Shawn said. "More like what the facts are hinting at. Or at least what Coules can make the fact look like."

Gus sunk down into a leather chair, which settled under him with a whoosh. "Shawn, if she killed those people, how are we ever going to prove that we weren't all part of a criminal conspiracy?"

"That's why we have to prove *she's* innocent," Shawn said. "And to do that, we've got to—"

"Figure out who the real killer is," Gus finished the sentence for him. "There's still that one small problem. What if she's the real killer?"

"I know she's not," Shawn said. "Look, we both know I'm not really psychic, but you have to agree I have a pretty good eye for detail. And those details say so much about who a person is. I've studied Tara in depth from the first moment I met her, and I've never seen a trace of malice or danger or cruelty in her. She can't be a murderer."

Gus had rarely heard Shawn speak this sincerely. And he knew it was true sincerity, since it was actually far less convincing than when he was faking sincerity. "We've got work to do," he said.

"Great," Shawn said. "What do we know about Tara?"

"You were the one making the list."

Shawn glanced down at his pad. "Hmm," he said thoughtfully. "Apparently all work and no play makes Gus a dull boy."

Gus grabbed the pad back and stalked to the desk, where he planted himself in front of the computer. "Maybe we should do a little research and figure out what Tara was doing before she was slavishly following your psychic orders."

Gus typed the words "Tara Larison" into a search engine. There were references to a couple of women with the same name, but since the Tara they knew was neither a housewife running an organization for the protection of songbirds in Mississippi or a teenage girl with a MySpace page devoted to resurrecting Vanilla Ice's career, this proved to be a dead end.

"I seem to recall she used to take care of her aunt Enid in Arcata," Shawn said. "Let's see what we can find out about a certain fat divorcée Realtor."

Shawn leaned in over Gus' shoulder and typed a string of words into the search engine, then hit ENTER. After a moment, they found themselves staring at a series of photos of large, middle-aged naked women. "Tara's aunt was a plus-size porn queen?"

"This is Fat Divorcée Realtor Dot Com," Gus said, muscling Shawn away from the keyboard. "Let's try actually entering her name."

Gus typed in the name "Enid Blalock." The first few hits were real estate listings she'd had in Arcata. The fourth was her obituary in the *Arcata Advertiser*. Gus clicked the link, and after a millisecond, the article loaded.

Enid Blalock, according to her obituary, was the queen of the Arcata real estate scene. Despite her short time in the profession, she was uniformly admired and even loved by the other agents in her office. She was on track to win the coveted Arcata Arrow Award for most sales in a single year when her life was cut short in a tragic accident. She had fallen down the stairs in an empty house she was trying to sell and broken her neck.

"There's nothing there," Shawn said.

"Yet." Gus clicked the button at the bottom of the screen and loaded the article's second page.

"Look." Shawn pointed to the screen. "In lieu of flowers, donations should be made to the Association for Divorcée Rights. I told you she was bitter."

"That's very helpful," Gus said.

"Okay, maybe not," Shawn said. "What about this?"

Shawn pointed at the last line of the obituary. Apparently, Enid was survived by a sister who lived in New Jersey and a niece, Tara Busby.

"She changed her name," Gus said. "I wonder why."

"Wouldn't you?" Shawn said.

Gus returned to the search engine and typed in "Tara Busby plus Larison". The handful of results seemed to have nothing to do with the woman they were looking for, with each of the three names drawn from long-separated sections of various texts.

"I guess she didn't marry someone named Larison," Gus said.

"That's good," Shawn said. "The last thing we need is to have a jealous husband coming after us. Then we'd really be in trouble."

Gus stared at the search engine. It was like one of those genies in a fairy tale. It would tell you everything you needed to know, but only if you asked exactly the right question. Unfortunately, there was no way to ask the one question he needed to answer first: What was the right question to ask?

"You'd think someone as crazy as Tara would have popped up somewhere before," Shawn said. "You don't just start out following psychic instructions to beat up burger chefs. You've got to work up to that. I can't believe she waited until she heard my voice to go completely nutso cuckoo."

Gus sat up straight. That was it—the clue he had been looking for. "She first heard you while she was listening to Artie Pine's radio show."

"So? Lots of crazy people listen to Artie Pine. In fact, I think it's required."

"Don't you see?" Gus said. "She was already interested in psychic phenomena before she met you."

"Because she was hearing voices in her head."

"So maybe you weren't the first psychic she decided was giving her orders."

"You're making me feel cheap," Shawn said.

Gus typed the words "Larison plus psychic" into the search engine. The screen that popped up listed hundreds of newspaper articles and Web sites referencing someone named Fred Larison who lived somewhere outside St. Louis. Gus clicked on the third listing, which appeared to be Larison's Web site.

Spooky music started playing out of the computer's speakers as the page loaded. Red text flashed over a black background: *Fred Larison, Psychic Detective*. The glowing ENTER HERE button was surrounded by pulsating skeleton hands.

"At least I don't feel that cheap," Shawn said.

Gus clicked the ENTER button, and the opening screen wiped away to reveal a black-and-white photo of a thin, balding man with a pencil mustache and a pronounced overbite staring directly into the camera. Underneath, more red type exclaimed that master psychic Fred Larison was available to solve the deepest mysteries of life, rates quoted on application.

"Sure, I'm going to trust him to solve the deepest mysteries of life when he can't tackle the basic mystery of finding a decent Web site designer," Shawn said.

Gus picked up the phone and dialed the number at the bottom of the page. After two rings, a recorded voice informed him that the number he'd dialed had been disconnected or was no longer in service.

"He also can't solve the mystery of how to pay his phone bill," Gus said. He hung up and keystroked back to the search engine. The next entry down was a news article titled "Psychic Solves Mystery."

"Does it mention if it was one of the deepest mysteries of life?" Shawn said.

"Let's find out." Gus hit the link, and a page popped up from the *Jefferson City Gazette*, "Central Missouri's News and Classifieds Leader." A picture showed the same man, still wearing the mustache but this time adding a cape to the look. He was holding an open jeweler's box with what appeared to be a large diamond inside.

" 'Renowned local psychic Fred Larison solved one of Jeff City's most perplexing mysteries yesterday when he used his mental prowess to find a two-carat diamond that had been lost since the days of the Civil War,' " Gus read. " 'The owners, Misses Bonnie and Eugenia Frakes, twin sisters, eighty-three years young, had searched their entire lives for the gemstone their late grandmother Prudence Winsocket had hidden from marauding raiders during the Civil War. But Prudence, living up to her name, went to her grave without ever telling a living soul where she had hidden the jewel. Larison's answer? Forget about talking to the living. He contacted Prudence directly at her address in the afterlife and asked her what she had done with the precious stone.' "

"I can't believe this," Shawn said.

"What? That there are other psychics working the same scams as you?"

"That anyone gets paid for writing this badly," Shawn said. "And this guy Peter Jones calls himself a reporter. I've never met Fred Larison, and I can tell from two thousand miles away that he's a fraud."

"Not everyone has your sharp eyes," Gus said. He pointed to the photo. Next to Larison, two old ladies stared at him with a look that would be considered indecent if the faces sharing it had even one unwrinkled square inch between them.

"Can you make that bigger?" Shawn said.

"Really? You want to see him better?"

"Not him. The person standing behind his left shoulder."

Shawn tapped the screen to show Gus what he was talking about. There was a hint of a face peeking out of the shadows. Gus centered the cursor on the face and clicked his mouse. The small section of photo enlarged. What had been a small blur of white was now a big blur of white.

"Okay, now focus in on that face," Shawn said.

"Okay," Gus said. "No, wait. I just remembered. This is reality, not *Mission: Impossible*. And this computer just shows me what's on a Web site. It can't make faces out of mush."

"Not much of a computer, is it?" Shawn said. "Let's see what else they say about Larison."

Gus clicked back to the search page and scrolled through the list of links. Many of them were references to the *Gazette*'s article on various sites devoted to psychic phenomena. At the bottom of the page, there was another *Gazette* article: "Local Psychic Wows Tough Critics."

"Let's see that one," Shawn said.

This story was also written by Peter Jones, and if anything it was even more breathless in its prose.

"They say that hardened cynics make the toughest audiences, but harder still are those minds that don't know enough to doubt what they believe. Such a crowd was faced by local psychic celebrity Fred Larison when he brought his bag of mental tricks to Suzie McKee's first-grade class at Harry S Truman Elementary School last Friday. By the end they were all won over by Larison's psychic stylings. Some had even decided to give up dreams of growing up to be policemen, astronauts, or nurses to follow him into the realms of worlds unknown.

"And they say public schools don't educate children," Shawn said.

"I don't remember my first-grade teacher being that hot," Gus said, looking at a woman who was partially hidden behind Larison's cape. "And I certainly don't remember her wearing hot pants to school."

"Mrs. Wilson had her charms," Shawn said, peering at the screen. "And since she was built like a cement mixer, not wearing hot pants was definitely one of them. But that's not Suzie McKee."

Gus craned his head to the screen to study the image. "How do you know?"

"I've spent a lot of time studying those legs," Shawn said. "That is definitely Tara. The question is, what's she doing there?"

"Maybe she was held back in first grade fifteen times," Gus said.

"Wait—here." Shawn scrolled down the page. " 'Larison was as always ably assisted by his lovely assistant.' "

"Tara was Fred Larison's assistant?"

"More than that," Shawn said. "It says here that Larison never needed to give her instructions. 'When asked how they worked together, the lovely helper, who chose not to give her name, said that she took her orders from Larison psychically.' "

"How does it feel to learn you weren't the first?"

"I'm devastated," Shawn said. "Let's find out why she left him."

Gus went back to the search engine and hit the button for a second page of hits. Shawn pointed to a listing halfway down the page. "I think I figured it out."

Gus clicked the link, which led to a page of funeral listings provided by a mortuary in central Missouri. " 'Memorial services will be held today for Fred Larison, noted local entertainer.' "

"Entertainer, ha!" Shawn said. "At least someone there wasn't fooled by that fraud."

Gus continued reading. " 'Mr. Larison died in St. Joseph's Hospital Tuesday night after suffering a broken neck in a freak accident.' Blah blah blah."

"No dependants." Shawn pointed to the end of the article. "I guess Tara took his last name without his permission."

"At least we know why she left him," Gus said. "He'd have to be a pretty good psychic to keep sending her orders even after he died."

"We know more than that," Shawn said. "We know that I was wrong. Dead wrong."

Gus noticed that Shawn's face had gone pale.

"When you say wrong, you mean about something unimportant, right?" Gus said. "Like pickles are really good on a burger, or *Gremlins 2* wasn't really better than the original."

"I mean I was wrong about everything," Shawn said. "I looked at Tara and saw innocence. I missed every sign. How could that be?"

"How could what be?"

Shawn waved weakly at the monitor. "How did Larison die?"

Gus glanced back at the screen. "In an accident. He broke his neck."

"Uh-huh. How did Enid Blalock die?"

"Didn't she fall down the stairs in an empty house?"

"And?"

Gus began to see the pattern that Shawn had already recognized.

"And John Marichal at the impound yard. His neck was broken, too."

Shawn and Gus stared at each other across the office. "She's not just a killer," Shawn said. "She's a serial killer."

Chapter Eighteen

" ' **B**ad to the bone! Ba-ba-ba bad to the bone!' "
Kent Shambling pounded the padded dash and wailed along with the stuttering scream of permanent rebellion. He *was* bad to the bone, damn it, and he was finally getting his chance to prove it.

Not that Nancy ever understood. She called him boring. Ungrateful bitch. Like he wanted to spend his prime years in an endless loop of office, home, Rotary, church, club, office. Like he didn't yearn to strap on a helmet, climb on a hawg, and live free or die trying. He did it for *her*. He gave up his youth and the opening chunk of his middle age to provide her with the security he knew she needed. And after all those years of sacrifice, she announced that because he was boring, she was leaving him for the barista at the local Starbucks. They were going to find a life of truth and commitment together in some hippie commune in the hills outside Ojai. And of course, because the barista barely made enough to cover his monthly weed bill, Kent would be expected to shoulder all her expenses.

If Kent were as boring as she claimed, that was exactly what he would have done. But Nancy's leaving revived the real Kent—the rogue, the rebel, the crazy cat who didn't play by anyone's rules. Instead of writing her that first check, he cashed out his 401(k) and put the bulk into a private account she'd never track down. He used the rest to buy the fastest, hottest, reddest car he could find with decent gas mileage and an above-average safety-and-repair rating from *Consumer Reports*.

That's right, baby. Ba-ba-ba-bad to the bone. Kent was blasting out of Moorpark, and he was never looking back. He didn't know where he was going, and he didn't care. A podiatrist with his mad skills could make a buck anywhere in this big country.

He was starting a new life. And this time he was going to do it right. No more rules for Kent Shambling. He was going to do what he wanted when he wanted, whatever it was. If anyone else got hurt, that was their problem.

Kent slammed out a one-handed drum solo on the Mustang's padded dash and peered out at the two lanes of freedom looming in front of him. He was saying good-bye to the dried brush and dripping eucalyptus trees of this dismal valley. In a few miles he'd hit the 101 and the coast. From there he'd go north or south; he'd make that call when he saw the sparkling blue of the Pacific.

As the song climaxed, Kent spotted a woman standing on the side of the road. She was wearing some kind of loose-fitting cutoff coverall, and even from a hundred yards away, she was the sexiest thing Kent had ever seen. He couldn't tell what she was doing besides watching the cars go by. But as Kent got closer, she stepped out to the shoulder and waved her tanned, bare arms at him.

If Kent had one inviolable rule of life, it was never pick up hitchhikers. You never knew what kind of psycho might be on the other side of that thumb.

But that was the old Kent. The new Kent lived to violate the inviolable. Ba-ba-ba-bad to the bone, baby. He flipped on his flashers and glided to the shoulder, where she stood. Reached over and opened the passenger door without even rolling down the window to ask where she was going.

The woman leapt into the car and slammed the door, then smiled up at him. Ice blue eyes burned out from under jet-black bangs. What Kent had thought was a cut-off coverall was actually torn off—she seemed to have ripped the sleeves and legs off a jumpsuit, uncovering yards of sleek golden flesh.

"I'm Kent," he said, putting out a friendly hand.

She took it in hers and held it warmly for a second. "I'm in trouble."

Kent's heart pounded. This was every one of his teenage fantasies coming true. Why had he wasted so many years with Nancy?

He gave her his most seductive smile. "Cops on your trail?"

Her seductive smile put his to shame. "Worse," she said. "Oprah." She pointed at a sign up ahead: *Road Maintenance Sponsored by Oprah Winfrey.* "I can't pick up one more Coke can or Big Mac wrapper, and I've got to get out of here before my shift supervisor comes back."

"Then let's find you a safe place to hide." Kent smoothly slid the gearshift into drive and, flipping on his blinkers, merged into traffic.

They rode in comfortable silence as Kent tried to think of something suitably cool to say. She didn't seem to mind the lack of conversation, staring tensely ahead at the road.

"So, Oprah," Kent finally said, "she must have some pretty tough enforcers."

The woman slid down in her seat, hiding her face with her left hand. At first Kent thought he'd said the wrong thing. Then he glanced across the divider and saw there was an accident on the other side of the road. A small gray bus had flown off the roadway and slammed into a eucalyptus. The driver, who was wearing some kind of uniform, dangled out his window, obviously killed in the collision.

"That must have been some crash," Kent said. "It looks like that guy's head is dangling by a thread."

The woman sank down farther in her seat. *Poor, sensitive soul*, Kent thought. *Can't even bear to look*. He tapped the gas, and the Mustang sped on toward his glorious future.

Chapter Nineteen

"My arms are getting tired." Gus' voice echoed out of the empty grave. "Why don't you climb down here and do some digging?"

"And get my cassock dirty?" Shawn peered down into the grave, his face gleaming in the light bouncing off his priest's collar. "Besides, you're doing great. You're a natural-born gravedigger."

Gus threw down the shovel and climbed out of the hole. "No, the bulldozer that dug this grave yesterday is a natural-born gravedigger. They haven't used shovels here in fifty years."

"Which is why your disguise is so brilliant. You don't have to worry about running into the real guy."

"I just want to run into the real woman so we can get out of here."

"Dude, it's all going to plan."

Which was true, although the fact that they were still only halfway through step one suggested there was still plenty that could go wrong. That and the gaping hole where step two of the three-step plan was supposed to go.

The fraction of a plan they had grew out of Shawn's realization that Tara was a serial neck breaker. While Gus was busy thinking back on things he'd said that might have inspired her to snap his spine like a twig, Shawn was furiously castigating himself. If only he'd read the signs, if only he'd noticed what must have been obvious. Now people were dead, and it was his fault. The only good thing was that Tara hadn't wanted Henry dead, so she had only tased him instead of snapping his neck, too. Because if Henry—

Shawn stopped in midthought. Gus looked over at him, thinking that the idea of his father murdered was too much for Shawn to take. But Shawn was smiling.

"What's funny?" Gus said.

"*Animal House,*" Shawn said. "On the other hand, if you want something that doesn't have big laughs, but leaves you with a wry smile, a warm chuckle, and that nod of recognition that we're all riders in the same cockeyed caravan of life, how about the fact that Tara didn't kill Dallas Steele?"

"You just said she did. You said she was a serial killer."

"And she may be. Which means she's got a pattern. She makes a friend, gets close, and when the relationship is over, she snaps his neck and moves on."

"So she would have killed you and not me."

"Can you stop thinking about yourself for one minute?" Shawn threw up his hands in exasperation. "She's got this whole neck-snapping thing down to an art. So why would she choose to stab Dallas Steele in the heart?"

"Variety?"

"Because she didn't do it. Which means we didn't tell her to do it. Which means we're off the hook."

Gus desperately wanted to believe Shawn. If only he could get past the one small flaw in his logic. "We saw her standing over him, holding the knife."

"Right," Shawn said. "So we know it was a perfect frame. Now who had a motive to want Steele dead?"

"Us?"

Shawn thought long and hard. He scrunched his eyes shut as he mentally replayed every moment of the case. Then he jumped up out of his chair. "Reynaldo!"

"Who?"

"The new wife's old lover, the handsome but poor artist. He couldn't stand to lose his true love to this arrogant billionaire, so he turned all his seductive powers on Tara. When she was completely under his control, he killed Steele and framed her for it."

By the time he was done, Shawn was practically glowing with amazement at his own genius. Gus wanted to share in the moment, but he was still stuck on logic issues.

"That's really good," Gus said. "Couple of small things. First, if anyone had Tara completely under his control, it was you. Remember?"

"She could have been using me to protect him."

Gus sighed. "Okay, maybe," he said. "But there's one other problem. Reynaldo doesn't exist."

"He doesn't?"

"You made him up when you were trying to figure out why Steele invited us to Eagle's View. Steele said he had a new wife, and you—"

Shawn jumped up from his chair. "Exactly what I meant! It's the wife!"

Of course it was. It had to be. Steele had no other living relatives either of them knew about, so she stood to inherit his billions. And there was clearly something strange about their relationship. Steele was willing to spend a hundred million dollars simply to win an argument. If she didn't have immediate access to that much cash, maybe a knife through the heart would have seemed like the appropriate response. If they could confront Mrs. Steele, Shawn was sure he could prove she was the real killer.

Gus didn't doubt Shawn's abilities. The trouble would be in finding her. They didn't even know her first name— Steele had always referred to her only as his bride. There was no announcement of the wedding in any newspaper, local or national. City hall had no record of their marriage. And somehow the wedding of *Forbes* magazine's Sexiest Billionaire Alive of 2007 and 2008 had managed to go unnoticed by tabloids that give saturation coverage to the nuptials of anyone who'd ever been in the same ZIP code as a celebrity.

After a fruitless afternoon of online searching and another hour wasted at the county's hall of records, Gus was almost ready to give up and say there was no Mrs. Steele. But Shawn would not let him quit. He was sure he was right. And besides, if he admitted Steele wasn't married, he'd have to come up with a new theory.

The next morning, armed with business cards identifying themselves as segment producers for E! Entertainment Television, they hit every florist, caterer, and bridal shop within a five-dollar cab ride's radius of their office. Even promises of a prominent role in a thirteen-week docu-soap about the wedding got them nothing but blank looks from the employees. They checked the gift registries of the most expensive stores on State Street, but the name Steele never appeared.

"This is useless." Gus dropped a wad of business cards into a wastebasket outside an art gallery. "No one's heard of this wedding. There is no Mrs. Dallas Steele."

"He said he was keeping it quiet," Shawn said, fishing the cards out of the trash and slipping them back into Gus' shirt pocket. "Billions of dollars buy a lot of privacy. But she'll have to show up sometime if she wants to claim her inheritance."

"That could be weeks from now," Gus said. "Months even. If she's smart, she'll wait until Tara is convicted."

"She may be smart, but she's got one weakness," Shawn said. "She loves the big dramatic moment. Why else would she stage her husband's murder for an invited audience?"

"So what are you suggesting? We should hold auditions for a phony musical, and see if she shows up to read for us?"

For a moment, Shawn actually seemed to be considering the idea. Then he shook it off. He rapped on the plastic screen of the *Santa Barbara Times* box. Beneath the scarred Plexiglas, the paper's front page was filled with a headline: "Private Services for Steele Tomorrow."

"We don't need to offer her a stage. She's already got one. We just need to make sure we've got good seats."

A quick scan of the part of the article visible above the fold strongly suggested those seats wouldn't be easy to come by. Admittance to the service was strictly by invitation; apparently Steele's fondness for privacy extended into the grave. To make sure there would be no press or other interlopers in attendance, the entire cemetery would be closed all morning, another one of the perks a few billion can buy. And while Shawn and Gus might have been able to make a plausible case for themselves as Steele's old high school chums, their more recent friendliness with the woman accused of his murder suggested they wouldn't be welcome.

Fortunately there was a costume-rental store within walking distance. Although tempted by a dented suit of armor—on the theory that if he was spotted, he could stand on a grave and look like a statue—Shawn ultimately decided on a Roman Catholic cassock, an ankle-length, close-fitting priest's robe. That way, he pointed out, if their investigation took them to the Vatican, he could use the costume a second time, getting value for their money.

Since there was only one cassock, and Gus refused to wear the matching nun's habit, Shawn dug through his own closet and dragged out a coverall he'd been issued on his first and last day working as a mechanic years ago. It was bright green and the embroidered name tag read LUBITY LUBE TRAINEE, but a quick pass with a Magic Marker blacked that out and brought an appropriately funereal accent to the ensemble.

Dallas Steele's memorial service was scheduled for ten o'clock the next morning. Shawn declared they should be there no later than eight, so they could see everyone arriving. Since their transportation issues hadn't improved overnight, that meant taking a series of local buses to reach the cemetery. Gus didn't mind riding the bus, especially since he was unclear on several parts of Shawn's plan, and looked forward to spending the time patching up the holes. But Gus hadn't anticipated how popular a Catholic priest might be on a Santa Barbara bus. Shawn spent the entire trip taking confessions and giving absolution to their fellow riders. By the time they reached the cemetery gates, Gus was no clearer on what they were doing next than when he first dropped his dollar twenty-five into the fare box.

Getting through the employee entrance was so easy that Gus forgave Shawn for the poorly fitting jumpsuit. He grabbed a time card at random and jammed it into the machine, then passed through. It took Shawn a little longer to persuade the gate guard to let him in, but after a few shouted "Begorrah"s and the occasional mention of a lake of fire, he joined Gus inside.

"Begorrah?" Gus said. "When did you become Irish?"

"When the guy at the gate was named O'Malley,"

Shawn said. "Besides, everything sounds convincing with an Irish accent. Now grab that shovel."

Following the road that snaked through the cemetery, they found an open grave on top of a hill that looked down over the entire park. At the center there was a large lake. Off to one side, a large area, the size of at least eight normal grave sites, was marked off with chains.

"I guess they're expecting a big crowd," Gus said.

"Give the people what they want," Shawn said. "Now get digging."

Gus glanced at the temporary marker lying next to the open grave. "I don't think Mrs. Lancashire is in any great hurry."

"No," Shawn said. "But that guy is."

He pointed down the hill, where an aging pickup truck was hauling a load of white folding chairs toward them. Gus snatched the shovel and jumped into the grave as Shawn piously crossed himself. If the maintenance man driving the pickup thought there was something odd about a priest blessing an empty grave while dirt flew out of it, he didn't stop to investigate. Shawn watched as the truck crested the hill, then chugged down toward the site of Dallas Steele's eternal repose.

"Isn't he gone yet?" Gus called from the grave after a few minutes had gone by.

"Better keep digging, just to make sure," Shawn said.

The truck puttered to Steele's site, and the maintenance man got out, unhooked the chain, and drove up to the open grave.

"If I dig any farther, I'm not going to be able to climb out," Gus said.

"At least you'll have Mrs. Lancashire to keep you company." Shawn stepped out of the way as a dirt clod flew up at him. Down below, the maintenance man got out of the truck again and opened the tailgate. He pulled one folding chair off the stack and set it up directly in front of the grave.

"What's he doing now?"

"Setting up the chairs for the memorial service."

There was a strangled curse from the grave. "And you want me to keep digging all that time? It's going to take hours."

"Maybe not."

The maintenance man shook the chair to make sure it was on level ground, then climbed back into his truck and started up the hill toward them. As soon as the sound of its engine faded away, Gus pulled himself out of the grave and looked down at Steele's site.

"Wow," Gus said. "When they said it was going to be a private service, they really meant it."

"At least we don't have to worry about picking the wife out of a large crowd."

"Or being inconspicuous in one."

Shawn and Gus watched the maintenance truck drive back toward the office. Gus nudged Shawn and pointed to the cemetery's main gates. They were swinging open to admit a battered Honda Accord.

"I thought the entire cemetery was closed for the private service," Shawn said.

"Maybe that's Mrs. Steele."

"If that's her car, no wonder she killed her husband," Shawn said. "Get back in the grave."

Gus pushed the shovel at him. "You get in the grave."

"That doesn't make any sense at all." Shawn pushed the shovel back at him. "What would a priest be doing in a grave with a shovel?"

"What would a maintenance man be doing in a grave with a shovel when there's a backhoe parked six feet away?"

"Maybe his driver's license was revoked for a DUI and he can't drive a backhoe. Maybe he's mentally retarded and they don't trust him with the keys." Shawn shoved Gus toward the grave.

"Maybe the priest is actually a phony in a rented costume." Gus shoved Shawn toward the grave.

"At least he's not a drunken, retarded phony." Shawn shoved again.

Gus grabbed Shawn and tried to drag him to the edge of the hole. Shawn dug in his heels, but felt the wet grass slipping under his feet. His big toes were just sliding over the lip of the grave when there was a discreet beep from behind them.

Shawn and Gus sprang apart to see the Honda idling beside the grave site. The window cranked down, and a cherubic pink face peered out above a priest's collar.

"Excuse me, Father," the priest said. "I'm a little turned around. Can you give me directions to the final resting place of Dallas Steele?"

Gus pointed down the hill. "It's right—"

Before he could finish, Shawn butted him out of the way. Arms cartwheeling for balance, Gus took one step backward and fell into the grave. Shawn leaned into the Honda.

"Now why would you be wanting to know such a thing?" Shawn said in the brogue he'd learned through careful study of Tom Cruise's accent in *Far and Away*.

"I'm supposed to be performing the memorial service," the priest said, reddening even further. "I'm afraid I'm running a little late."

"Sure and the service doesn't start until ten," Shawn said.

"That was the public announcement to fool any reporters who might want to crash the ceremony," the priest said. "The real service begins, well, almost immediately."

Gus glanced down the road and saw the main gates swinging open to admit an immaculately polished hearse. Right behind it was a familiar black Bentley. Shawn knew that car well, having ridden in it up to Eagle's View. Suddenly the middle step in his three-step plan became clear.

"Sorry, Father, but your services won't be required. I've been sent to replace you."

The priest goggled at him. "Sent by whom?"

Shawn reviewed everything he knew about the hierarchy of the Catholic Church. Since the vast majority of his knowledge came from repeated viewings of Britney Spears removing her Catholic schoolgirl uniform in the "Baby One More Time" video, that left him plenty of time for staring blankly at the priest.

"Begorrah," Shawn said.

"Excuse me?"

"Erin go bragh?" Shawn tried. "Shillelagh?"

A voice floated up from the grave behind him. "Tell him it was the cardinal."

"The cardinal," Shawn said.

"Which cardinal?"

Shawn thought. "Excuse me for one moment." He took two steps backward to the grave and whispered down into it, "He wants to know which cardinal."

"There's more than one?" Gus said.

Shawn stepped back to the car and leaned in. "Stan Musial?"

The priest glared at him, then shoved the gearshift into reverse. "I'll be speaking to the archdiocese about this."

The Honda executed a neat three-point turn and sputtered back the way it had come. Shawn reached a hand into the grave and pulled Gus out.

"I appreciate your help," Shawn said, "especially after the whole 'knocking you into an open grave' thing."

"I didn't do it for you. I did it so I wouldn't be sent to the gas chamber," Gus said. "But if I'm called to testify against you, you're on your own."

The gate had finally opened wide enough to admit the Bentley. "Let's go," Shawn said.

Shawn and Gus sprinted down the hill to the site of Steele's memorial. Gasping for breath, Shawn positioned himself between the open grave and the sole folding chair. "Quick, get in the grave," he said.

"They're going to put the coffin in there."

"Hey, you were the one who wanted to get close to that phony."

"Not close enough to spend eternity with him," Gus said.

"Fine," Shawn said. "Go maintain something."

That was harder to do than it sounded. The section of the cemetery Steele's widow had chosen for his burial was reserved for the richest of the rich. Service fees were double here what they were everywhere else, and the grounds were immaculate. There were no weeds to pluck, no grass that needed reseeding, no trash to pick up. As the hearse led the Bentley up to the grave site, Gus turned his back to the cars and started polishing the chain that surrounded the plot.

Gus heard the hearse pull to a stop. After a moment, doors opened, followed by the rear gate. Out of the corner of his eye, he watched two men dressed in black carry an elaborate mahogany coffin to the grave site and lay it across bands of nylon attached to a metal frame fitted over the hole. The two men got back into the hearse and drove slowly away. A minute passed, and then Gus heard the driver's door of the Bentley open.

Gus risked a glance over his shoulder and saw Shepler, his gray pinstripes traded for simple black, go around and open the passenger door. After a moment, a woman's legs emerged.

They were probably not the most attractive female legs Gus had ever seen. That honor still went to Tara. But they were close enough that Gus started formulat-

ing a theory on the relation between a woman's append-
ages and her propensity toward homicide.

Gus glanced toward the grave and saw that Shawn
was also watching as the widow emerged from what was
now her car. Her hair and face were covered by a black
hat and veil, her hands and arms by long gloves. Her
black dress was simple and classically elegant, except for
the neckline, which plunged almost to her shoes. Gus
kneeled down, picking an imaginary flake of paint off
the ground, and tried to get a glimpse under her veil, but
all he could see was her tight, firm jawline.

The widow seemed to be lost in a fog of grieving. Paying no attention to Shawn or Gus, she walked directly to
the coffin that rode astride the empty grave and draped
herself over it.

Gus ordered himself not to look. It was bad enough to
find his eyes moving involuntarily toward any cleavage,
no matter how slight the exposure. This was much worse.
The poor woman was here to mourn. It was positively
indecent for Gus to be taking advantage of her.

But the part of the male brain that ordered eyes to
cleavage had been around far longer than the notion
of decency, and Gus could no more keep himself from
looking than a dog could choose to ignore a steak someone had dropped on the floor.

At least he was enough of a gentleman to feel guilty
about it. Apparently wearing a priest's garb didn't have
any effect on Shawn's behavior, because he was not only
staring straight into Mrs. Steele's cleavage—he was waving at Gus with one hand and pointing with the other. If
his own sense of propriety wasn't enough to keep Gus
from sneaking a peek, Shawn's schoolboy behavior certainly was. He crossed his arms, lifted his head, and con-
spicuously refused to look where Shawn was pointing.

Shawn grabbed a dirt clod from the lip of the grave
and chucked it at him, then pointed again, this time even

more urgently. Silently he mouthed a word. Gus tried to read his lips.

"Stag party?" Gus guessed. "This is a funeral!"

"Strawberry!" Shawn said.

Stunned, the widow straightened to stare at him. But not before Gus caught a glimpse of the familiar birth-mark, and the freckle on top that looked like a stem. She whipped off her veil, revealing the red hair and green eyes they'd last seen in the Santa Barbara courthouse.

"Veronica?" Shawn said.

Chapter Twenty

"I knew I couldn't hide from your psychic powers forever," Veronica Mason Steele said, sinking into the one folding chair that had been set up for her. "I never should have tried."

"No, you shouldn't," Gus said.

If she heard him, she didn't show any sign of it. Those deep green eyes never left Shawn. "Can you ever forgive me?"

Gus had so many responses to that. He struggled to pick the right one. He was trying to decide between "As soon as you pay us" and "Not until you confess" when he noticed that Shawn had gone over to her, knelt at her feet, and taken her hand.

"There's nothing to forgive," he said, "although I don't think I'm supposed to say that when I'm wearing this suit."

She seemed to notice for the first time that he was dressed as a priest. "Is this what I drove you to? Subterfuge, disguises, lies, all because I couldn't trust anyone with the truth."

...in the same desperate, breathless tone Gus ...ound so much more convincing when she was describing her great love for Oliver Mason. Although her performance was no less emotional now, Gus was having trouble overlooking the coincidence of a second dead, rich husband in one year. To say nothing of the weeks of unreturned phone calls.

Shawn didn't seem to share any of Gus' misgivings. "Of course," he said. "I can see it now. During the days of your travails, a phone call out of the blue. A colleague of your late husband's, reaching out to give you condolence. A brief conversation that led to a meeting between two people facing challenges the masses could never understand."

"Yes!" she said.

"You mean the challenges of living with the burden of hundreds of millions of dollars?" Gus said. "Give me a break."

Shawn and Veronica didn't seem to hear him.

"And then that understanding turned into love," Shawn said. "A love that had to be kept secret from the prying eyes of a world that would unfairly judge these two souls. That's why your entire relationship was a carried out in secrecy. Why you got married in the only place you knew no reporters could follow you—your private island."

"Yes," she said.

"You mean Oliver Mason's private island," Gus said.

"Which she inherited after her tragic loss," Shawn said. "Try to keep up here."

Gus grabbed Shawn and pulled him away from Veronica. "Don't you realize what's happening?"

"Yes, it's a chance meeting," Shawn said. "Although maybe it would be better to call it fate. Destiny. Kismet."

"Don't you dare think of Kismet—or any other kind of kissing," Gus said. "This woman killed her husband."

"Impossible. We already proved she's innocent."

"Not that husband." Gus leveled an accusing finger at the mahogany box in front of them. "*That* husband."

Veronica Mason took a lace handkerchief out of her tiny black purse and dabbed gently at her eye. "This is why I kept my marriage to Dallas a secret. Because if even close friends like you, Gus, can't believe me, who can?"

Shawn patted her hand consolingly. "You can't help it if you're attracted to rich men with abnormally short life spans."

A tear trickled down her cheek. "You do believe me, Shawn?"

"Absolutely."

"Then will you help me? Will you find my husband's real killer and prove I didn't do it?"

"I guarantee it," Shawn said.

"No, *we* don't," Gus said. "If you killed Dallas Steele, we're going to expose you."

"I accept those terms," Veronica said. "Thank you, Gus."

"For what?" Gus reran the conversation in his head to see what he might have said that she'd find helpful. "What terms?"

"You'll investigate Dal's death, and if you find evidence that I did it, you'll turn me in to the police," she said. "I accept that because I know I'm innocent—and you two are the only ones who can prove that."

Gus didn't remember making that deal. He didn't remember making any deal. He knew somehow that this wasn't what he'd meant, but he couldn't find the spot where her logic diverged from his own. "And you'll pay us."

"Every penny I owe you, and a big bonus on top," she said, those huge green eyes lighting up in relief. "I felt terrible about not paying before, but Dal was so jealous of the way I gushed about you, he wouldn't let me give you a penny, not even out of my own personal funds. Every time I brought it up, he just muttered something about shoelaces."

Shawn glowed with triumph. "I knew it!"

"When he offered you that consulting position, he told me it was to reward you for saving me from prison," she said. "He didn't tell anybody what his real plan was. If only I had known . . ."

Veronica spared them the bus ride back to their office. As Shepler drove, she told them the full story of her whirlwind romance with Dallas Steele, their instant wedding, and the brief, troubled marriage that followed. Dal was not what he seemed. He always came across as a happy, confident, genial person, but inside there was darkness and insecurity. Somehow all of that had become focused on Shawn and Gus. Although he was grateful that they had rescued the woman he loved, it made him crazy that he wasn't the one who could save her. He had to punish them for doing what he couldn't.

Gus didn't listen too closely. For one thing, he knew that Shawn would be repeating every syllable of it on a regular basis for the next few weeks. And while Shawn was too busy having all his prejudices validated to think it through, Gus couldn't stop focusing on the huge problem this new development created for them. Their only hope for clearing Tara and thus themselves of Steele's murder was to find the real killer. But they'd just promised their most promising suspect—their only suspect—that they'd prove her innocent, too.

As the Bentley dropped them off outside their bungalow office, Veronica promising to send Shepler back with a check as soon as possible, Gus tried to explain what a problem they were now facing.

"Either Tara killed Dallas or Veronica did," Gus said. "And we're working for both of them."

"That's terrific," Shawn said. "They can't both be guilty. So whatever happens, we're coming out of this one with a win!"

Before Gus could begin to formulate the corollary of that theory, Henry Spencer's pickup squealed up to the curb, and Henry jumped out.

"You must think this is pretty funny!" Henry said, grabbing Shawn by the arm and dragging him toward the truck. As Henry turned, Gus saw the seat of his khaki pants was striped green.

"I can see the humor in many situations," Shawn said, pulling his arm away. "Those pants, for example."

"That means a lot coming from a man in a dress, *Father*," Henry said through clenched teeth. "They painted my lawn chairs. They painted every room in my house. They painted the exterior. They painted my house number on the curb. If I hadn't driven away, they would have painted my truck."

"I thought you'd taken care of that elf problem," Shawn said.

"These elves were sent by your friend Dallas Steele, and they won't stop until he tells them personally. Which he can't, because, as I understand it, you hired a psychopath to kill him."

"I did not hire her."

"No, you just enabled her."

"And she didn't kill Dallas Steele," Gus added, although he knew neither Shawn nor his dad would hear anything he said until their argument was over.

Henry pushed Shawn toward the truck. "Meanwhile,

I can't breathe in my house for fumes. I can't step anywhere, in case they've painted the floor. They have taken over my home."

"And I have two women to prove innocent of murder," Shawn said. "Maybe after I rescue them both from the gas chamber, I can help with your interior-decoration issues."

"Oops, phone's ringing," Gus said, more for the record than in any hope they'd notice. "I'd better answer that."

He slipped away before either father or son could enlist him in his cause. Gus knew how their arguments ran, and he figured he had time to go inside, get out of the filthy jumpsuit, wash his hands, put on his street clothes, and maybe even catch up on e-mails before they'd finish. But as he stepped into the office, the phone actually did begin to ring. Gus hit the SPEAKER button as he unzipped his grave-digging uniform.

"Psych Investigations. Burton Guster speaking."

"Guster, you and Spencer have to get out of that office right now." Lassiter's voice sounded even tighter than usual. "Come down to the police station. We'll find a safe place for you."

"Like a jail cell?"

"Unless you'd prefer a pine box. We've done some checking on Tara Larison."

"So you've figured out she didn't kill Dallas Steele."

"If she didn't, that puts him in a distinct minority. She's left a trail of broken necks across the country. And most of them belonged to phony psychics."

"Phony psychics?" Gus said, already feeling the vertebrae in his neck cracking. Then he remembered who he was talking to. "In that case, we're perfectly safe."

"Whatever. She meets a psychic, declares that she's his mind slave, does whatever she thinks he wants. And then at some point she decides he's betrayed her, and

somehow he falls down the stairs or trips on a skateboard or crashes his motorcycle."

Gus could practically hear the sound of his own spine
snapping. Which proved that you could find good in any
catastrophe. As terrible as Dallas Steele's murder was,
at least it put Tara in jail before she could turn on them.

Or did it?

"That, um, matches our findings," Gus said. "But why
are you warning us now? She's in jail."

"She never made it," Lassiter said. "Somehow she
managed to break out of the prison bus. She killed the
driver and disappeared."

"You let her get away?"

"The SBPD didn't let her out. The idiots who handle
prison transportation did," Lassiter said. "If she comes
back into our jurisdiction, we'll put her away again. Until
then, the chief feels you two need protection. Because if
Tara was ever going to feel betrayed by a psychic over-
lord, it would be the one who sent her to prison. Do you
need us to send a squad car to pick you up?"

Gus glanced out the window and saw Shawn still arguing with Henry. "We're okay," he said.

"Not as long as that psycho is out there," Lassiter said.
There was a click as he hung up.

Gus looked out the window again. Shawn and his
father were still at it, arguing over something either
of them could have resolved with a simple apology or
kind word. If they knew how close Shawn had come to
sudden, violent death, would they keep on like this?
Gus took a step toward the door. He was about to find
out.

Something grabbed Gus around the neck and yanked
him backward. His heels dug for purchase on the slip-
pery hardwood, but he couldn't keep his balance. He
was going down.

At the car, Henry glanced up to the bungalow's window and saw Gus waving at them with both hands. "I think Gus wants to say something."

"You know how he is," Shawn said. "Can't stand to see Mom and Dad fighting. Needs to make peace."

Gus pounded the window with both fists, his mouth contorting as he struggled to pull a breath of air to his lungs.

"Poor Gus," Henry said. "That soft streak is what's always let you take advantage of him."

"I don't take advantage of Gus."

Inside the bungalow, Gus was sliding back from the window. He grabbed the windowsill and tried to pull himself forward.

"If you want to make it as a priest, you're going to have to learn to be honest with yourself," Henry said. "Look at that poor kid. He's got the same naive, trusting spirit he had when you were ten. The same bright, hopeful attitude."

Gus slammed his head against the window, then was dragged back again.

"He didn't always have three arms, though, did he?" Henry said.

Shawn looked at the window. Gus did seem to have three arms. But the new limb was tanned bronze and wrapped around his neck.

"It's Tara!"

Shawn sprinted to the office and kicked the door open, Henry right behind him. Gus was bent over, trying to shake Tara off his back.

"Let him go!" Shawn shouted.

At the sound of his voice, Tara jumped back. Gus grabbed his throat, grasping for breath.

"She tried to kill me!" Gus wheezed.

"No, it was an accident," Tara said. "He fell down the stairs and broke his neck."

"This is a bungalow," Shawn said. "There are no stairs."

"And we saw you with your arm around his throat," Henry said.

Tara backed away, tears forming in her eyes. "No, I'd never hurt anyone. It was an accident. Shawn, you have to believe me. Please!" Her last word extended into a howl of pain.

"I can see how she fooled you, Shawn," Henry said. "No way I'd ever guess she was crazy."

Shawn took a step toward Tara, holding out a hand to her. "It's all right, Tara. We know you didn't mean to hurt anyone."

She sniffed back a sob. "I knew you'd understand."

"And now we have to make the police understand."

"No!" She stepped back from him. Her back was up against the wall.

"Come on, Tara," Shawn said as gently as he could. He reached out and took her hand. "Everything's going to be all right."

She seemed to melt under his touch.

"Easy, Shawn," Henry said. Gus gasped his agreement.

Shawn waved them back. He had this under control. Slowly, calmly, he took her other hand in his. "It's all going to be okay," he said.

She gazed up into his eyes, and he felt a buzz of electricity running up his arm. Then she squeezed her hand shut, and he got the entire shock.

Shawn collapsed to the ground, his arms and legs twitching uncontrollably.

"Shawn!" Henry shouted, rushing over to him.

"Ack!" Gus agreed, still trying to regain control of his vocal cords.

Tara let out a piercing scream and ran right at them, waving the stun gun wildly. Gus and Henry fell back on the floor, trying to avoid the crackling weapon, and she blasted out the front door. Scrambling to their feet, Gus and Henry got to the door just in time to see a red Mustang screaming away down the street, a blur of orange jumpsuit all they could make out of the driver.

Shawn let out a groan and managed to pull himself to his feet. "I do not want to know where she was hiding that thing when she was in jail," Shawn said.

"I'm thinking she picked up a new one since she got out," Henry said. "You'd be on the ground for an hour if she hit you with the same one she used on me."

"We have to call the police," Gus said. Actually, it came out sounding more like, "We ah oo leese," but both Spencers were able to make sense of it.

"We do have to call the police," Shawn said. "And tell them we now have proof that Tara is innocent of both murders."

The outrage flooding Gus' body was enough to bring back his power of speech. "She just tried to kill me!"

"Absolutely," Shawn said.

"Not to mention Aunt Enid and Fred Larison and all the other phony psychics who broke their necks in tragic accidents," Gus said.

"Phony psychics?" Henry said, cocking an eyebrow at Shawn.

Gus filled them in on what Lassiter told him. Henry's scowl got more disapproving with every new detail. But Shawn was completely undaunted.

"Exactly what I was saying," Shawn said.

Henry's cell phone trilled. "Hold that thought. Or whatever it is that passes for thought in your head." Before he could flip the phone open, the ringing stopped. Henry glanced at the incoming number. He pressed the CALLBACK key and let the phone on the other end ring five times before he disconnected, looking troubled.

"One of my clients," Henry said. "No answer when I called back."

"Maybe we can deal with that when the serial killer

stalking us is back behind bars," Gus said. "How are we going to stop her, Shawn?"

But Shawn wasn't listening to Gus. He was deep in thought. "Which client?" he said finally.

"The first one," Henry said.

"That was the widow of the tackle shop guy who used to be a cop?"

"Yes," Henry said. "Not that it makes any difference."

"It might make all the difference in the world," Shawn said. "Let's go."

"Go where?" Gus had given up trying to follow Shawn's logic.

"You heard my father," Shawn said. "There's a scrapbook emergency out there, and we're the only ones who can help."

During the ten-minute drive into the hills, Gus tried repeatedly to get Shawn to explain what they were doing. Or why he was now so completely convinced that Tara was innocent despite witnessing her trying to kill him. But for once Shawn seemed to have nothing to say. He drummed his fingers on the truck's seat, fidgeting nervously. His anxiety even seemed to affect Henry, whose foot got heavier as they got closer to Betty Walinski's house.

When they finally arrived, Shawn jumped out and ran to the front door. It was slightly ajar. As Henry and Gus joined him, Shawn held up one finger for silence. He pointed to Henry and waved toward the back of the house. He tapped Gus' chest and indicated that he should stand under the open kitchen window and be prepared to dive through it. Then he jabbed a thumb toward himself and wagged it back at the open front door. He'd handle this one personally.

"Whatever," Henry said, and pushed past Shawn through the open front door. "Betty?"

Shawn sighed heavily. "I spent a long time coming up with those hand signals."

Gus clapped him on the shoulder, then followed Henry into the house. As soon as he got through the door, Henry barked at him, "Stay back!"

Henry was crouching in front of the sofa. Betty Walinski was lying on her stomach, but her head was looking up at the ceiling.

"Damn it, Shawn," Henry said as his son came into the room. "If you'd just done the right thing from the first instead of trying to be so clever. You knew this woman was crazy, but instead of helping her, you used her. And now another innocent person is dead."

Shawn stepped up to his father. "This isn't my fault."

Henry wouldn't even look up at him. "You enabled Tara for—"

"Absolutely," Shawn said. "But Tara didn't do this. And now I know for sure she didn't kill John Marichal."

"You said you knew that before," Gus said.

"Yes, but at the time what I meant was, I had a gut instinct about it," Shawn said. "Now it's a fact."

"You're going to have to explain this to the police." Henry pulled out his phone and started to punch in the number.

"I will," Shawn said. "But not here."

"Then where?" Henry said.

"Think back," Shawn said. "Where did someone try to kill us?"

"In our office," Gus said.

"Before that," Shawn said. "The first time."

Gus remembered the searing pain as he grabbed Marichal's shotgun. "The impound lot."

"And the second time?"

Gus heard bullets thwocking into abandoned cars. "The impound lot."

"So where should we go to find the solution?"

"The impound lot?"

"Eagle's View!"

Gus and Henry stared at him. "What does Eagle's View have to do with any of this?" Henry said.

"Nothing," Shawn said. "But that impound lot is a dump. Who'd want to waste any more time there?"

Chapter Twenty-one

When Shawn called Veronica Mason with his request, he didn't have a chance to finish the question before she agreed. The call to Detective Lassiter wasn't quite as friendly. In fact, Lassie hung up on him three times before Shawn finished explaining what he needed the Santa Barbara Police Department to do.

"Don't make me go over your head, Lassie," Shawn said when Lassiter picked up the fourth time.

"If you're thinking about calling Chief Vick, be my guest." Shawn could practically hear Lassiter's smug grin through the phone. "She and Detective O'Hara will be happy to spend a couple of hours explaining how demeaning they find it to be treated as sex objects instead of law enforcement professionals. God knows they've already spent most of the day on the subject."

Shawn put a hand over the speakerphone's mike and turned to Gus. "How did Chief Vick know what I said about her?"

"I don't know," Gus said. "Maybe the same way Tara knew which BurgerZone outlet you prefer. Maybe sound can actually travel between the front and back seats of an automobile."

Shawn leapt out of his seat. "That's it!"

"Umm, yeah," Gus said. "It was pretty obvious to anyone who's ever ridden in a car."

Shawn sank back in his seat and folded his hands across his desk like a third-grade teacher trying one last time to explain fractions to a particularly slow student. "No, Gus, it's the final piece of the mystery," he said patiently. "I know who killed Dallas Steele."

Lassiter's voice squawked out of the speaker. "So do we, Spencer. That's why the entire force is out hunting for your former mind slave before she kills again."

"They're wasting their time," Shawn said.

"Good point," Lassiter said. "The way she's going, she'll run out of civilians to murder, and she'll have to come to the police station just to find another victim."

"I'll make you a deal, Lassie," Shawn said. "You do what I ask, and I'll deliver the real killer to you within an hour. And if I can't, I'll confess to every single one of the murders myself."

There was a long silence on the line. Gus was beginning to think the connection had been cut when Lassiter's voice came back. "Fax me what you need."

Four hours later, Shawn and Gus were standing outside the magnificent front door of Eagle's View. A stream of squad cars delivered all the people whose presence Shawn had requested, then headed back to the city.

The first to arrive were Chief Vick and Detective O'Hara. They glared at Shawn as they came up the walkway.

"You have exactly one hour, Mr. Spencer," Chief Vick said. "Where do you want us?"

"And I'd think very carefully before I answered if I were you," Juliet O'Hara added.

"Where I really want you—"

"Shawn!" Gus whispered. "Don't do this."

"—is at the top of a hierarchy that for far too long has been exclusively male-dominated. But for now, the grand ballroom will do. Mr. Shepler will show you."

Shawn snapped his fingers, and Shepler appeared from the entry hall. He stood frozen before them as his mind processed the new information; then he gave a short bow. "Please follow me."

As O'Hara and the chief followed Shepler down the hall, Henry Spencer came up to Shawn and Gus. "Are you sure you know what you're doing?" he said.

"Like I always do," Shawn said.

"That's what I was afraid of." He went inside as a middle-aged woman in a black dress stepped up. A uniformed officer followed, dragging a huge black plastic case. Shawn waved them both in.

"Who was that?" Gus asked. "And what's in the box?"

"The most important element of all."

"That can't be," Gus said. "Because we went over this plan together, and you never mentioned whatever that thing is. So how is it that we agreed exactly what we were going to do, and I still don't know about the most important element of all?"

"Because you're not paying attention?"

Gus was about to respond when he noticed another squad car disgorging its passenger. Tall and blond, blue eyes sparkling almost as brightly as her white teeth, bronzed skin only slightly covered by her crop top, short shorts, and tiny green apron.

"Wait a minute," Gus said. "You brought—"

"The girl from that coffee place," Shawn said.

"Why?"

"We're here to solve a series of mysteries," Shawn said. "So we might as well answer the greatest one of all—who does she like, you or me?"

The girl stepped up to Shawn and Gus, gazing in astonishment at the house towering above them. "Cool," she said. "You guys live here?"

"In a manner of speaking," Shawn said.

She looked puzzled. "What manner?"

"The one that means no," Gus said.

She thought that one through, then let it go. "Hey, I know you guys," she said.

"You certainly do," Shawn said.

"You're that creepy guy who hangs out at the Coffee Barn for hours yapping about everything and never tips," she said to Shawn.

"I'm sure you're confusing me with someone else," Shawn said, but she just shrugged.

"The creepy guy, eh?" Gus said. "I guess that's one mystery solved."

She turned to Gus. "And you're the guy who talks so quietly I can never hear your order, but you take whatever I give you, anyway."

Gus felt his face flushing. All those times she'd given him a special drink—a triple caramel chocolate malto-latte instead of the plain cappuccino he'd ordered—he had assumed she was demonstrating her affection. Now it turned out she simply didn't care enough to ask him to speak up.

If Shawn was embarrassed, he didn't show it. He leaned in close enough to see his reflection in her gleaming teeth. "So you've got a loud pushy guy and a timid stalker—which one do you like best?"

Gus found himself leaning in for the answer, too. But while she was still looking blankly at them, Shepler appeared and guided her down the hall.

"You going to do that good a job of solving the rest of the mysteries?" Gus muttered. "Because if you are, I've got dibs on the top bunk in our cell."

The rest of the guests filed past Shawn and Gus without comment, casting them only puzzled stares or hostile glares—first Bert Coules, the prosecutor, and then, led in handcuffs by Detective Lassiter, Arno Galen, who was still awaiting trial on pet-napping charges. When everyone was inside, Shawn pulled Gus through the massive front doors. Shepler locked them with an ornate antique key, then brought them down the hall to the grand ballroom.

Under any other circumstance Gus would have paused in the doorway to study the ballroom's ornate design, which put even the theater to shame. The floor was polished granite, inlayed with another mural celebrating some aspect of Adler's domination over human history; the walls were hand-carved *boiserie* taken from a French château. But Gus' attention was immediately riveted on the cluster of people in the center of the room, none of whom seemed to notice them when Shawn threw the doors open.

The detectives were prowling on opposite sides of the room so they could keep an eye on all the suspects at once. Chief Vick had positioned herself between Veronica Mason and Bert Coules, apparently trying to referee an argument. Arno Galen stood next to Veronica, his eyes shifting between the cops guarding him and the low-cut dress his hostess was wearing. Henry Spencer was lost in conversation with the coffee girl, who stared up at him rapturously. Gus couldn't see the unidentified mystery woman, but her black case was in the back of the room, and it was possible she was hidden behind it.

Shawn cleared his throat loudly. Still no one seemed to notice him. He coughed theatrically. Veronica glanced up from her argument and noticed them standing in the doorway. Her face lit up as she stepped away from Coules.

"Finally here's the man who can tell us who actually killed my husband, instead of casting vague, unsupported allegations," she said. "Come in, Shawn, and let us share in your genius."

Coules scowled at her. "That's one way to keep him from pointing the finger at you."

Shawn and Gus stepped into the room. All the other conversations stopped as the guests turned to look at them.

"Thank you all for coming," Shawn said.

"As if we had a choice." Arno Galen rattled his cuffed hands. "Only way you could get an audience, you cheap phony."

"Detective, silence that man," Shawn barked to Juliet O'Hara, who stood beside Galen.

"Silence him yourself," O'Hara said.

"Just get on with it," Lassiter said from across the room.

Shawn cast O'Hara a reproachful look, then turned back to the crowd. "You're probably wondering why I've brought you all together."

"No, we're not," Coules said. "We've all suffered through your shtick before."

Veronica whirled on him. "You mean freeing an innocent woman you were trying to convict? Is that what you call 'shtick'?"

Gus stepped forward. "People, please, we're trying to solve a series of murders here!"

The coffee girl peered at Gus. "Did he say something? I can never understand that guy."

"That's two of us, honey," Henry said.

The room dissolved into cross talk. Gus looked over to see if Shawn had noticed how completely he'd lost control over the situation, but Shawn didn't seem concerned.

"Ahem!" Shawn waited until the various conversations died down. "I've brought you all here for two reasons."

"What's the one besides keeping your neck out of the noose?" Coules said.

Shawn clapped his hands sharply, and Shepler opened a door in the back of the ballroom. The crowd turned to see four tuxedoed waiters emerging from a service corridor, each one carrying a silver tray laden with crystal glasses filled with what looked like iced cola. They moved through the room until every guest was holding a drink. One waiter approached Gus with the last glass. Gus reached for it, but Shawn stepped in front of him and snagged it off the tray.

"Sorry," Shawn said. "My plan, my beverage."

Shawn knocked it back in a couple of gulps as the waiters retreated from the room; then he handed the empty glass to Gus.

"We are here tonight to correct a terrible injustice," Shawn said. "But first, enjoy your drink."

Those who hadn't did. Some of the glasses were already empty.

"It tastes kind of like coffee," the coffee girl said. "But it's not."

"This, my friends, is the elusive Coca-Cola Blāk, one of the greatest inventions in the history of mankind," Shawn said. "I admit, it's not the standard commercial version. It's Dallas Steele's special blend. But through an injustice of global proportion, even the normal American version of Blāk is unavailable anywhere in this country. I bring you here today to unite you all in my cause to force the Coca-Cola company to bring back Blāk!"

Shawn's arms shot in the air like Richard Nixon at the end of a speech. Somehow the gesture didn't bring a wave of cheers from his audience.

Gus sniffed the glass. It smelled like Coke with a hint of coffee grounds emanating from the ice cubes. He had a hard time imagining why anyone would get so excited over a soft drink, but then he'd never actually tried the stuff. Maybe he could request it with his last meal if Shawn kept talking about Coca-Cola products instead of producing a killer.

"You have thirty-nine minutes left, Mr. Spencer," Chief Vick said. "I urge you to use them wisely."

Shawn dropped his arms to his side. "Fine. We're also here to solve a bunch of murders."

"Murders?" the coffee girl squealed. She looked around, frantic. "No one told me anything about murders."

Henry draped an arm around the girl, protectively. "Why is she here?"

"For one thing, I've seen the women you've been dating lately," Shawn said.

Henry pulled his arm away from the girl, embarrassed. But she grabbed his hand and wrapped it around her, then snuggled close to him.

"As I said, we are here to solve a series of baffling crimes," Shawn continued. "Who killed John Marichal? Who killed Dallas Steele? Who killed Betty Walinski?"

"Tara Larison," Coules said. "Can we go home now?"

"Impossible," Shawn said. "Tara couldn't have killed all those people."

"Why not?" Lassiter said.

"Because she's the most obvious suspect," Shawn said.

"Right, because she's killed a bunch of people before," O'Hara said.

"But the most obvious suspect is never the killer," Shawn said. "Otherwise, what's the point?"

Gus stared at him. "This is all you've got?"

Shawn shrugged. "It sounded good when I came up with it."

Gus stared down at the ice cubes in his glass. Maybe

if he studied them hard enough, he'd find a subliminal picture of the real killer. Because that looked like the only thing that was going to keep the police from taking Shawn's confession in a couple of hours.

"Actually, Mr. Spencer, the likeliest suspect is almost always guilty," Chief Vick said. "That's what makes them obvious—evidence they've created in their commission of the crimes."

Coules and the detectives muttered their agreement. Shawn held up a hand to silence them.

"Then let me give you another reason why I know Tara didn't kill John Marichal and Betty Walinski," Shawn said. "Because she did kill Fred Larison and Aunt Enid. Because this very morning she tried to kill Gus."

"Well, I'm convinced," Lassiter muttered. "Can we go home now?"

"Every one of those killings was staged to look like an accident," Shawn said. "A fall down the stairs, a trip over a skateboard. At first I assumed, like you, that this was the work of a canny criminal covering up her crimes. But then she tried to kill Gus, and even though we caught her in the act, she insisted that it was an accident."

"That's right," Gus said. Maybe there was hope outside of the dream of an ice-cube portrait. "She claimed I fell down a flight of stairs in a one-story building."

"So she's nuts," Coules said. "Big deal."

"It is a big deal. She needs to believe she's not a killer, just the victim of a series of tragic accidents. That's why she fooled me for so long. Because even though she had killed several people, she was completely convinced in her own mind that she didn't."

"So when you read her aura, it proclaimed her innocence," Veronica said.

Shawn shot her a grateful smile. "Exactly. But for her to keep up the illusion, when she killed, she arranged the scene to look like an accident. Whoever killed John

Marichal and Betty Walinski didn't bother to make them look like anything other than victims of cold-blooded murder."

Shawn turned to Gus to see how he was doing. Gus gave him a quick thumbs-up.

"What about Dallas Steele?" Arno rattled his handcuffs for emphasis. "I saw her kill him. And I'm willing to testify—as long as they reduce these ridiculous charges against me."

"I'm glad you brought that up," Shawn said. "And so is Fluffy, by the way."

Arno made a move toward Shawn, but Lassiter pulled him back.

"You didn't see Tara kill Steele. You saw her standing over him with a knife."

"The knife forensics proved was the murder weapon," Coules said.

"She made no attempt to hide or to claim Steele's death was an accident," Shawn said. "So we can all agree that Tara is innocent."

Chief Vick held up her watch. "The one thing we can all agree on is that you have twenty-eight minutes left."

"If Tara didn't kill these people, who did?" Shawn said. "Before we can answer that question, we have to understand what an ex-con, a tackle shop widow, and a billionaire venture capitalist who didn't know how to tie his shoes in kindergarten had in common."

"Nothing," Lassiter said.

"Do you think so?" Shawn said. "Let's go back to the beginning and figure out where it all began. At first I thought it was the towing of Gus' car. That's what took us to the impound lot."

"He was parked illegally," Lassiter snapped.

"But that's not what kept us at the impound lot." Shawn ignored Lassiter as he plowed on. "Six thousand dollars of parking tickets did that. So we have to go back a little further to discover where this story really begins. To find our killer, we need to understand who is responsible for those tickets."

"Umm, you?" Gus said. There was one ice cube that seemed to be growing a face as it melted.

"Only in a technical sense," Shawn said. "I accuse . . . *her*." He pointed a finger at the coffee girl, who gazed back at him, perplexed.

"Me?"

Henry pulled her to his side. "Shawn, this is ridiculous."

"Is it really?" Shawn said.

"Yes," Gus said. The face on the cube was looking more like an elephant and less like a suspect. Gus rattled the ice, hoping to find another image. Instead, he saw something on the bottom of the glass. It looked like a shard of gray plastic.

"Think about it," Shawn said. "She's a seemingly insignificant player in the drama. We never even saw her once over the course of the investigation, but somehow her name kept on coming up."

"We don't even know her name," Gus said.

"It's Mindy," the coffee girl said. She looked up at Henry adoringly. "Mindy Stackman. I'm in the book."

"Why do you think there were all those constant, subtle, seemingly meaningless references to a character we never see? To establish her as a plausible suspect. And then she appears here for reasons no one understands."

"She's here because I brought her here," Lassiter said. "And I brought her here because she was on your list."

"And now she's finally unmasked as the real killer," Shawn concluded. "Can you imagine an ending more satisfying than that? More technically perfect? Even Joe Eszterhas would approve, and he wrote both *Jagged Edge* and *Basic Instinct.*"

"He also wrote *F.I.S.T.*, which is what you're going to get in your face if you don't stop saying things about me." Mindy looked around at the accusing faces. "What? You've never seen a film major working at a coffeehouse before?"

"Fourteen minutes, Mr. Spencer," Chief Vick said.

"Is there one reason why we shouldn't think Mindy is the killer?"

"There's no evidence," O'Hara said.

"There's no motive," Lassiter said.

"There's no connection," Coules said. "Except some arbitrary pattern you imposed on a series of events because it's convenient for you."

"And that's a bad thing?" Shawn said.

"Obviously," Coules said.

"So why wasn't it just as bad when you assumed that Dallas Steele's murder was connected to the killings of John Marichal and Betty Walinski?"

Gus stopped trying to fish the thing out of the glass. Shawn actually seemed to be on the verge of a point. "The only reason to accuse Tara is a pattern. And the police created that pattern."

"She was holding the knife!" Coules said.

"And because of that, you created this pattern that said she must have committed those other two murders," Shawn said. "Because she's the one person who could have had any reason, no matter how vague, for killing all three victims. But if you stop assuming there's only one killer, there's no reason for her to have done any of it."

"Are you saying there are two killers, Mr. Spencer?" Chief Vick tapped her watch significantly.

"Disappointing, isn't it?" Shawn said. "Classically, it's much more satisfying to wrap up everything together. So if you want to go that way, I'll understand and I'll testify against Mindy."

"That's it," Mindy said. "You are so banned from the Coffee Barn."

"But if we want the truth, we have to dig a little deeper. Let's think back to the first time Gus and I went to the impound yard."

Shawn stopped. The others began to murmur their irritation as he stood silently, his head slightly cocked, his hands frozen in the air.

Gus nudged him. "What are you doing?"

"I'm waiting for the flashback."

"We don't have flashbacks. This is real life, not *CSI*."

Shawn looked crushed. "Really?"

"Get on with it!"

Shawn sighed. "I've been informed that the flashbacks aren't working. So while I go through this, please try to picture it in grainy black-and-white, maybe with a slight blurring effect on the action. Alicia?"

A harp glissando filled the room. Gus turned and saw that the woman in black had unpacked her case and taken out a full-size harp, which she was now seated in front of.

"What the hell is that?" Lassiter said.

"If we don't have different film stocks, how are we going to differentiate past and present? Please, when you hear the harp, assume the image is dissolving away."

"My life is dissolving away," Galen said. "What am I doing here?"

"Quiet, you," Lassiter snapped.

"I thought we went over the plan," Gus said. "You didn't mention any of this."

"I was born to improvise."

"When you call hours in advance to request the services of a harpist, that's not improvising anymore?"

"It's not?"

Chief Vick cleared her throat. "Your time is up, Mr. Spencer."

Shawn checked his own watch, then cast a glance around the room.

"Okay, fine, you're right," Shawn said. "No drama, no flashbacks, no suspense, no craft. If all you want is the killer's identity, it's yours. Bert Coules did it. Come on, Gus."

Shawn headed for the door. Walking behind him, Gus saw that his feet seemed to be dragging on the floor.

"That's outrageous," Coules shouted. It seemed like he was shouting, anyway. The words came out slowly and hesitantly. "You can't accuse me of killing three people and just walk out of here." He turned to the detectives. "Stop him."

The detectives seemed frozen to the ground. They stared blindly into space. Gus looked around the room and saw that the others all appeared to be imitating department-store mannequins.

"There you go again," Shawn said. His feet were barely lifting off the ground with each step. His words were beginning to slur. "Not three people. Just John Marichal and Betty Walinski. Although I might suggest revisiting her husband's autopsy, just in case."

"What's going on here, Shawn?" Gus said. "And who killed Dallas Steele?"

"Look in your glass," Shawn said, the words coming out with obvious effort. "The killer just revealed hims . . ."

Shawn's voice trailed off. He stared blankly into space. Gus nudged him, but Shawn didn't react. He seemed to be in a coma, like all the others.

What had happened to them? And why wasn't it happening to Gus? He dumped the glass on the ground and scrabbled through the ice cubes to find the piece of gray plastic. It wasn't the broken shard he'd assumed it to be. It was a tiny model of a gun. The kind you'd find mounted on a toy warship.

The kind you'd find mounted on a toy ship that transformed into a robot. And that would come off easily, since the glue holding it on, when exposed to water, dissolved into a hallucinogenic drug.

Someone must have spiked the Blāk Shawn served here. And, Gus realized, it wasn't the first time. Whoever it was must have also drugged Dallas Steele before killing him, and drugged Tara before putting the knife in her hand. That would explain why Tara seemed so lost and so docile when she was discovered standing over the body, and why she couldn't remember anything about the killing. That was what Shawn had been trying to tell him.

It could have been Veronica. But Steele told her he'd given them the consulting position to help them. He wouldn't have revealed the truth about the toy boats. And even if she wanted to kill her husband, how would she know about Tara? Gus could ask her, but she was as frozen as her guests.

At least Gus knew the crucial question to ask: Who knew both about Tara and the toy boats? And how had they found out?

Something was tickling the back of Gus' brain. Something Shawn had said earlier. When he'd jumped up and announced he knew who killed Dallas Steele.

Except it wasn't something Shawn had said—Gus had said it. That sound traveled between the front seat and backseat of a car.

Devon Shepler knew all about Tara, because they'd talked about her on the way up to Eagle's View. And he knew about the disastrous investments because he'd been waiting to lead them up to the tower when Dallas revealed the truth. If he'd caught Tara breaking in to the house looking for them, it would have been easy to manipulate her into ingesting some of the drug—and even easier to slip it into Steele's late-night beverage.

But why would Shepler kill the man to whom he seemed so devoted? To whom he had dedicated every minute of his waking day? Who relied on him for everything?

Gus tried to put himself in Shepler's mind—and discovered it was frighteningly easy. He could feel the man's resentment at being constantly needed and never rewarded, or even acknowledged. At being taken advantage of.

How blind Gus had been not to see this all along. The way Shepler would freeze before answering a question or following an order—it wasn't the pause of a methodical brain searching for the correct response. It was the moment he needed to get his rage in check before acting like the proper gentleman's gentleman.

Maybe Shepler tried to build a little something for himself. When Dallas told him that he'd hired a psychic genius to invest his money, it would have seemed like a perfect chance to get some for himself. How much of his life savings did he pour into their ridiculous investments? How much of Steele's had he borrowed without permission? And then when he found out the truth that Dallas had casually destroyed him as collateral damage in a cruel scheme to humiliate Shawn, how great would his rage have been?

And then Gus realized something else. Shawn had stopped him from drinking the Blāk. Stopped him by drinking it himself. At the time, Gus attributed it to his typical self-centeredness. Now he realized that Shawn had sacrificed himself for his friend. He was giving Gus the chance to get away—or to save the day.

Gus patted Shawn on the shoulder. "Don't worry, buddy," he said. "I won't let you down."

The door the waiters had come through swung open. Gus froze in position as Shepler led Tara in. Her eyes were blank, her steps unsteady. Gus suspected he knew how she'd disappeared after trying to kill him. Shepler found her and started feeding her small doses of the drug, not enough to paralyze, but sufficient to keep her extremely pliable.

"Here we are, Tara," Shepler said cheerfully. "All your friends are in one place." He turned to the paralyzed crowd. "No, just stay where you are. No need to bother yourself for me."

Chuckling, he reached into his pocket and came out with the ugliest handgun Gus had ever seen. It had a wooden handle and black steel barrel, and when Shepler unfolded the front grip down, it looked like some kind of evil alien insect. Gus didn't know enough about guns to identify the make or model, but he was pretty sure it would be able to take out everyone in the room.

Shepler walked through the room, studying his victims like they were statues in a gallery. He stepped up to Veronica and leered in her face.

"All this time you've thought I was just that useless little servant. You thought—" Shepler broke off. He raised the gun and pressed it to her temple. "Why am I making a speech? You'll all be dead in thirty seconds."

"No!" The word was out of Gus' mouth before he could stop it.

Shepler wheeled around. "Who said that?"

Gus tried to stay absolutely still. Shepler watched them all carefully for a moment, then shrugged. He turned back to Veronica, raising the gun to her head.

Gus dived for the ground and grabbed the only weapon he could find. Before Shepler could aim the gun, Gus hurled the glass directly at his head. The throw was perfectly aimed, the force was enough to take his head off his shoulders. Unfortunately, before it connected with its target Shepler stepped out of the way, and the glass sailed past him, shattering against the far wall.

"That was a special Baccarat pattern made solely for Mr. Steele," Shepler said as he aimed the gun at Gus.

"Now I can only have two hundred forty-nine people over for dinner."

Shepler's finger tightened on the trigger. Gus rolled along the floor until he could scramble to his feet. He bolted for the door, but the handle wouldn't turn.

"Don't you remember? Shawn asked me to lock you all in." Shepler leveled the gun at Gus.

"Don't you want to explain your master plan?" Gus said, still trying to make the door work. "Or maybe make me watch you execute all my friends before you lock me in the dungeon to suffer for hours with the memory burning in my brain?"

"Because I care so much about what you think? Are you always this arrogant?"

Shepler was moving closer. Not so close that Gus had any hope of grabbing the gun, just near enough there was no chance of missing.

Gus only had one prayer. Shawn. Maybe he was coming out of his trance. Maybe he'd been faking all along. Maybe he could be sneaking up on Shepler as they spoke.

Gus risked a glance in his direction. He wasn't. He hadn't. He couldn't.

But one part of him was moving. Shawn's eyes were shifting back and forth urgently. Gus followed his gaze and let it lead him to the harpist.

"He doesn't even want to give a speech. He's not going to go for a flashback," Gus said.

Shawn's eyes widened slightly and shifted quickly back toward the harpist. Now Gus saw what he was indicating. The harp case stood open behind her.

Shepler took another step toward Gus. There was no chance he could miss from this distance. "I've seen that movie, too. You pretend to talk to someone, I turn around to see who it is, blah blah blah."

"Shawn?" It was Tara's voice. She was blinking slowly, as if trying to focus.

This time Shepler did turn his head, and Gus took advantage of the moment. He dived to the ground, sliding across the slick marble like a puck on an air-hockey table, crashing into the harp and toppling it with a musical crash. As bullets smashed into the wall behind him, Gus rolled over and pulled himself behind the open case. He crouched down, wishing that Shawn had brought someone who played an even bigger instrument.

"Do you really think they make harp cases bulletproof?" Shepler said. "It's not like there's a big demand for them in war zones."

There were three shots, and three holes appeared in the top of the case. "Nope, not bulletproof," Shepler said. "Let's see if you are."

There was nowhere to run. There was nowhere to hide. There was only one chance, and it was as slight as they come.

"Tara!"

"Gus," Shepler said wearily, "when a drugged-out zombie is your only hope, you might as well pack it in."

"Tara, Mr. Shepler put pickles on Shawn's burger!"

Gus pulled his head down to his knees and waited for the impact of the bullet into his body. And waited.

There was no gunshot, just a muffled crack, and then a thump. And after a moment, Tara's pleading voice.

"Gus, I think Mr. Shepler fell down the stairs."

Chapter Twenty-two

Santa Barbara chilled under a blanket of fog. Across the city, smoke was pouring out of fireplace chimneys, furnaces were roaring for the first time in months, and the homeless who had moved here for the weather were bundled in multiple copies of the *Times*.

Somehow, however, the impound office was as hot as ever. It seemed to be made out of a miraculous new kind of tin that would let heat in but never allow it out.

Of course that could be partly due to the fact that it was crammed full of people. The day after the Eagle's View affair, when the hallucinogen's twelve-hour effectiveness had worn off and all its victims had been released from the hospital, Bert Coules demanded that Shawn be arrested for his outrageous accusation. Chief Vick wouldn't accede to that, since there was no law against maligning public officials. But she did strongly urge Shawn to either prove what he'd said or take it back before Coules found some statute to hold him on.

Gus thought this showed a good deal of ingratitude. After all they had solved the murder of Dallas Steele and had helped bring his killer to justice. Or, if not exactly justice, death. Either way Shepler wouldn't get what he'd been planning on, which was complete control of the Steele estate once it passed to the Dallas Steele Foundation, of which he had been the executive director.

Tara had been captured, and was undergoing observation at an upscale spalike psychiatric hospital where she'd probably spend the rest of her life, thanks to Veronica Mason Steele's generosity. If she ever stood trial, she might easily be sentenced to multiple centuries in prison. But it would be hard for even the toughest prosecutor to find her sane enough to stand trial when she honestly seemed to believe that the dead podiatrist in the trunk of her stolen car had ended up there by falling down a flight of stairs.

Even so, the police refused to take Shawn's word that the city's district attorney was also a murderer. So Shawn had arranged a demonstration, and because of—or maybe despite—the results of his last gathering, this one was well-attended. Chief Vick had brought Detective Lassiter, Detective O'Hara, and several uniformed officers, while Coules had come on his own. Henry Spencer was there with a large scrapbook in one arm and Mindy in the other. And of course, Alicia the harpist had set up her instrument in the corner. Arno Galen was nowhere to be seen since, as Shawn cheerfully admitted, he'd only had him brought to Eagle's View to annoy him.

"Before we start," Shawn said cheerfully, "who wants a beverage?"

The others glared at him. Even Gus struggled to find the humor.

"Get on with it, Spencer," Coules growled.

"Okay, but I'm warning you, we're going to need flashbacks. Are you ready, Alicia?"

From the corner, she let loose a series of glissandos.

"That's enough." Shawn held up a hand to stop her. "We're only going back a few weeks. Now I need a volunteer from the audience." He scanned the crowd packed into the tiny space, then pointed at Lassiter. "You, sir, step up behind the counter, please."

Lassiter didn't move. Chief Vick leaned over and whispered in his ear. He scowled, but he shuffled over to take the place of the attendant.

"First I want you to assure the audience that we've never met and that I haven't given you any direction on what to do," Shawn said.

"We have met more times than I care to count," Lassiter said. "And, in fact, you've not only told me what you wanted—you typed out a script. There's only one 's' in 'gcnius,' by the way."

"Sorry. The key sticks," Gus said.

"Can we just get on with this farce?" Coules said. "I have criminals to prosecute."

Shawn turned to his audience and bowed. "Allow me to set the scene. We're in a tin shack that passes for an impound office. It's well over a hundred degrees inside. And two intrepid young sleuths come in on a desperate rescue mission. Alicia!"

The harpist let loose with a brief glissando. Shawn and Gus stepped up to the counter. Lassiter glared at them.

Shawn rapped on the counter. "My good man, we are here to collect a car. Prithee, hasten and fetch it!"

"Prithee?" Henry said. Mindy, who had wrapped most of her limbs around him, beamed at his interruption. "Are we flashing all the way back to the sixteenth century?"

"First, all good drama includes the word 'prithee,' " Shawn said. "Second, you should be ashamed of yourself. That girl's a third your age." He turned back to the counter. "Hasten already."

Lassiter glanced at his script. "That will be six thousand dollars."

Gus clapped his hands to his cheeks in full Macauley Culkin. "I don't have that kind of money."

"Then get lost."

Shawn touched his fingertips to his forehead. "Wait. I'm getting an emanation from the beyond. The spirits are speaking to me. They're telling me you're not who you claim to be. You are not the legal holder of this position in an impound lot licensed to serve our fair city. You are in fact a convict who has recently escaped from a chain gang."

Lassiter checked his script, then dropped it on the counter. "I am not going to say this."

"You have to," Shawn said. "Gus stayed up all night working on that script."

"You'd think it was easy, but it turns out good dialogue has to advance both the story and the character, while providing a break from straight exposition," Gus said.

"Just say it," Detective O'Hara said. "We're never going to get out of here until you do."

Lassiter muttered something under his breath, but he picked up the pages and read from them. "Oh, you are indeed a wise and powerful psychic. How it pains me to know that my own master plan depends on depriving the rest of the world of your geniusssss."

He took a shotgun out from under the counter and aimed it at them. Shawn motioned to Alicia, and she glissandoed them back to the present.

"End scene!" Shawn said. "I'd like a special round of applause for our volunteer from the audience."

No one clapped. Chief Vick said, "Mr. Spencer, what was the point of that? We already know what happened when you came to get Mr. Guster's car."

"Do we?" Shawn said. "Do we really?"

263

"Yes," Gus said. "We already told them."

"Oh," Shawn said. "Sorry we wasted your time, then. Come on, Gus." He pushed through the crowd of astonished and angry faces to the door.

"I'm waiting for my apology, Spencer," Coules shouted at him.

Shawn stopped and turned back. "You know, I don't think we did tell you what this refugee from a chain gang was doing here."

"I don't believe we did," Gus said.

"Remember, he was serving time in Arizona," Shawn said. "After he escaped he came directly to Santa Barbara and murdered the real impound lot attendant so he could take over his position. It's a safe bet that a second-generation criminal with a history of armed robbery wouldn't be that excited to land a minimum-wage job. He was here for a specific reason."

"Yes, Mr. Spencer, the police were also able to reach that astonishing conclusion." Chief Vick was finding it hard to hide her frustration in the heat of the shack. "We simply couldn't figure out what that reason was."

"That's because you weren't looking in the right place," Shawn said. "Alicia!"

Lassiter raised the shotgun. "I swear, Spencer, if you start another flashback, I will beat you to death with this. And I guarantee you there won't be a single witness who'll say they saw me do it."

"No more flashbacks," Shawn said. "Just a little traveling music." He signaled to Alicia, and she launched into a jaunty tune. Shawn took a moment to appreciate the music, then walked around the counter and out the back door to the impound lot. The others followed.

Shawn waved at the acres of cars in front of them. "John Marichal came all the way across the country to die here."

"If you consider the next state over to be all the way

across the country," Coules said. "He escaped from a chain gang in Arizona."

"Only because he was caught holding up a liquor store to finance the rest of his journey," Shawn said. "He originally came from Florida. Miami. Isn't that where you're from, Bert?"

"Me and Detective O'Hara and eighteen million other people."

"Good point. And among those eighteen million people were Herman and Betty Walinski."

"Didn't he used to run the tackle shop down on the pier?" Lassiter said.

"Before that, he ran a small fleet of tow trucks," Shawn said. "Which he then contracted to the city, and used that connection to open the impound yard, later expanding it into one of the few combined impound-and-wrecking yards on the West Coast. When he'd made his fortune here, he used some of it to open his tackle store, where he spent a happy retirement."

"Thanks for the lesson in local history," Coules said. "Is there a point?"

"Dad?" Henry stepped up and handed Shawn the scrapbook. Shawn flipped it open to the picture of Herman as a young police officer. "It turns out that before Herman moved to Santa Barbara, he was an officer on the Miami PD. He went undercover with some bad cops and managed to bust them for participating in the biggest race track heist in Florida history, the Calder Race Course robbery of nineteen seventy-two."

Shawn flipped the pages over and showed them headlines about the robbery from Miami newspapers. "But after that heroic act, Herman turned his back on law enforcement. He quit the force, took a long vacation in Europe, and then settled here, where he never told anyone he used to be a cop. Wonder why."

"Because cops don't like cops who inform on their fellow officers, even if they deserve it," Detective O'Hara said. "That robbery happened before I was born, but there were still people upset about it in the department when I was there."

"That's what my dad assumed," Shawn said. "It's probably what any cop would assume. But Gus and I aren't cops."

"And we can all thank the city of Santa Barbara for that," Coules said.

"The money from the race track robbery was never recovered," Gus said, trying to get things back on track.

"Three million dollars," Shawn said. "You can bet that the people who planned the heist never stopped looking for it. But all the crooks were caught, and no one had a dollar. Imagine what it would be like to spend twenty-some years in jail with nothing to do besides trying to figure out who'd taken your money. And when you finally did, to know there was nothing you could do about it until your sentence was up."

Shawn stopped to take a breath, and Gus stepped into the breach. "Then, when you got out, you were too old and too feeble to go after the SOB who stole your money. But if it couldn't help you, at least you could pass the information to your son, who'd followed you into the armed-robbery business."

Lassiter stared at them suspiciously. "You're saying that John Marichal's father was part of the Calder heist?"

"It'll be pretty easy to check out," O'Hara said. "I can call one of my buddies out there."

"So let's go with it for now," Shawn said.

"And he was looking for the money here?" Henry said. "You're not going to try to tell us that Herman was one of the thieves. He was a friend of mine."

"And yet in all those years of friendship, he never mentioned his past in law enforcement," Shawn said.

"Because the fewer people who knew about it, the fewer people would think to connect him to the money. But John Marichal's father did, and he sent his son to get it. Unfortunately, by the time the lad got off the chain gang, Herman had died of cancer, so John was going to have to search for the loot himself."

"Here?" Chief Vick said.

"Where better to hide three million cash than in acres of abandoned automobiles? Marichal killed the original attendant and took his place so he could take his time and search every car in the yard. He would have started with Florida plates and tried to move on from there."

"This is ludicrous," Coules said. "Why would the money still be there after all this time?"

Shawn turned to his father. "I think you can figure out why."

Henry thought back on the Herman Walinski he knew. He was kind and gentle and happier with his life than anyone he'd ever known. All Heman had wanted to do was sit behind the counter in his tackle store and design lures. "Because Herman didn't need it. Maybe he never did. Maybe he just stole it to keep it out of the hands of the thieves. Either way, he made his own fortune in the towing business, and never had to touch the loot."

"And so here it sat for almost forty years, until Old Man Marichal got out of jail," Shawn said. "He told his son what he had figured out, and young John headed west. He must have told someone else, too."

"Someone he was scared of," Gus said. "Why else would he talk?"

"And what would frighten this old man more than the threat of spending his last few years back in jail?" Shawn said. "I wonder who'd have the power to do that."

"Say," Gus said. "Didn't Bert Coules used to work in the Miami DA's office?"

"I believe he did," Shawn said.

All heads swiveled to stare at Coules. He took a step backward. "You can't believe this fraud."

"I've often started off with that attitude, Mr. Coules," the chief said. "But by the time he's done, I almost always find myself convinced."

"I am not going to put up with this." Bert Coules started back toward the street, but Lassiter and O'Hara stepped in his way.

"Just for a little while longer," O'Hara said.

"If it makes you feel any better, we're rooting for him to get it wrong, too," Lassiter said.

"Bert Coules came to Santa Barbara, settled into the community, and began a yearlong search for the money. He'd break into the impound lot after hours and search the cars, one by one."

"He was even searching for the loot while you all were staring at a corpse in the shack. Remember the oil stains on his slacks? If you crawl around on the ground here, you'll end up with spots just like that," Gus said.

"So he kept on searching," Shawn said. "Until one night he broke in and found someone there. He must have recognized young Marichal—and no doubt Marichal recognized him. There was a fight, and Marichal ended up permanently staring backward."

"Like I could take on a giant like that," Coules protested.

"You're the one who said that someone as small as Tara Larison could break his neck with the proper technique," Gus said.

"A technique I'm sure you learned during your time in the Special Forces," Shawn said. "You stole the office's computer in hopes that Herman had kept a record of where he hid the money. But it didn't help."

"Maybe it was in Herman's private code," Gus suggested. "Or maybe it wasn't in there at all. Something drove you to see Betty Walinski and try to force the truth out of her. You snapped her neck, which not only kept her quiet about you, but also helped convince the police that Tara Larison was a mad dog who needed to be killed on sight."

"And if I may say, that might be the worst crime of all," Shawn said.

"What do you mean by that, Shawn?" Gus said.

"To depend on our Victorian stereotypes of the madwoman in the attic, to play on our prejudices about women as unstable and vengeful, is to reduce countless individuals to gender-based cartoons whose entire selfhood is determined solely by their reproductive organs. It diminishes me as a man simply to hear such canards recited."

Henry, Lassiter, Coules, and the other men in the shack stared at Shawn baffled. But Detective O'Hara and Chief Vick regarded him warmly for the first time since Tara had tried to forcibly exchange saliva with Juliet, apparently on Shawn's psychic orders.

"Do you mean that, Shawn?" Detective O'Hara said, finally treating him to one of her warm smiles.

"I always have," Shawn said. And it was actually true, if by "always" he meant since this morning when he'd memorized the passage from a Web site of feminist literary theory.

Coules waited for them to go on. When they didn't, he broke out into a smile. "So aside from sisterhood being powerful, is that it?"

"I think so. Gus?"

"Sounds about right?"

"You don't have anything," Coules said. "It's all supposition and theory. You don't have one shred of proof."

Shawn turned to Gus, suddenly troubled. "You know, I think he's right."

"Definitely. We've got no proof at all."

Coules tried to push past the detectives. They didn't move out of his way.

"They don't need proof, Mr. Coules," Chief Vick said. "They're not police. We're the ones who need to show proof. And if you'll be so good as to accompany us back to the station, we'll make a couple of calls and find out if you ever handled a case involving Mr. Marichal Senior. That should be enough to hold you while we start checking some of these cars for your prints. Mr. Spencer, you say we should start with the Florida plates?"

"It's still all ridiculous speculation!" Coules shouted. "It's all based on the idea that Walinsky and Marichal were involved in the race track robbery. And there's no evidence of that."

Chief Vick turned to Shawn. "He does have a point there. Do you have any evidence that Herman Walinsky had anything to do with the Calder Race Course robbery besides catching its perpetrators?"

"None at all," Shawn said.

"Unless you count the three million dollars," Gus added.

"We can't count it if we can't find it," Lassiter said.

"Then you should check out a yellow nineteen sixty-five Ford Thunderbird with Florida plates about three hundred yards west of here," Shawn said.

"If you'd be so good as to lead us, Mr. Spencer," Chief Vick said.

"Yes, do," Coules said. His smile had turned into a smirk.

Shawn and Gus led the group through the maze of cars until they came to the rusting T-Bird.

"This is your brilliant idea?" Coules said. "If half of what you said was true, this is one of the first cars Marichal would have checked."

"You, too," Gus said.

"Fine. Whatever. Go ahead and check it."

Shawn rapped sharply on the trunk. With a groan of hinges, the lid began to lift slowly. The others crowded around to see what was inside.

"It's empty!" Mindy said.

"Just like this clown's head," Coules said. "Can I go home and start preparing my defamation suit now?"

Shawn stared into the empty trunk. "Dad?"

Henry Spencer sighed wearily. "Yes, son?"

"What was the name of Herman Walinsky's legendary lure?"

"I really don't think that fishing tackle is going to do you much good right now."

"Humor me."

"Please humor him," Mindy said. " 'Cause he can stand here and keep talking if he wants. Believe me, I know."

Henry took the scrapbook back from Shawn and flipped it open to a page with a photo of a fishing lure fastened securely in its center. He held the book open so everyone could see. "It was called the YTBL3."

"Did he ever say what that stood for?"

"No," Henry said. "I always assumed it came after the YTBL2 and before the YTBL4."

"Good thought," Shawn said. "Here's a better one. Y—Yellow. TB—Thunderbird. L—Left." He turned theatrically to his left. "Three—well, three." He walked down three rows of cars and stopped next to a decaying nineteen sixty-one Olds Cutlass. "Does anyone happen to have a crowbar?"

Gus bent down and picked one up from off the ground. "Look, Shawn, it seems that someone has graciously left one for us right here."

"Then let's accept their generous gesture." Shawn took the crowbar and used it to pry open the Cutlass' trunk. Inside were a dozen fraying canvas bags. Shawn lifted one out of the trunk. With a sound of ripping cloth, the bottom tore out and bundles of cash poured out on the ground.

Coules stared at the money. "So close. All this time, it was right there."

O'Hara pulled out her cuffs and snapped them on his wrists. "And this is as close as you're getting to it."

Chapter Twenty-three

Gus cranked down the window and let the wind blast him in his face. This was what life was all about: speed, freedom, and the open road.

Veronica Mason had finally come through with the reward she'd promised, and the first six thousand dollars had ransomed the Echo. The rest of it would let Shawn and Gus live safely and securely no matter how much profit the Psych agency was generating.

At least it would if Shawn managed to persuade the rest of the nation to drink Blāk. Although Gus had begged him to put the money into T-bills, Shawn had insisted on investing the entire post-Echo sum in a new Bulgarian Blāk bottling company. Odds were, they'd never see a penny of it again. But they were young, they were free, and for the first time in ages, they didn't have the prospect of execution in their near future.

Gus tapped the brakes to let a BMW slip in ahead of him. There was an anguished scream from the seat next to him.

"What are you doing?" Shawn forced the words out through a throat choked with frustration.

"Thought we'd draft for a bit."

"*Draft?* You thought we'd *draft*?"

"What I said."

"As in ease out of the headwind and take advantage of the Beemer's slipstream?"

"That's what it means."

Shawn chose his words with extreme care, as if fearing that the wrong ones were lurking in his mouth and threatening to leap out and pummel Gus over the head.

"We've been in this drive-through line for twenty-three minutes," he said. "We haven't moved in twenty-two. The only headwind is coming from that kid blowing straw wrappers at us."

Gus cranked down the window another notch and let the warm breeze fill the car. "You drive your way, and I'll drive mine."

Shawn reached for the door handle. "I'm going to go inside, place my order, receive my food, eat my delicious BurgerZone burger, place my refuse in the receptacle, and when I come back out, you'll still be sitting in exactly this place."

"Quite possibly true, except for one thing."

"What's that?"

"Remember this?" Gus reached into the glove box and pulled out the xeroxed flyer. Across the top it read: *Attention All BurgerZone Employees.* On the bottom it warned in stern letters: *Do Not Serve.* And in the middle, a police artist's sketch of Tara. And another one of Shawn.

"If you even want to sniff the aroma of those delicious BurgerZone burgers, you'll do it my way."

Shawn crumpled up the flyer.

"You're going to sit here forever because you're so happy to be back behind the wheel of this car."

"Yup."

"And you're going to make me sit here because you don't like to be alone."

"Uh-huh."

"Don't you think you're taking advantage of the fact that I've been banned from BurgerZone? That you're taking advantage of my own personal weakness?"

"Don't think of it as me taking advantage of you," Gus said, patting Shawn on the knee. "Think of it as a win-win."

Acknowledgments

Many thanks to Steve Franks for the loan of these wonderful characters and to Kelly Kulchak and Chris Henze for making sure that my versions of Shawn, Gus, and all the rest stayed true to Steve's vision. Thanks as well to Kristen Weber and Jeff Gerecke for their faith, support, and encouragement.

And even if Lee Goldberg had not been my friend and partner for a quarter of a century, and even if he had not helped to make this possible, I'd still owe him the same debt that all tie-in writers do, for setting the bar so high and raising it higher with every book.

About the Author

William Rabkin is a two-time Edgar-nominated television writer and producer. He has written for numerous mystery shows, including *Psych* and *Monk*, and served as showrunner on *Diagnosis Murder* and *Martial Law*.

Also available in the new series based on
the hit USA Network television show!

PSYCH
Mind Over Magic

by WILLIAM RABKIN

When a case takes Shawn and Gus into an exclusive club for
professional magicians, they're treated to a private show by the
hottest act on the Vegas Strip, "Martian Magician" P'tol P'kah.
But when the wizard seemingly dissolves in a tank of water, he
never rematerializes—and in his place there's a corpse.

Eager to keep his golden boy untarnished, the magician's
manager hires Shawn and Gus to uncover the identity of the
dead man and find out what happened to P'tol P'kah. But to do
so, the pair will have to pose as a new mentalist act, and go
undercover in a world populated by magicians, mystics,
Martians—and one murderer...

And don't miss
Psych: The Call of the Mild
Psych: A Fatal Frame of Mind
Psych: Mind-Altering Murder

**Available wherever books are sold or at
penguin.com**